Table of Contents

A Place to Call Home
Roberta Grieve

Print ISBNs
Amazon print 9780228632863
Ingram Spark 9780228632870
Barnes & Noble 9780228632887
BWL Print 9780228632894

BWL Publishing Inc.

Books we love to write ...
Authors around the world.

http://bwlpublishing.ca

Copyright 2024 by Roberta Grieve
Editor Victoria Chatham
Cover artist Pandora Designs

Chapter One

The smell of damp and mould permeated the cabin and Emily shivered. She should have been used to the conditions on board the former ship 'Dunkirk.' They had moved here when she was just a toddler, and she had little memory of their life in London. Life on board the rotting hulk, moored alongside the mudbanks bordering the naval dockyard at the northwestern tip of the Isle of Sheppey was all she really knew. After the defeat of Napoleon, the old ships had been used to house workers re-building the naval dockyard. Now the workers and their families were moving to proper houses, making way for criminals from the overcrowded London prisons.

Emily finished packing the last of the bags and straightened up, looking around at the dismal place that had been her home for most of her short life. She had shared this tiny cabin with her parents and younger siblings, making the best of things and taking over the care of her brother and sister after the death of their mother.

Her father was at work in the dockyard, leaving Emily to look after eight-year-old

Joey and toddler Cissie while packing up their belongings.

At last, they were leaving this awful place, having been allocated one of the new dwellings in nearby Blue Town.

A place of our own, Emily thought, her lips curving in a smile, a smile which disappeared as a wave of grief swept over her. Her mother had passed away a year ago, victim to the fever which swept through the hulks from time to time. If only she could be here to share this momentous day with them.

Until now, the de-commissioned warships had been used to house the workers on the new dockyard buildings. Her father had told her that when the last of the families left, the hulks would be fitted out with cells to house prisoners awaiting transportation to Australia. Looking back at the cramped cabin that had been her home for so long, Emily thought that the damp and mouldy quarters would be more fitting as a prison.

She and her family were among the last to be moved out and she was excited at the change in their fortunes. But, as she gave one last look around the cabin, she felt a pang of nostalgia. Despite the damp and cold, they had been happy here. Her mother had done her best to make the place into a home, making curtains from old clothes to hang at the tiny portholes and hooking rag rugs for the floor of their cabin. She had also spent hours cleaning and scrubbing to drive away the foul smells. Best of all though, Emily thought, Mother had showered them with love, singing to them or telling stories, teaching her and Joey to read. Oh, how she missed that loving presence.

'Hurry up, Joey. We need to be gone,' she said sharply, thrusting the sad thoughts away.

'Are we going to the house?' he asked. 'Our house? A real house?'

'Yes, Joey. Now, help your sister and take one of these bags.'

'Is Dad coming too?'

'Of course he is.' Emily hastened to reassure the little boy, who still missed his mother and worried that his father would leave them too. 'He'll come to the new place when he finishes work.'

Joey took Cissie's hand and picked up one of the bags. Emily hefted the other two and led the way along the narrow passage and down the gangway onto the mud bank. They passed several hulks before reaching the road with its high brick wall which wound past the dockyard. Occasionally, they glimpsed the tops of the masts and spars of the ships moored in the harbour, as well as the tower of the Dockyard church.

Emily hoped she could remember the way to St Paul's Close. All these little closes and alleyways looked alike.

'Is it much further,' Joey asked. 'My legs hurt.' He tugged on Cissie's hand. 'Cissie's legs are hurting too.'

'Never mind. We're nearly there,' Emily said, sighing with relief as she spotted the sign for the Red Lion and remembered her father's instructions. 'It's this way.' She led them down the narrow alleyway between the pub and a butcher's shop. It came out onto a lane and she spotted the entrance to the Close.

She hoped the carter who had promised to deliver their pitifully small amount of furniture had arrived. She was especially anxious about her mother's old trunk, which held their most precious belongings. The glasses and china ornaments, mementoes of happier more prosperous times, had been carefully wrapped in several of her mother's silk dresses. Emily remembered her holding up the blue silk and saying, 'This was my wedding dress. We must keep it for when you get married.'

Emily choked back yet another sob. She couldn't imagine ever getting married, let alone wearing that beautiful dress or meeting a man as good and kind as her father. When she'd said so, her mother had replied, 'You'll know when you meet the right one, just as I did when I first saw your father.'

She sniffed and hefted the larger bag onto her shoulder. She should have put that on the cart as well, she thought.

The entrance to the close was shrouded in shadow. It was getting late. She hoped she would be able to sort out their belongings and make up a bed for the children before it got too dark.

'Here we are then.' She tried to inject a note of optimism into her voice, telling herself that the change from the familiar must be for the better.

She led the children through an archway into a cobbled courtyard. The little cottages ranged on two sides, and along the back were the privies and coal sheds.

She crossed the yard and opened the door to number one in the far corner. It was almost dark now and she could just make out the heap of furniture in the centre of the room. The carter had just dumped it there, making no attempt to arrange it or to take anything upstairs. To her relief, the trunk was there too.

'Wait there,' she instructed Joey and Cissie. 'I'll just find some candles.' She fumbled in the bag, finding them at the bottom along with some matches. 'I hope they're not damp,' she muttered. She struck one, sighing with relief as it ignited. She lit the candle and dripped some of the wax on to the mantelpiece, pushing the candle into it to anchor it safely.

Joey put down the bag, rubbing his arm. 'Is this really ours,' he asked, looking around the single room. 'It's big.'

'And that's not all. Look.' Emily went to a small door in the corner of the room and opened it to reveal a curving staircase.

'Whoopee – stairs,' he exclaimed, running across the room. Pushing Emily aside, he ran up, laughing.

'Careful,' his sister warned. 'Let me light a candle.' She lit another from the first one and followed him up, pausing as Cissie started to cry. 'It's all right, love. I'll be down in a minute,' she called, turning to Joey who was standing in the middle of the bedroom, looking around in amazement. 'Come on down now. We need to sort Cissie out.'

'Two rooms. Lucky us,' Joey said, following her downstairs.

'Yes, we are lucky.' And they were, she thought – a living room downstairs twice the size of their cabin on the hulk, as well as a separate bedroom. She looked around, not sure where to start. It was a good-sized room with an iron kitchen range along the wall next to the stair cupboard. A stone sink stood against the tiny window next to the entrance. There was no tap, just a drain to take away the water. She would have to fill a bucket at the outside pump before they could wash.

Cissie had stopped crying and was sitting on a pile of bedding, her thumb in her mouth. Her eyelids were drooping and Emily decided to leave her where she was. 'Joey, help me with the beds. Cissie's tired, so we must get her settled before we do anything else.'

'I'm hungry.' Joey scowled.

'Well, the sooner we get things done, the sooner we can sit down and eat.'

Emily didn't usually speak so sharply but she was tired and hungry, too. She felt a guilty pang at Joey's shocked expression.

'Dad's bringing fish and chips when he finishes work,' she said.

The little boy's scowl disappeared. 'My favourite,' he said.

'Well, come on then, let's get the bedding upstairs.' She tugged at one of the straw-filled pallets. On the hulk, they had slept on wooden bunks with only these thin mattresses to sleep on. They would do for now, Emily thought, but she promised herself she would find work and earn enough to buy proper beds. For the time being, Dad would have to sleep in the armchair downstairs. His wage was enough to feed, clothe, and keep them warm in winter, but little was left over.

Together, she and Joey managed to get the pallets upstairs and then the blankets. Tomorrow she would hang curtains at the little window. And she would have to learn how to operate the kitchen range so they could have proper hot meals.

Fortunately, although it was only March, the weather had been mild and the children would be warm enough.

As Emily laid the pallets out on the floor and arranged a couple of blankets over them, she thought how fortunate they were to be away from the stinking hulks and the ever-present fear of catching some foul disease in their overcrowded quarters.

She was about to carry Cissie upstairs when she heard the door downstairs open.

'Dad,' Joey cried, rushing downstairs.

Emily hurried after him.

Joseph Williams stood at the bottom of the stairs, his arms outstretched. 'Come to me, my boy,' he called in his deep booming voice.

Joey jumped the last few stairs into his father's arms, and they tumbled into the room laughing.

'Shush. Don't wake Cissie,' Emily said quietly. But it was too late. The little girl stirred on her blanket and let out a thin wail.

Joseph put his son down and leaned over the toddler, picking her up and making soothing noises. 'There, my pretty one. Don't cry.' He turned to Emily. 'Well, how do you like it?'

'It's fine, Dad. We'll be happy here.'

'I hope so, love. It's good to get away from that awful place.' He put Cissie down and said, 'Let's eat. I'm sure you're all hungry.'

He handed her the paper-wrapped parcel from which the appetising smell of fried fish filled the room. Emily rummaged in one of the bags and found plates. 'I can't find any forks,' she said. 'We'll have to use our fingers for now.'

There was only one seat, a high-backed armchair with faded upholstery, left behind by a previous tenant. 'Sit there, Dad,' Emily said. She folded the tatty blanket over the lid of the trunk and directed Joey and Cissie to sit on it.

She shared out the food and soon the only sound in the room was the munching of crisp batter and chipped potatoes. Even Cissie had shrugged off her tiredness and managed to eat a few of the chips.

Emily looked round at her family, their faces lit by the flickering candle and her heart filled with love. A little lump formed in her throat. Mum should be here with us, she thought. If we'd had a place like this to live, she wouldn't have caught the fever. So many had died a year ago when the disease had rampaged through the hulks. They were lucky to have escaped. But Sally Williams, weakened through childbirth and the loss of two babies, hadn't stood a chance.

Emily stood up, gathering the paper the food had been wrapped in and putting it in the sink with the plates. She would sort it all out in the morning. Now, it was time for the young ones to go to bed.

* * *

Emily was woken by a soft whimpering and she sat up abruptly, unsure for a few seconds where she was. Grey light outlined the small window, and memory returned.

They were here, really here, in their own little house. She sat up, easing the stiffness from her back, and crawled over to the makeshift bed in the corner, sitting Cissie up and patting her back.

'All right, lovie, I'm here. Shush. Don't wake Joey.'

'Em'ly. I couldn't see you,' Cissie whispered.

'I know. It's all strange, but you'll get used to it. Let's go downstairs and see if Pa's awake yet.'

'Stairs?' Cissie murmured, her brow creased in confusion.

'Don't you remember? We're in our own house all to ourselves.'

Emily struggled upright, lifting her little sister and carrying her downstairs.

The room was empty, and her heart thumped. For a second, she feared that Dad had deserted them. How would she manage without him – and his wages?

She set Cissie down in the battered armchair and, sighing, went over to the range. To her surprise it was warm and the kettle was singing on the hob. Dad must have lit the fire. But where was he?

Perhaps he'd gone to work, although she'd hoped he would be at home today to help her get the house straight. She shrugged. Better get breakfast for the children, she decided.

At that moment the door opened, bringing a blast of cold wind. Cissie wriggled out the chair, shouting 'Dada.' She toddled towards her father and Emily smiled her relief.

'Well, lass,' Joseph said. 'Seems you all slept well last night. I was up with the lark, chopping kindling, lighting the range, pumping up water and you slept through it all.'

'Sorry, Dad. I meant to be up early. There's so much to do.'

'Not to worry. You were exhausted. Plenty of time to get the house straight.' He looked around. 'Now, where's that son of mine?'

'I let him sleep in. He worked so hard yesterday. We couldn't have managed without him.' Emily smiled. 'The way he lugged those heavy bags – and not a word of complaint.'

'Aye, he's a good lad.'

'He was talking about finding work, but he's too young.'

'Much too young. He needs to go to school.' Emily knew that her father set great store by education. He'd not had much learning when young and was determined that his children would not miss out which was why he had encouraged his wife to teach the children to read.

Joey came downstairs and heard his father's words. 'I don't need school,' he protested.

'Yes, you do,' said Joseph. 'I hear there's a new one opened here - just round the corner.' He turned to Emily. 'I'd take him along but I must get back to the dockyard. They've kept me on – labouring, building the new dry dock for the big ships.'

'I'll take him,' Emily said. 'But first, you need some breakfast. There's some bread – a bit dry but I'll toast it on the range.' She busied herself preparing the food while Joseph lifted Cissie on to his lap.

After breakfast, Joseph shrugged on his jacket, tied a muffler around his neck and stepped outside. 'Sure you'll be all right, lass?' he asked.

Emily nodded.

He put his hand in his pocket and drew out a few coins. 'Get some food in. There's a shop around the corner, near the Red Lion.'

'Thanks Dad.'

He ruffled Cissie's hair, said goodbye and strode across the cobbles, disappearing under the archway.

Emily watched him go. Time for me to get to work, too, she thought. But first, she must see about getting Joey into school.

She cleared the dishes, stacking them in the stone sink under the window. 'Now then, Joey, get your shoes on.'

He protested at first. 'Do I have to go to school?' he whined.

'Yes, you do. You need to keep up with your letters and numbers. Education is very important.'

'I don't see why. What good is book learning?'

'Like Dad said, if you do well, you'll be able to get a good job, maybe get a shipwright's apprenticeship. You don't want to spend your life struggling, do you?'

Joey shrugged and slowly put on his shoes and his jacket. Emily took down a broken piece of comb from the shelf above the range and made a passable effort at smoothing down his riot of black curls, so like their late mother's. He was going to grow up into a fine-looking young man, Emily thought with a smile.

Joey submitted for a few minutes, then wriggled away.

Emily picked Cissie up and opened the door, shivering as cold air gusted into the cottage. She pulled her shawl more closely around herself and her little sister, seized Joey's hand and set off across the cobbled yard, wending her way between the lines of laundry flapping in the wind.

'You don't need to hold my hand,' Joey protested. 'I'm a big boy now.'

'All right, but promise me you won't run off. I know you're not keen on school, but Dad says you have to go.'

'All right,' Joey muttered, kicking a stone into the gutter.

The school was a couple of streets away, and Emily looked up in awe at the brick building, which seemed huge to her. She had been very young when the family left London to live on the Sheerness hulks, and she was unused to seeing the large buildings springing up around the dockyard.

There were two entrances, the words 'Boys' and 'Girls' carved in stone over the doors. She hesitated, unsure which one to use. The sound of children chanting came to her. Lessons must have started already. She was late. She was almost tempted to turn away but, mindful of her father's words, she hefted Cissie up onto her hip and walked towards the door marked 'Boys.'

As she reached to open it a man came round the corner of the building.

'Well, who do we have here?' he asked, a smile on his face.

'I've brought my little brother to start school,' Emily said, stammering a little. He was a big man, bigger than her father, with a red face, chestnut hair and matching beard and moustache. She was a little in awe of him but took a deep breath and continued, 'We've just moved here – to St Paul's Close, and Dad said Joey must go to school.'

'Quite right, too. I'm Mark Thompson, the headmaster here,' said the man. He bent down towards Joey. 'Now then, young man what's your name?'

'Joey Williams.'

'And how old are you?'

'Eight, nearly nine.'

The school master straightened and addressed Emily. 'Has he had any schooling?'

'Our mother taught us to read and do sums.'

'That's good,' said Mr Thompson. 'We'll put him in Miss Cook's class. Follow me.' He led them round the side of the building and through a door opening on to a corridor. 'This is my office,' he said, opening a door. 'We'll get you registered, and then I'll show you the classroom.'

While he entered Joey's name into the register, adding birthdate, address and next of kin, Joey fidgeted, casting nervous glances at his sister.

Mr Thompson put down his pen and rose from his desk. 'Now then, Joseph. Say goodbye to your sisters.' He turned to Emily. 'We provide dinners for a few pennies a week, or he can go home as you live near enough. But be sure to get him back by twelve thirty.'

Emily fished in her pocket for a few of the coins her father had given her, saying, 'I'd like him to stay for his dinner.' She felt she might have trouble getting her little brother to return if she let him come home. Besides, she felt better knowing he would have at least one good meal today.

Cissie had fallen asleep, and Emily's arms were aching. She said a hasty goodbye to Joey, promising to be there to meet him when it was home time.

Outside, the chilly wind woke Cissie, and she began to wail. Emily set her down on the pavement and took her hand. 'You'll have to walk for a bit,' she said.

A leaf blew across the path and Cissie tried to grab it, chuckling. Emily smiled, grateful that her little sister had such an equitable temperament. Looking after her was no hardship. Joey was a different story, growing up fast and developing a mind of his own.

They reached the main road with its line of shops opposite the grim dockyard wall and Emily made for the butchers with rows of rabbits and chickens hanging outside. She paused in the doorway, counting the coins left after paying for Joey's dinners. Not enough for a whole chicken but she could make several meals from half of a carcass if she put some vegetables with it.

Shopping done, she trudged back through the maze of alleyways and closes to St Paul's Close, ignoring Cissie's pleas to be carried. The bag was heavy enough. Through the archway she spotted a woman taking laundry off the line.

'Hello,' the woman called. 'Just moved in?'

Emily nodded. She didn't want to stop and talk but the woman seemed friendly and she would have to get to know her neighbours.

'I'm Agnes, number five.' The woman nodded to the door on the other side of the Close.

'Emily – Williams, number one.'

'You come from the hulks?' Agnes asked.

Emily flushed, embarrassed, unwilling to admit that she'd lived in such terrible conditions.

'Don't be shy, love,' Agnes said. 'Most of us here were on the hulks. Good to have a proper roof over our heads, such as it is.'

Cissie tugged on Emily's hand before she could reply, and Agnes said, 'Better get inside before the little one catches cold. We'll have a chat later – when you've settled in.'

'That'll be nice,' Emily replied.

Indoors, she gave Cissie a crust of bread to chew on and made herself a cup of tea, using the leaves from their morning brew. It was weak but warming and better than nothing, she told herself.

She was relieved when her sister fell asleep and she was able to get on with sorting their belongings, such as they were.

She placed the trunk against the wall with the table in front of it. The children could sit on the trunk to eat their meals. She would make do with the footstool their father had made and Dad could have the old armchair.

She opened the trunk and unwrapped the trinkets and ornaments, arranging them on the shelf above the range. She left her mother's dresses, thinking that one day she would have to cut them down to make clothes for Cissie, who was fast growing out of what she was wearing.

When she'd finished unpacking, she glanced around at the room with satisfaction. They didn't have much, but she had done her best to make the house more homelike. The curtains she'd brought with them were too short but she could use them for patchwork and the rag rugs made a splash of warm colour on the cold flagstones.

She must try to find work if she wanted to buy proper furniture, curtains and more bedding. Her father's wage just about kept them in rent and food but there was very little left over. She bent and stroked Cissie's hair. How could she get a job when she had this little one to look after?

Cissie stirred and Emily shrugged. She'd work something out.

Chapter Two

Emily reached for another sheet and helped Agnes peg it on the washing line. Her friend earned a little money doing laundry for the officers' wives who lived in Admiralty Terrace within the dockyard walls. Her hands were swollen and painful after years of immersing them in water, and she was grateful for Emily's help.

Emily had seen her struggling to turn the handle of the mangle and rushed to help. Since then, she had regularly worked with Agnes, who paid her a little out of her hard-earned wages.

The two had become real friends over the months she had lived here. The families in the little close were a close-knit group, willing to help each other with child care and odd jobs.

Emily had to admit she was a bit envious of her friend, whose cottage was a little larger than her own. Being at the end of the row, the builders had managed to fit in a small extension which Agnes referred to as the scullery and used as a kitchen. In one corner was a brick-built copper with a wooden lid. At the bottom was an opening for the fuel for the fire to be inserted. When the laundry was done, the hot water was bailed out into buckets and poured away down the sink. It was still hard work but better than heating water on the range as she had to.

Emily wasn't afraid of work. She enjoyed helping her friend and appreciated the little extra she earned.

Together, they finished hanging up the washing and sat down for a bit of a rest. Emptying the copper could wait for a while. Cissie was playing with a couple of other children in a corner of the yard and Agnes said she'd keep an eye on her while Emily went indoors to make a cup of tea.

When she took the drinks across to Number Five, Agnes had set out two chairs so that they could catch the warmth of the sun.

'What's your Joey up to today?' Agnes asked after taking a sip of her tea.

'He's off with that Bobby. Goodness knows what they get up to.' Emily sighed. Joey had settled in to school and was doing well at his lessons, according to the headmaster, Mr Thompson, but she worried that he would run wild during the summer break, pleased to be free from the discipline of school.

'He's a good boy,' Agnes said, 'always ready to run errands and look how good he is with Cissie.'

Emily had to agree. 'I can't blame him for wanting to play with his mates. The other day he disappeared for hours.' She smiled at the memory.

He'd returned home sunburned and dirty, and she'd been ready to scold him. But he'd looked up at her with a grin.

'Look what I found,' he'd said, holding out a bundle of something wrapped in a torn piece of cloth. 'Bobby says they're good to eat.'

He unwrapped the cloth to reveal a handful of shellfish.

'Cockles,' Emily exclaimed, smiling. She had a faint memory of her mother buying them from a stall when they had lived in London. 'Where did you get them?' she asked, suddenly concerned that he had been stealing.

'Down by the water,' Joey said. 'I didn't pinch them. The tide was out, and Bobby showed me how to dig them up from the mud.'

'We'll have them for tea.' She took the cockles and put them in a basin of water to keep them fresh. It suddenly occurred to her that she had no idea how to cook them. But Joey was obviously proud of contributing to their meal. 'Keep an eye on Cissie, love,' she had said. 'I need to go and talk to Agnes. I'll get tea ready when I get back.'

She'd hurried across the yard and knocked on her friend's door. 'I need help,' she'd said.

Agnes had explained that cockles and other shellfish didn't take long to cook but needed to be washed well in several changes of water.

Emily laughed. 'I soon learnt. We've enjoyed them several times since.' She sat up straight and looked across the yard. 'Here he is now.'

Just then, Joey ran up to them, showing them a bucket full of cockles. 'I got some more. Can we have them for tea, Em?'

'Oh, Joey, I wasn't planning to cook. It's too hot and I'm worn out with all the washing.'

'I'll do it – if you show me how.'

'All right then. You can help me.' She turned to Agnes. 'I'll bring some over to you.'

'Thanks, Em.'

She took the cups and followed Joey into the house. She showed him how to clean the shellfish, explaining that it wasn't just to get the mud off. 'They can make you ill if they're not properly cleaned,' she told him

By the time their father came in from work, the cockles were simmering in a pot on the range and Emily had cut some bread to go with them. She put some in a bowl and sent Joey over to Agnes with them.

'That was great,' Joseph said, wiping his plate with a piece of bread.

'I'll go and get some more tomorrow,' Joey said.

'Good idea, son,' said Joseph. 'But you be careful out there. Don't go too far out. It can be dangerous when the tide turns.'

'Bobby always goes with me. His dad's a fisherman. He knows the tides.'

'Make the most of it,' Emily told him. 'You'll be back at school next week.'

Joey pulled a face and mopped up the juice from the shellfish with the last of his bread, stuffing it into his mouth.

Emily was pleased Joey had made a friend, but she was relieved that the holidays were nearly over. She felt more relaxed knowing her little brother was safe in school where he could not get into mischief. She had enjoyed the cockles though and looked forward to more. Free food was a bonus too.

* * *

The summer was over, and Joey was back at school. Joseph worked long hours in the dockyard and often returned home in the evenings exhausted. It fell to Emily to draw water, tend to the range and do all the myriad tasks to keep the household running. If it hadn't been for Agnes, she didn't know how she would manage. She had become a good friend.

Agnes, a widow, had two grown sons. One was in the navy and was away from home for months at a time. The other worked in a papermill on the mainland and lodged in Sittingbourne.

'I hardly see them,' she told Emily. 'I had hoped they would have married and given me grandchildren by now.' She sighed.

Emily sympathised. She could not imagine living in their little cottage alone, although sometimes she longed for some time to herself.

As they got to know each other better, she was pleased to let Agnes take care of Cissie while she got on with her own chores. She in turn was happy to help her friend with the mounds of laundry that Agnes was finding it hard to manage these days.

It had started to rain and Emily rushed outside to take the sheets off the line. 'Bring them in here,' she said, as Agnes struggled to help her.

They draped the sheets over the wooden clothes horse that Joseph had made from scraps of wood salvaged from the building work in the dockyard.

'I don't know how we'll manage when winter comes. It's always been a problem getting it all dry and ironed,' Agnes said.

'Perhaps Dad will make you one of these,' Emily said, indicating the clotheshorse. 'It's a godsend on wet days.'

* * *

By the time Cissie had woken up from her after-dinner nap, the sun had come out again, but it was too late to rehang the washing. It would soon be time to meet Joey from school. Emily was pleased that he had willingly returned after the summer holiday. He had settled in well and seemed to enjoy his lessons. He was confident enough now to walk home on his own, but Emily liked to meet him when she had time and they would walk down to the water and look at the ships anchored out in the estuary.

She brought Cissie downstairs and put on her shoes and coat. There was already an autumn chill in the air.

By the time she reached the school, the doors were open, and children were streaming through, laughing and calling to each other, revelling in their freedom after hours confined to the classroom.

Joey ran towards her, closely followed by his friend Bobby. 'Can we go down to the water?' he asked.

'Only for a little while,' Emily said. 'I've got lots to do when we get home.'

'Can Bobby come? We want to show you where we find the cockles.'

Emily nodded, and the boys ran on in front. She followed slowly, holding Cissie's hand.

To Joey's disappointment, the tide was in. 'No cockles today,' he said.

'Never mind. There'll be other days.'

They strolled along the bank separating the roadway from the estuary until they reached the newly built pier. In the summer, pleasure boats from London stopped here to pick up passengers and take them to Margate or Ramsgate.

Today, only a couple of Royal Navy frigates were anchored out at sea.

'I'm going to sail in one of them when I'm big,' Bobby announced, pointing.

'Me too.'

Emily's heart sank. It would be years before her brother was old enough to leave home, but she dreaded the thought of losing him.

'Come on. It's time we went home,' she said, turning away from the water. She glanced across to where the prison hulks were beached against the dockyard wall. The narrow stretch of water between them and the pier was known as Rats Bay. She shuddered. It wasn't the thought of rats that troubled her but the inhabitants of the grim hulks that had once been her home. 'Murderers and thieves,' her father had said.

She clutched Cissie's hand tighter and quickened her steps. 'Come along, boys. Time for tea,' she called.

Reluctantly, they followed her down the steps and crossed the road to the Royal Fountain Hotel. A narrow road down the side of the impressive building led to the warren of alleys and closes that made up the little settlement known as Blue Town.

As they neared home a loud boom made them all jump. Cissie started to cry and Emily clutched her hand and bent down to calm her. The boys laughed and Joey said, 'That scared you didn't it, Em.'

'Of course it didn't,' she protested. 'I was worried about Cissie.'

'I bet one of those prisoners has escaped,' Bobby said. 'They always fire the guns to tell people to watch out.' He seemed more excited than scared.

'He'll be caught in no time,' Emily said. 'He can't get off the island.' She said it as much to reassure herself as the children.

'He could steal a boat,' Bobby said.

'Don't talk daft,' Emily told him. She didn't want Joey to get any ideas. 'Time you were getting home,' she told Bobby, ushering Joey through the arch and into the close.

Bobby raced off. 'See you tomorrer,' he called.

As they entered the cottage, the guns boomed again. Emily hastily shut the door and set about getting the meal ready. Joey kept on talking about the escaped prisoner, and Emily shivered. The prisoners were desperate men and she hoped she was right about him being caught soon. Where could he go? Beyond the small town the treacherous marshes stretched for miles towards the narrow Swale which separated the island from the mainland.

'There goes the gun again,' Joey said. 'He must be still out there.'

'Shut up about it,' Emily scolded. 'You're frightening Cissie.'

'Sorry, Cissie,' Joey said, going to his little sister and giving her a hug. 'Don't worry, he won't come here. He'll be miles away by now.'

Cissie continued to snivel and Emily tore a crust off the loaf of bread. She dipped it in the opened tin of condensed milk which stood on the table and handed it to the little girl.

Her tears ceased as she sucked on the sweet treat and Emily sighed with relief. She was still cross with Joey though and sent him outside to draw another bucket of water while she got the meal ready.

The appetising aroma of frying bacon filled the little room and Emily sniffed appreciatively. How she longed for a couple of thick rashers but she was grateful for the fatty scraps she had managed to get at the grocer's for only a few pennies. They would add flavour to the fried potatoes.

She was about to dish up when Joseph came in. 'Something smells good,' he said.

Emily smiled and moved the pan off of the hotplate. 'Just in time,' she said.

'Did you hear the guns, Dad?' Joey asked.

'Course I did. Anyway, they caught him. He's back in chains now.'

'Thank goodness.' Emily slid a heap of potatoes and a few scraps of bacon on to her father's plate. She divided the rest between herself and Joey, took the soggy crust of bread away from Cissie and gave her a piece of bacon to chew on.

A contented silence filled the room as they ate. When they'd finished, Joey helped Emily to clear away and their father took

Cissie on his lap and rumpled her blonde curls.

Joey sat on the floor beside his father, and despite Emily's warning look, he could not contain himself any longer. 'Dad, did you see the bad man?' he asked. And without waiting for a reply, he went on, 'I wasn't scared when I heard the guns. I knew they'd catch him.'

Cissie looked up. 'Where bad man?' She stuck her thumb in her mouth.

Joseph stroked her hair. 'He's gone. You don't have to worry about him anymore.' He looked at Joey and frowned. 'Let's have no more talk about it. I don't want you upsetting your sister. Besides, it won't happen again. They've put more guards on.'

He turned to Emily. 'Everything all right here?'

'I helped Agnes with the laundry. She can't manage on her own now. She's going to pay me. And Joey earned a few pennies before school running errands for the butcher.'

'Good lad,' Joseph said. 'But don't you go missing school just to earn money. We're doing all right.'

'Don't worry, Dad. Mr Thompson says I'm doing well.'

'Well, like I said, education's important.'

Joey shrugged. 'I s'pose so. But I won't need no book learning if I join the navy.'

'What put that idea in your head, son?'

'That's what my mate Bobby's going to do.'

'Well, plenty of time for that,' Joseph said.

Joey was about to protest, but he caught Emily's frown. She didn't want an argument.

When the younger children were in bed, Joseph said. 'What about this lad our Joey's friendly with? I don't want him getting into bad company.'

'He's alright, I suppose. They're a big family, a bit rough. I think that's why he wants to join the navy – get away from home.'

'I don't want him influencing Joey. I've been thinking of him working with me in the dockyard when he's old enough. Maybe get an apprenticeship as a shipwright.'

Emily agreed, although she felt a little envious that her brother might have a career and make something of himself. If only there were similar opportunities for girls, she thought.

* * *

Another damp, cold day. Winter had come early this year. Emily turned the handle of the big mangle which stood outside Agnes's door while her friend grabbed the damp sheets and carried them indoors. They wouldn't dry outside today. She had come to hate doing laundry, especially on days like this. If only there were some other way to earn money, but she was grateful to Agnes for giving her the work. The few coppers she'd earned over the past few months had meant the cottage was beginning to look more homely. She'd bought a rather battered dresser and a kitchen chair from a second-hand furniture dealer in the High Street.

Soon, both cottages were filled with the aroma of drying washing, which hung in front of the range on the clotheshorses Joseph had made. A line stretched across the ceiling carrying more sheets.

Agnes had gone indoors for a rest, and Emily would have liked to sit down, too. But she had to tidy up and start thinking about getting a meal for her father and the children. I shouldn't complain, she thought. At least I'm not down on my knees scrubbing floors in the Red Lion like Gladys across the way or plucking and gutting chickens for Mr Burston, the local butcher. Her other neighbour Doris had said that he had plenty of work available. Emily was pleased that she could tell truthfully that she was too busy.

She opened the back door to see that it was still drizzling. As she shook the mat, shivering a little, she heard the church clock striking the hour. Joey would be home from school soon. He'd keep Cissie amused while she got on with her chores.

She had stoked the fire, peeled the potatoes, and rearranged the laundry to make the most of the range's heat when she realized Joey had not yet come home.

'I bet he's off messing around with that Bobby,' she muttered.

Just then, the door opened, and Joey came in. 'Where have you been? And look at the state of you.' She grabbed his shoulder and shook him. 'You're supposed to come straight home.'

Joey twisted away. His wet hair was plastered to his skull and his socks were wrinkled and muddy. 'I'm sorry, Em. I stayed behind to help Mr Thompson.'

Emily's anger evaporated as suddenly as it had flared up. 'Help him – how?'

'The door fell off the book cupboard, and I helped him fix it'.

'Really? You're not fibbing?'

'No. He said I was a handy lad.'

'Well, I suppose that's all right then. But he really shouldn't keep you after school. I'll have to have a word with him.'

'Oh, please don't, Em.'

'All right, not this time. But he shouldn't be giving you jobs like that. You go to school to learn.'

'Yes, Em.'

'Well, get those wet things off and help me lay the table. Dad will be home in a minute.'

Emily wasn't sure how she felt about Mr Thompson taking an interest in Joey. She supposed it was kind of him and, of course, while her little brother was doing odd jobs for the teacher he would not be getting into mischief with Bobby.

When Joseph came in from work, looking very tired, she decided not to mention it to him. She was worried about him. He'd always been a robust man, used to working hard in all weathers, but he had recently developed a bad cough which, despite her efforts with homemade remedies, would not go away.

She encouraged him to sit by the fire and carried his plate of stew over to him instead of insisting he sat at the table as usual. She was even more concerned when he did not protest. Emily's mother had always impressed the importance of good manners on the family and Joseph had tried to keep up her standards. 'Being poor is no excuse for slipping into bad habits,' he'd said.

When Joey started telling his father about helping the schoolmaster, Emily shushed him. 'Dad's tired. Let him rest,' she said.

Joseph shook his head. 'No, let him tell me. It's good to hear he's making himself useful.' He reached over and ruffled Joey's hair. 'Just don't neglect your lessons, son,' he said.

They had finished their meal and Emily was clearing the table when a loud boom made them all jump.

'Oh, no. Not again,' Emily gasped.

'Must be another convict on the run,' Joseph said. He glanced at Cissie, who was on the brink of falling asleep. She rubbed her eyes and said, 'Big bang.'

Joey had rushed to the window and pulled the curtain back, but before he could say anything, Emily gave a warning shake of her head. 'It's all right, Cissie love. Nothing to worry about,' she said, lifting her little sister out of her chair. 'Come along, time for bed.' She carried Cissie up the stairs and settled her under the covers. 'I'll be up soon,' she whispered.

She hurried downstairs, determined to have a word with Joey about frightening his sister. She didn't blame him. He was at that age where everything was exciting. He didn't understand that what was thrilling for him was frightening to a four-year-old.

She needn't have worried. Her father was gently explaining to his son and Joey was nodding thoughtfully. 'Those men are dangerous,' Joseph said. 'Let's hope they're caught soon.'

'I wanted to go and help catch them,' Joey said.

'There are plenty of marines looking for them. You're far too young to go chasing over the marshes.'

Chapter Three

Harry Jones curled up in the corner of the cell willing himself not to cry. He almost vomited from the pain in his jaw but he managed to keep it down. He ran his tongue around his mouth and found that one of his teeth was loose. Abe Lucas packed a hefty punch.

'You wait till I'm big,' Harry muttered. 'I'll get you.' Brave words from a skinny, undernourished lad of sixteen. And it was brave words that had earned him the punch on the jaw from Abe. He should learn to keep his mouth shut, he told himself, especially when Toothless Tony, the gang leader dished out orders.

The thought almost made Harry smile ruefully. If they carried on like this, Tony would lose his nickname and Harry would be 'Toothless' instead of 'Ginger'. He probed the loose tooth with his tongue. He'd heard that Tony had lost his teeth in a gang fight in which he had come off best, leaving two of his rivals dead. Now he wore the nickname like a badge of honour.

The pain was slowly receding and Harry pushed himself to his feet. Standing up to

Toothless's gang was no good. He'd never win. There was only one thing for it – escape.

Could he manage it? Discipline on the prison hulks was harsh, and the more desperate criminals were kept in chains for much of the time. Harry was one of the lucky ones, not chained and trusted enough to run errands for the warders or help to dish up the gruel that made up their meals. Looking younger than his years had its advantages.

If he kept his nerve, it should be easy enough to hide somewhere until darkness fell. Then he'd slip over the side and make his way across the marshes which lay to the south and east of the little hamlet of Blue Town. He hoped that the whispers he'd heard about the surrounding terrain were true. But he'd listened carefully to the gang's plans for their own escape. Sid had lived on the island before going to London and getting involved with Toothless and his mates. He'd been the one to come up with the escape plan. He'd told them he knew his way across the marshes to where they could find a boat to the mainland.

Harry hadn't wanted to become involved but Toothless had bullied him into helping them. 'It's easy for you, Ginge. No one takes any notice of you - you can get in anywhere,' the gangster had said. 'All you have to do is get the keys for us, and we'll be away. We'll take care of you.'

Harry shook his head. 'I can't do it,' he said.

'Oh, yes, you can or it'll be the worse for you, boy.'

'No. I won't.' Harry was defiant although his heart was hammering and his knees weak. 'I've only got four more years to serve.'

Abe, Sid and Mac, along with the gang leader, had been sentenced to transportation to Australia. Harry knew that if he helped them and they got caught, he would be making that long, desperate voyage with them, that's if they weren't hanged.

Abe shook his fist. 'You will – or else.'

Foolishly, Harry had stood up to him, shaking his head. 'I won't. You can't make me.'

Abe's fist shot out and Harry crumpled to the floor. The big man grinned. 'We'll leave you to think it over,' he said.

Now, here he was, still weak from the blow, but determined not to suffer another. Toothless and his mates were planning to get away after dark. He must escape before them. He hoped they wouldn't discover he'd gone before he had a chance to get across the marshes. Sid had said it would be easy to find a boat to carry him to the mainland. After that, he had no clear plan.

He hauled himself to his feet, staggering a little and felt his way along the gangway to a storage locker. He would hide here till nightfall. Hope fled as a shout stopped him in his tracks.

'Oy, lad, what you up to? Your work's not done yet. Get clearing up those dishes.' The warder cuffed him round the head.

Harry bobbed his head. 'Yes, sir.'

There was still time to get away, Harry told himself as he gathered up the wooden bowls and returned them to the galley. He decided not to wait for darkness and crept along to the steps leading up to the deck. As he reached for the handrail, a hand shot out and grabbed his collar. He hadn't heard the rattle of the chains around the gangster's ankles.

'Where you off to, Ginge? Deserting us, are you?' Abe growled, raising a threatening fist.

Harry shook his head. 'No. Abe. Just finishing my work'

'A likely tale. So, where are the keys? Did you get them?'

'I'm just going to.'

'Well, get a move on. It'll be lock-up soon.' He gave Harry a shove and the lad scurried away. No chance of escape now. He'd have to get those keys or suffer another beating.

He not only knew where the keys to the chains were kept but also knew the routine of the hulk. It only took a minute before he was able to hand them over and retreat to his own cell. No chance to hide now. He could hear the warders shouting, 'Lock up. Back to your cells.'

He hoped he would be locked in and could claim no knowledge of the gang's escape. Surely, they would have climbed overboard and got away by now. But to his dismay, he realised Abe and his mates were still on board when Toothless Tony suddenly appeared, pulling at his arm. 'Come on,' he growled.

Harry tried to wriggle away, but the gang leader picked him up and threw him over his shoulder, scrambling up the gangway onto the deck.

It was almost dark now but he could make out Abe and the others standing on the muddy bank alongside the hulks and Toothless threw Harry down to them.

'What you bring him for?' Abe whispered.

'Don't want him telling tales. We'll dump him when we're well away.'

Harry scrambled to his feet and tried to run.

'Oh, no you don't.' Toothless grasped his arm and Harry knew it was useless to struggle.

Dragging him along, the gang crept through the maze of alleyways, passing the newly built church and finding themselves in an open area that seemed to stretch for miles in front of them. The area was lit only by a pale moon that occasionally peeped between the clouds. A gleam of water showed in the distance.

'Which way?' Mac asked.'

'Don't ask me,' Toothless hissed. 'Hey, Sid. You know the way.'

'I'm not really sure,' Sid mumbled.

'But you used to live on this god-forsaken island – how do we get off?'

Sid waved vaguely. 'Across the marshes. There's a ferry.' He set off into the darkness, and the others followed.

As they left the houses behind, the going got harder. Their feet sank into the water-logged ground. Harry, still held fast in Toothless's grip, stumbled along behind. Abe and Mac grumbled as they slipped and staggered through the boggy terrain, cursing as they tripped over unseen obstacles.

They'd been walking for about an hour when they all stopped, staring back the way they had come as they heard the boom of the guns echoing through the darkness. Their escape had been discovered. Before long, the town and surrounding marshes would be crawling with marines and prison warders.

Mac voiced their thoughts, shuddering. If they were caught, it would be the hangman's noose for him, not Australia.

'Better get moving then,' Toothless snapped, chivvying them on. 'If we can reach the mainland, we won't be caught.' His grip tightened on Harry's arm. 'As for you...', he snarled.

The first hint of dawn was showing to the east, and Toothless swore as they resumed their walk. The boggy ground made it impossible to run. 'I hoped we'd be off this damned island before now,' he muttered, giving a painful tug on Harry's arm.

Abe turned round. 'He's slowing us down,' he growled, shooting a baleful look at the lad. 'Leave him. With a bit of luck, he'll freeze to death out here.'

'He's coming with us. Think what he could tell them if he's caught.' Toothless pushed Harry ahead and started walking again, only to shout an oath as he slid in the mud and landed on his backside. Letting go of Harry's arm, he floundered in the mud, trying to haul himself upright.

Harry seized his chance and ran, only to tumble into a ditch. As the muddy, foul-smelling water closed over his head, he heard Abe laughing. Then Toothless snarled. 'Leave him to drown. And help me up, one of you. We're wasting time.'

Fighting his way to the surface, Harry realised the water wasn't as deep as he'd thought. I'm not going to drown, he told himself. And I'm not going with them. Trying not make a noise, he edged himself to the bank and ducked down into a clump of reeds. He stayed there for what seemed like hours, shivering uncontrollably. He could still hear the gang arguing.

'We're not going to find him,' Mac snarled. 'He's probably drowned.'

Toothless laughed. 'Let's hope so.' He turned to Sid. 'And why didn't you tell us there were canals, rivers, or whatever you call them here?'

'I didn't know,' he snivelled.

'You're as useless as Ginger. Why didn't you drown instead?'

The others laughed.

It seemed Sid didn't know the island as well as he'd boasted, Harry thought as he crouched in the freezing water. Maybe there wasn't even a ferry. At last, their voices faded away and he dared to crawl out onto solid ground. It was starting to get light, so he stood up and looked around. There was no sign of Tony and his gang, and he hoped that, even if there wasn't a ferry, they had managed to find a boat and get off the island. The bare marsh stretched away on all sides, broken by tussocks of tough grass and an occasional animal, which he thought might be a sheep, although he'd only ever seen dead ones being manhandled in Smithfield Market.

Which way was the town? The thought of being caught out here with nowhere to hide was more daunting than trying to make his way back to civilisation to find food and shelter. A biting wind had sprung up, and he shivered in his wet clothes. Glancing back the way they had come, he saw a light in the distance.

He set off, trying to keep the light in sight. But lights meant people and he almost changed his direction. He didn't want to get caught. No one would believe he hadn't been involved in the escape. But people meant food and warmth and shelter. He was sure to find somewhere to hide. Then he could decide what to do next.

* * *

It was just getting light when Emily woke next morning and there was a chill in the air. She snuggled down under the covers hoping to snatch a few more minutes before the children stirred.

She was just drifting off to sleep again when she heard Joey getting out of bed and going to the window. She sat up and saw him lift a corner of the curtain.

'Wow,' he murmured. 'Look at that.'

'What is it?' she asked.

'I can't see anything. The fog's hidden everything.'

Emily got out of bed and went to the window. They were used to mist and fog, especially at this time of year, but she had never seen it this thick. The cottages opposite were practically invisible. A faint light from Gladys's cottage shone through the mist.

Her neighbour was up early as usual. As Emily watched, the older woman stepped outside, a shawl over her head. On her way to the Red Lion to start her cleaning job, Emily thought, turning away. Time I was getting up, too.

'Get a move on, Joey,' she said.

Joey dressed quickly and followed her downstairs. 'Good job I pumped some water before bed,' he said. 'Don't fancy going out there in this weather.'

'Don't worry. I expect it will clear soon.' She got the range going and boiled water for tea, then woke her father.

She handed him a cup of tea, set Joey to make toast and went upstairs to fetch Cissie. When she came down, carrying her little sister, her father was once more telling Joey not to keep talking about the escaped prisoners.

'I haven't heard the guns again, so they've probably been caught. So let's hear no more about it.' He turned to Cissie and smiled. 'How's my princess this morning then?'

Cissie chortled and waved her fingers at him.

Joseph finished his toast, drained his cup and fetched his jacket from the hook behind the door. 'Better get off,' he said, ruffling Joey's hair. 'Don't be late for school, lad.'

'I'll try not to get lost in the fog, Dad,' the boy said with a cheeky grin.

The fog was even thicker when it was time for Joey to leave for school. Emily decided to walk with him but first she knocked on Agnes's door and asked her to look after Cissie.

'I'll only be gone a few minutes but I don't want her catching cold if I take her out in this. She's only just got over the last one.'

'That's all right, Duck. She'll be fine with me.' Agnes took Cissie's hand. 'Come on in the warm love.'

Emily thanked her and called to Joey, who was stuffing the remnants of his breakfast into his mouth.

'You don't need to walk with me,' he said.

'I know – you're a big boy now.' She grinned. 'I just want you to be safe, especially as the guns went off last night.'

'I'm not scared. Besides, they're probably miles away by now, and the marines won't be able to find them in this fog.'

Emily didn't answer. Joey had an answer for everything. They reached the school just as the bell stopped.

Mr Thompson greeted her. 'Good to see you, Miss Williams.' He turned to Joey. 'And well done, Joseph, for making it this morning. Quite a few absentees today.' He gave Joey a gentle push in the direction of the boys' entrance.

As Emily went to walk away, he said, 'Do you have a minute to spare? There's something I'd like to discuss with you.'

Emily's heart sank. It could only be about Joey. What had he been up to?

She turned back. 'Yes, Mr Thompson?'

He was smiling, and her anxiety dissipated.

'Nothing to worry about,' he said. 'I just wanted to tell you how well Joseph is doing. He is a very bright lad.'

'Thank you.' Emily didn't know what else to say. She wanted to get home – so much to do.

But he continued. 'And you, Miss Williams. How are you managing?'

No business of yours, she thought, but she managed a smile and said, 'Very well, thank you.'

'Joseph tells me your father works in the dockyard, but I wondered if you might need to earn a little extra money. I could offer you some work.'

Cheek, Emily thought, her face reddening. She was about to refuse but he carried on speaking. 'I need someone to help in the school. Miss Cook and I are so taken up with actual teaching. We need someone to collect the dinner money, maintain the register and maybe look after any child who is sick, all that sort of thing.'

Emily found her voice. 'That's very kind of you, sir. But I already have a job, and then there's Cissie to look after.'

'I hardly think helping your neighbour with her laundry counts as a job,' he said.

'It suits me,' she retorted and started to walk away.

'The offer's still there if you change your mind,' he called.

She carried on walking.

Chapter Four

The fog was beginning to lift, and Harry could see the outline of buildings in the distance. He was exhausted from stumbling over the boggy and tussocky ground and having to keep stopping to listen for any sound of the gang. He hoped they had managed to get right off the island and was beginning to feel a bit safer.

He staggered on, relieved when his feet struck a stony trackway. He had to find somewhere to hide, although he was past caring if he got caught. If Toothless and his gang had got away, being sent back to the hulks wouldn't be so bad, he told himself. At least he wouldn't have to worry about them beating him up or worse.

He turned a corner and found himself in a narrow, cobbled street. A couple of men loomed up out of the mist and he shrank back into an archway. Workers on their way to the dockyard he guessed – not marines.

He was shivering, his wet clothes clinging to his body. Hungry too. He'd have to steal some food from somewhere, although he rebelled at the idea. He wasn't a thief, despite having been accused and convicted of stealing an apple which had rolled under a market stall back in Bethnal Green. He'd just picked it up and was contemplating taking a bite when a Peeler grabbed his collar. His protests that he hadn't stolen it went unheeded, and he was dragged before the Magistrates. Sentenced to transportation and incarcerated on the hulks to wait for a ship, he'd come to the notice of Toothless and his gang.

Now, here he was, cold, tired, and hungry. He crept under the archway and glanced around him. Six little houses were ranged on either side of a cobbled square. In the centre was a pump, and in the back wall were four doors – privies or storage, Harry thought, reminded of similar courts or closes in London. Could he hide here, he wondered.

He crept across the square and tried one of the doors, gasping as a cottage door opened behind him. Quickly, he slipped inside the building. Not a privy he realised thankfully. The shed was piled high with coal, logs and kindling, maybe shared with the inhabitants of the close. As quietly as he could, he shifted some of the logs and made a space at the back to lie down. If someone opened the door, he hoped he wouldn't be seen in the gloom.

He strained his ears for sounds from outside. Everyone would be waking up now, getting ready for work, lighting their fires. He prayed no one would come in here. He had to rest for a while, get his strength back before moving on in search of food.

Gradually, he drifted off to sleep.

* * *

Joseph had gone to work early but not before he had lit the range and pumped up a bucket of water.

Emily thanked him and wound his scarf around his neck, kissing him on the cheek. 'Thaks, Dad. That's a great help.'

'Least I can do, lass. You have enough to keep you busy.'

When he had left, Emily wished she hadn't mentioned Mr Thompson's offer of work the previous evening. Dad had been against the idea, saying he earned enough to keep them warm and fed. He was grateful for the extras that the money from helping Agnes brought them but as he'd said again this morning, she had plenty to do. No need to get a proper job.

Emily didn't want to go against her father's wishes but she had been tempted by Mr Thompson's offer. The job sounded interesting – more so than turning the heavy mangle and wrestling with wet sheets on cold and windy days. Of course, she could still find time to help Agnes, though.

As she bustled around the tiny cottage, sweeping, washing dishes, caring for her little sister, she couldn't get the idea out of her head. In the end she sighed and mentally shook her head. She couldn't expect Agnes to look after Cissie while she worked. Maybe later, when Cissie started school and she had more time.

As she fed her sister some soup she'd made from bones and leftover vegetables, she thought it was a good job Joey had his dinner at school. She hoped he'd be given something more substantial than soup. He was growing fast, already filling out, with the promise of becoming a fine young man. She puffed with pride, picturing him in navy uniform and hoped Dad would change his mind about paying for a dockyard apprenticeship. They couldn't really afford it anyway. Of course, she would miss Joey if he went away but it would be a good life for him. Still, she wouldn't have to worry about that for a few years yet.

She spooned the last morsel of soup into Cissie's open mouth and wiped her face with a damp cloth.

'Time for your nap, lovey,' she said, looking forward to a quiet hour, sitting in Dad's armchair and doing her mending.

Cissie's eyes drooped, and Emily carried her upstairs and settled her in bed, tucking the blankets around her. She planted a kiss on the child's cheek and stroked her hair, pleased that she settled down to sleep straight away.

She pulled the curtain across the window, glancing out into the yard. The fog had disappeared, but it was still grey and damp. Thank goodness there was no washing today, she thought.

Downstairs, she poked the fire in the range, trying to coax a bit more warmth from it. No good, she'd have to venture out into the cold and fetch some wood from the store. They had used up their share of the coal.

She flung her shawl around her shoulders, grabbed a basket and stepped out into the chilly air.

Agnes was shaking a mat outside her door and she called across to Emily. 'Did you hear – they caught those convicts.' She laughed. 'They didn't get far, got lost in the fog, Bill Brent told me.'

Constable Brent was the local policeman who lived on the High Street near the Magistrate's Court. Agnes knew everyone in their little town. Emily smiled and said, 'Good.' Her friend gave a final shake to the mat and hurried indoors.

There was nobody else about – the neighbours were all either at work or trying to keep warm indoors.

She went to the corner of the shed where Dad had piled a load of wood. They were lucky he managed to bring home offcuts from his work in the dockyard. All perfectly legitimate, he assured her when she had queried it. He paid for what he took, pleased it was cheaper than coal.

She filled her basket and straightened up, gasping as a movement caught her eye. Rats, was her first panicked thought. But then she caught a glimpse of a pale face peering through the gloom.

'Joey, what are you doing hiding in here?'

The figure shrank back into the shadows, but not before she saw that the boy had a shock of ginger hair, nothing like her brother's dark curls.

Her voice softened. 'Don't be frightened,' she said, holding out a hand to him. She could see that he was terrified, shaking with fear and cold. She put down the basket of firewood and stepped towards him, still extending her hand.' Are you hungry?' she whispered.

The lad nodded his head. 'Come on, then. Come indoors in the warm.'

He crawled slowly out of his hiding place and inched towards her. As he straightened up, she saw he was much older than she'd thought. He was taller than her brother, but skinny, his face pale beneath the grime.

She picked up the wood basket and went to the shed door, looking around. There was still no one about, and she beckoned him to follow her.

Shuffling his feet, he crossed the yard behind her, hesitating as she opened the door. 'Come in, then. There's no one here. You're quite safe – only my little sister asleep upstairs.'

He slowly entered and stood by the door, looking around him, his eyes wide.

'Sit on this stool by the fire. I'll go up and get you a blanket, then you can get those wet things off.'

She hurried upstairs, hoping Cissie was still sleeping. But as she entered the bedroom, her little sister stirred and sat up, rubbing her eyes.

Emily wanted to leave her there while she questioned the lad downstairs. She was already regretting her impulsive decision to invite him into her home. He looked harmless enough but you couldn't really tell from his bedraggled and unkempt appearance. It suddenly occurred to her that he might be one of the escaped prisoners. But hadn't Agnes said they'd been caught? Besides, he looked far too young. Perhaps he had run away from home.

Whoever he was, he was cold and hungry and she could not find it in her heart to turn him away. She pulled one of the blankets off the bed and turned to go downstairs, but Cissie was fully awake now, so she followed Emily to the head of the stairs.

'Stay here, lovey. Just for a little while,' she whispered.

Cissie shook her head. 'Come down, see Joey,' she said.

'Joey's not home from school yet,' she replied.

'I want to come down,' the little girl insisted, screwing her face up. She was usually obedient, but sometimes she could be stubborn, and this was one of those days.

Emily couldn't cope with a tantrum right now so she sighed and said, 'All right then.'

She took Cissie's hand and helped her down the stairs, the blanket trailing behind her.

The boy was huddled on the stool, holding his hands out towards the fire. He looked up as Cissie toddled towards him and stood staring, her thumb in her mouth.

Emily handed him the blanket and said, 'Take off those wet things. You'll soon warm up.' She lifted Cissie away from him, still a little wary. 'Sit in Dad's chair,' she told her sister.

She went to the range and stirred the embers, then added a couple of logs. There was soon a good blaze and she picked up the pan. There was a little soup left from their dinner and she put it on the hob and stirred it. While she waited for it to heat, she arranged the boy's wet clothes on the clothes horse and moved it closer to the range.

'Now then,' she said. 'Tell me why you were hiding.'

The boy began to shiver again but not from cold this time. 'They said they would kill me,' he blurted.

'Who?'

'The gang. They made me help them, but I got away.'

'What gang?' Emily knew there were a few criminals on the island, rough types who tried to get away with robbery. But she hadn't heard of any gangs outside London.

The lad shook his head. 'I can't tell you. They'll kill me if they find out I peached.'

Emily didn't ask any more questions as it dawned on her that he must mean the escaped prisoners. She busied herself, stirring the soup and pouring it into a bowl. As she handed it to him, he looked up at her, his eyes filling with tears.

He shook his head. 'You mustn't help me. You'll get into trouble.'

'Never mind about that. Just eat up. We'll decide what to do when you're warm and fed.'

Hesitantly, he took the spoon she offered and took a mouthful. He swallowed then took another and another until he was scraping the bottom of the bowl.

Emily took it from him, regretting there was no more to offer him. But already she could see that it had done him good. The colour had returned to his cheeks, although he was still pale, and the haunted look in his eyes was gone.

'Now then, lad. Tell me your name and what you were doing out in that awful fog.'

The boy shook his head, looking scared again.

Emily glanced across to Cissie, who was still huddled in Dad's chair, staring at the boy. 'That's my little sister,' she said. Her name's Cissie – and I'm Emily.'

Cissie took her thumb out of her mouth and pointed at her sister. 'Em'ly,' she said, then pointed at the boy. 'Joey?'

Emily laughed. 'That's not Joey.'

The boy leapt up from the stool, knocking it over. 'Who's Joey? Where is he?'

'Hush, lad. No one's going to hurt you.' Emily righted the stool and persuaded him to sit down again. 'Joey is my brother. He's at school, but he'll be home soon, so we must hurry up and decide what we're going to do with you.'

'You'll turn me in, won't you? They'll take me back to the hulks.' He started to shiver again. 'They'll kill me, I know they will.'

So he was an escaped prisoner then, as she'd surmised. 'I won't let them,' Emily said, with more confidence than she actually felt. 'I'll help you. But you must tell me who you are and what happened.'

'My name's Harry. They call me Ginger.'

'Go on,' Emily encouraged. 'What about this gang?'

'There's four of them, right hard cases they are. They say Tony's a murderer.'

Emily gasped. She knew from her father that the prisoners on the hulks were real villains, murderers among them. She wondered what the boy's crime could have been to be incarcerated with those hardened criminals. She didn't dare ask.

After a pause to swipe his hand across his nose, Harry stammered, 'I ain't done nothing, miss. It was all a mistake, but no one believed me. They say I'm bound for Australia.'

'So, how did you get mixed up with this gang?'

'They picked on me, miss. Because I'm small I can get in places they can't. They made me help them get away.'

'You went with them?'

'I tried to hide but they made me.' He sniffed again.

Gently, Emily coaxed him to tell the rest of the story – the stolen keys, the flight across the marshes, his fall into the ditch and being left to drown.

'They thought I drowned – I heard them laughing.' He looked up at her and said, 'I'm sorry - I just needed somewhere to hide. I hoped they'd got away. Have they really got caught?'

'So my neighbour said.'

Harry shuddered. 'I can't let them catch me. They'll send me back to the hulks, and Tony and his mates will kill me.' He looked into Emily's face, his eyes imploring. 'Can't I stay here for a while?'

'Not possible. My dad would never allow it.'

'He'll turn me in, won't he?' He glanced at the window. 'When does he get home?'

'Later. You can stay till then.' Emily knew she shouldn't have promised, but she didn't know what to do. And what about when Joey got home from school? She felt sorry for the lad, but her family came first. She couldn't turn him in, and she couldn't hide him either. She would try to persuade him to leave. Maybe he could escape the island. The marines wouldn't be looking for him now, and the gang thought he'd drowned.

Cissie started fussing and asking for Joey and she knew her brother would be home soon. The boy had to be gone before then, and if not, definitely before her father returned.

* * *

Harry was still scared, but he felt better with some food inside him. He pulled the blanket around him, grateful for the comforting warmth. He knew he couldn't stay, but where could he go? It was a life on the run or giving himself up.

He watched the girl – Emily, nice name, and so pretty with her wavy blonde hair and cornflower blue eyes, he thought. She was tenderly caring for her little sister, washing her face and hands, reassuring her about their unexpected visitor. The little girl thought he was one of Joey's friends come to play.

Emily had been so kind to him. If only he could stay here. Don't be daft, he told himself. He couldn't get her into trouble. He had to leave.

While Emily was occupied with Cissie he inched forward on the stool and grabbed his clothes. They were quite dry, warm from the fire. He started to dress, trying to be quiet.

He would slip out of the door while she was busy.

As he reached for the door handle, it flew open, and a small boy tumbled inside, rearing back in shock at the sight of him.

This must be the brother, Harry thought, a thought confirmed as a voice cried, 'Joey' and the little girl toddled across the room, her arms outstretched. The boy scooped her up in his arms and turned to Harry.

'Who's this, then?'

Emily turned round and said calmly, 'This is Harry. He's just visiting.'

Joey put Cissie down and looked him up and down, understanding dawning.

He knows, Harry thought.

'Just visiting? Em, have you gone mad? You know who he is, don't you.'

'I've told her everything,' Harry interrupted. 'Don't worry – I'm just going. I don't want to cause any bother.'

'You're already in trouble, mate. My dad will be home soon, and he'll sort you out.' Joey made a dive for him, but Emily's voice stopped him.

'Stop. You don't understand. He's giving himself up.'

'Really? I don't believe you.' He glared at Harry. 'Is that true?'

Harry glanced at Emily and nodded. In that moment he understood she was right. Besides, she had been so kind, he couldn't risk her getting her into trouble.

'I'll go,' he said, pulling the door open.

'Wait till Dad gets home,' Emily pleaded. 'He'll know how to go about it. If you just walk out of here and someone sees you, you'll be hauled back to the hulks with no chance to explain.'

Harry didn't like the idea of talking to Emily's father but he nodded and sat down again. 'All right. I'll wait.'

* * *

Emily busied herself preparing a meal, glancing from Harry to Joey as she worked. The lad leaned towards the fire, clasping his hands in front of him, avoiding Joey's eyes. Joey had pulled Cissie on his lap, cuddling her close as if to protect her from the intruder. He glared at the unwanted visitor, muttering threats under his breath.

Emily ignored him. If only Dad would get home soon, she prayed.

A few minutes later the door opened, and Joseph entered, stamping his feet before taking off his boots.

'Ooh, blooming cold out there,' he said, rubbing his hands together. 'Hope you've got a good blaze going.' He moved towards the range, only then noticing the lad crouched on the stool. 'Hey, who's this then?'

Before Emily could reply, Joey burst out, 'He's an escaped convict.' He pushed Cissie off his lap and rushed across the room. 'Turn him in.'

'Wait a minute, lad. I thought the convicts had been caught.' He turned to Emily. 'Well, girl. What's going on here?'

'Dad, he's just a boy. Look at him.' Emily's voice was pleading.

Harry stood up and pulled his shoulders back, standing tall, facing Joseph. 'It's true. I am a convict. I escaped with the others but...' His voice fell. 'They were going to kill me.'

Joey scoffed. 'A likely story.'

'Hush, Joey – let the lad speak,' his father said. He turned to Emily. 'How did he end up here?'

'He was hiding in the shed.' She proceeded to relate what Harry had told her.

Harry kept quiet, edging towards the door. Emily spotted him and called out. 'Don't run away. We want to help you.' She turned to her father. 'That's right, isn't it, Dad?'

'You're not going to let him go free?' Joey protested.

'No, son. We must do what's right.'

Harry spoke up. 'I don't want any trouble. I'll give myself up.' He moved closer to the door.

'Wait, lad. Let me think.' Joseph gestured to Harry to sit down again and seated himself opposite. After a few moments, he sighed and ran his hands through his hair. 'There's only one thing for it. We must fetch Bill. Joey, run along and see if he's home – and don't tell him why we want him.'

Harry's brow creased. 'Who's Bill?' He asked.

'He's the local bobby.' Before Joseph could say more, Harry leapt up from the stool, knocking it over again and rushing towards the door.

'I'm out of here.'

'No, Harry,' Emily shouted. 'He's a friend. He'll help.'

She went over and took his arm, persuaded him to resume his seat by the fire.

Joseph squatted down in front of him. 'You want to give yourself up, you said. But if you go marching down to the dockyard, you'll be nabbed and clapped in irons without having a chance to tell your side of things.'

'They'll hang me. That's what Toothless Tony said.'

Emily gasped. 'They wouldn't. He's far too young…'

Harry gave a mocking smile. 'I'm not. I'm sixteen – nearly seventeen. I know I don't look it. Anyway, I thought if I turned myself in and told them Toothless forced me to help, I might not….' He swiped his hand across his face.

'Who's this 'Toothless' you mentioned?' Joseph asked

'He's the gang leader. Everyone's scared of him, except his mates.' He hesitated. 'Well, they're his mates if they do what he says.'

'And did you do what he said?' Joseph asked.

'No – not always. But he beat me up, and he made me help them.' Harry hung his head. 'You can't send me back there,' he muttered.

Emily's heart went out to him, and she turned to her father. 'You're right, Dad. Let's wait for Bill. He'll know what to do.'

Harry nodded agreement but he remained perched on the edge of the stool, poised for flight. When the door opened and Joey came in with the policeman, he leapt up but Joseph took his arm and calmed him down.

'Well, Bill, we've got a bit of a problem here,' he said, indicating the trembling lad.

'Your boy told me. Off the hulks, isn't he?'

'I believe so.'

'Well, they caught four of them but I heard another of them drowned in the dike over the marshes. So, who is this then?'

Emily went across to Harry and squatted in front of him. 'Tell Bill what you told us – about the gang.'

Hesitantly, with many pauses to sniff and swipe his hand across his nose, Harry told his story. 'You've got to believe me, sir,' he implored. 'They made me help and they said they'd kill me if I told.'

Joey scoffed. 'Pity you didn't drown instead of bringing trouble to my family.'

'Now then, Joey, give the lad a chance,' said his father.

'Your dad's right,' said Bill. He turned to Harry. 'I believe you, son, but you'll need to convince the magistrate. And then, whatever he decides, you'll have to go back – finish your sentence at least.'

'You can't send me back,' Harry cried, his face paling.

'It will go better for you if you go willingly. Mr Williams will speak up for you, young Emily too. You didn't steal from them, and no harm came to them.'

'She was kind,' Harry muttered.

'Come on then, let's get you to the police station. It'll have to be a night in the cells, but it's better than facing your mates back on the hulks.'

'They ain't my mates. I told you. I 'ate them.' He spoke violently but Emily could see he was still terrified.

'Bill will take care of you,' she said gently.

The policeman took the boy's arm and led him outside. He turned at the door. 'I'll let you know what happens,' he said.

When they'd gone, Joseph sighed. 'I hope they treat him well,' he said. 'The lad's gone through enough, I should say.'

'He's a convict. He must have done something wrong to be sent to the hulks,' said Joey.

'It doesn't matter. He's been punished. It's up to the law now what happens to him.'

'Dad, I don't think he's really bad.' Emily told her father about Harry being accused of stealing an apple from a market stall. 'Just an apple, Dad. He was hungry. And they sentenced him to seven years.'

Joseph nodded. 'It's that gang are the baddies. Did you see the bruises on his arms?'

'On his back, too,' Emily said.

Emily was pleased her brother seemed somewhat mollified hearing this. She understood how he felt and was proud of him in a way – he'd sounded so grownup speaking up in defence of his family. She smiled at him as he shrugged and sat down near the fire.

'Nothing we can do now.' Joseph rubbed his hands. 'Well, what about some supper. I'm starved.'

Emily went to the stove and stirred the stew she'd begun to prepare. 'Sorry, Dad. I meant to have it ready for when you got home. Sit down. It won't be long.'

Joseph went over to his chair where Cissie had fallen asleep. He picked her up and set her on his lap. 'She didn't seem bothered by our visitor then?'

Emily smiled. 'She thought it was Joey at first, but no, she accepted him. Must have thought he was one of Joey's friends.'

'No friend of mine,' Joey said.

'Enough of that. You don't want to go frightening your sister with talk of convicts and bad men. And another thing – no word of this at school tomorrow.'

Joey stared defiantly at his father but, after a moment, he nodded.

Emily hoped he would obey. She didn't want any gossip about harbouring an escaped convict in their home, especially as she had started to make friends with her neighbours.

She didn't sleep well that night, worrying about the lad. Despite being a convicted criminal, she had sensed something innocent about him. The haunted look in his green eyes told of a hard life - and not just on the hulks. She'd seen the remains of old bruises when he'd taken his shirt off as well as the signs of malnutrition on his skinny body.

Sending him back to the hulks and from there to the penal settlement in Australia would not do any good. She sighed and turned over in bed. Nothing she could do about it but oh, how she wished she could help him. There was something about Harry Jones that had stolen a piece of her heart.

The next morning, Joseph had gone to work, and she was helping Cissie to dress while chivvying Joey to get ready for school when there was a knock at the door.

'It's me – Bill.' The policeman opened the door and came in. 'Come to tell you what we decided last night,' he said.

'Dad's not here,' Emily said.

'No, it's you I wanted to see.'

'Me? I'm not in trouble, am I?' Emily's heart began to thump. After all, she had helped a known convict. Bill was so friendly it was sometimes hard to remember he was a policeman.

'No, of course not.' Bill hastened to reassure her.

Emily gave a relieved sigh. She turned to Joey, who was hovering in the doorway. 'Time you was off to school,' she said sharply.

Joey scowled but after a glance from Bill, he started to walk away.

'And don't forget what Dad said – no gossip,' Emily called after him. She closed the door and invited Bill to sit down.

'Am I really not in trouble?'

'You did the right thing – the lad said it was you persuaded him to give himself up.'

'He was going to anyway – but he was so scared.'

'He was right to be. That gang are ruthless. It's my opinion they should have been hanged.'

'So, what will happen to them – and to Harry?' Emily put a hand to her throat. 'He hasn't been sent back to the hulks, I hope.'

'They'll be on the next ship to Australia.'

'Not Harry, too?'

'Don't worry. I think the magistrates believed his story of being bullied into helping them.' Bill paused. 'He'll have to stand up in court, though, while they decide. And he'll probably have to complete his sentence. But my sergeant told me they'll keep him in the cells here until there's another ship. With any luck, the gang will be long gone before the court case is done. If they think he drowned, they won't come looking for him out there in the Colony.'

Emily sighed. 'So, he'll still be transported then?'

'I'm sure of it. If he's lucky they won't add years to his sentence like they did with those gangsters. He's already done three years so by the time he gets to Botany Bay he'll only have less than four years to serve.'

Four years – a lifetime, thought Emily. 'Will he be able to come back to England then?'

'I doubt it. But let's wait and see what the court decides.'

Emily tried to hide her disappointment. Would she ever see him again? Something about the lad had struck a chord in her. Despite his small stature and unkempt appearance, he was well-spoken and polite. If she had met him in any other circumstance she would have thought him from a good family. What had happened to turn him into a convicted criminal? Stealing an apple couldn't be the whole story, she thought.

Bill stood up. 'I must be on my way,' he said. 'I'll let you know if there's any more news.'

Emily thanked him and said goodbye. As she went about her household tasks she couldn't stop thinking about the boy. Not a boy though, she thought. Harry was about her own age, almost a man. She wished that she could see him before he went away to let him know she'd be praying for him.

Chapter Five

After the excitement of the escaped prisoners' recapture and their subsequent appearance at the magistrates' court, life in St Paul's Close had settled down. Even Joey stopped talking about them and Emily, relieved that the gang who had terrorised Harry were now on their way to Botany Bay, tried to put the incident out of her mind.

She couldn't stop thinking about Harry though. Constable Brent had told her father that he was still being held in the cells below the court house, awaiting the decision of the magistrate. At least he was safe from the gang now, whatever happened to him. She had accepted that he would most likely be sent to Botany Bay. At least it was warm there she thought, shivering.

It had been several weeks, and winter now had the whole island in its grip. The wind whistled around the little cottage, and even from here, they could hear the huge waves battering the shore. Thanks to Joseph keeping them supplied with fuel for the range, the little cottage was reasonably cosy, although sometimes, with the wet washing draped over the clothes horse, the dampness in the air brought on Cissie's cough. Emily worried about her, remembering their mother's constant ill health when they'd lived on the hulks.

Cissie was a happy little girl though, and now that she was walking well, she had her hands in everything.

'Help, Em'ly,' she said, pulling towels off the clothes horse and attempting to fold them before they were dry. Emily tried not to get impatient, but some days, she was exhausted. She thanked God for Agnes, who was happy to look after Cissie while she went to the shops. She often wondered how the older woman had managed with two lively sons and a sick husband to look after.

Emily was relieved that Joey came straight home from school these days instead of going down to the shore with Bobby and getting into all sorts of mischief. He was becoming more responsible, bringing in wood for the fire and pumping buckets of water without being asked.

She was peeling potatoes for their dinner when there was a knock on the door. She wiped her hands on her apron and called out, 'Come in,' expecting to see Agnes. Her face paled when she saw Constable Brent on the doorstep.

'What's Joey been up to now?' she asked.

The policeman smiled. 'I'm not here about Joey,' he said. 'I thought you'd like to know that Harry Jones is up before the magistrate this morning.'

Emily gasped. 'What will happen to him?'

'I think they'll go easy on him. After all, he did turn himself in.' Bill Brent paused. 'I think he needs someone to speak up for him. I was wondering if you...'

'Will they let me?'

'I think so. You'll have to get there soon.' He pointed at Cissie. 'What about your sister though? They won't let you in the court house with her.'

'My neighbour will look after her.'

'Come along then.'

Today, there was a bitterly cold wind, and Emily wrapped Cissie up in her shawl before running across to Agnes's cottage and knocking on the door. Her friend opened it a crack, smiling when she saw who was there. 'Come in out of the cold,' she said, ushering them in and closing the door firmly.

She picked Cissie up and kissed the tip of her nose. 'Ooh, let's get you warmed up,' she said, turning to Emily. 'Cup of tea, love?'

'I haven't time. I'm going to the court.'

'Court?' Agnes gasped.

Emily reassured her. 'I'm not in trouble. It's Harry, he's up before the magistrate.'

Agnes knew the whole story and was concerned about Emily's involvement, but Emily had been able to reassure her. 'I'll tell you when I get back,' she said.

Bill Brent was waiting for her at the entrance to the close, and they hurried through the narrow streets to the imposing court house in the High Street.

Emily was pleased she had Bill with her as they were ushered into the court room and tried to ignore the Court official's suspicious looks.

When it was her turn to give evidence, she took a deep breath and spoke up clearly. The magistrate let her speak and didn't interrupt until she'd told the story of finding Harry, half-drowned and frightened out of his wits. 'They'd beaten him – I saw the bruises,' she said.

The magistrate nodded. 'Go on,' he said.

'He was bullied into going with that gang,' she said. 'He wanted to give himself up.' She looked up at the dock and gave Harry an encouraging smile.

The magistrate pursed his lips and turned to Bill. 'Is this true?'

Bill nodded. 'The family called me in and asked for my help. They are a respectable family, sir. The father works in the dockyard.'

After a brief consultation with his fellow court officers, the magistrate told Emily to stand down and wait outside.

* * *

Harry woke in his cell in the court basement with a sick feeling in his stomach. Today was the day his fate would be decided. He had been locked up here for weeks, but no one had told him what was to happen to him.

He stood up and stretched, took a deep breath and told himself it wouldn't be too bad. That policeman friend of the family who had helped him had said the worst that could happen would be for him to have to complete his sentence. He shuddered at the thought of going back to the hulks, but at least he wouldn't be bullied by Toothless and his gang. Constable Brent had told him they were on their way to Australia so he was safe.

The trembling in his stomach started to ease but the sound of the key turning in the lock brought back the queasiness. All very well the Williams family and even the constable being kind to him. He would have to face a magistrate and they were known for their harsh judgments. He was no stranger to the law and he dreaded the verdict.

He shrank back as the warder entered the cell, leg irons clanking in his meaty hands. 'Come along then. No use struggling,' the man said as he clamped the irons around Harry's ankles.

He had no intention of struggling. He wanted this over as soon as possible.

With the warder gripping his arm, he shuffled along the hallway and up the stairs to the dock, his head bent.

'Stand up straight,' the warder barked and pushed him forward.

Harry grasped the bar in front of him and raised his head, looking around the

Court with its high ceilings and dark wood furnishings. A gallery ran along one side of the huge room, and Harry wondered at the number of people gathered there.

The face he was hoping to see wasn't there, and his heart sank. So, Emily, the girl who had persuaded him to give himself up, had forgotten him. He couldn't blame her. He had been sure that once he was warm and dry with food in his belly, he could have got away again. But these weeks in the cell had given him time to think, and he acknowledged that Emily had been right. If only he could thank her for her kindness.

He trembled inwardly as he imagined making his way alone across those treacherous marshes pursued by dogs and marines with guns. Here, whatever the Court decided, he was safe from Toothless Tony and the gang.

He scarcely took in the magistrate's words. If only they would get on with it and give the verdict. His mind wandered, and he started to feel faint. As his eyes drooped, the policeman behind him nudged him in the ribs.

'Stand up straight,' the man whispered harshly.

Harry stood to attention, his heart racing when he heard the Magistrate's stern words, 'You do realise, young man, that the sentence for escapees is death by hanging?'

Harry's knees sagged, but the policeman grasped his arm and hauled him upright.

He became aware that the man was still speaking, and his knuckles whitened on the bar in front of him.

'You are a very fortunate young man to have friends speaking up for you. The jury will now retire to consider their verdict.'

Fortunate? Friends? Harry lifted his head and looked around, his heart thumping as his eyes met those incredible blue ones that had haunted his dreams. Emily? Was it really her? But there was no mistaking that smile.

Before he could react, he was hustled away. It seemed hours before the jury returned and he was once more in the dock. He looked around. Where was Emily? Had he imagined she was there?

The warder pinched his arm, and he stood to attention, aware that the magistrate was speaking.

'However,' the official continued, 'I have been assured that you gave yourself up voluntarily and that you were coerced into assisting the other escapees. Therefore, the sentence of this court is that you will be returned to the hulks to await a ship and complete your sentence in Australia.'

'Thank you, sir,' Harry whispered.

A court official stepped forward, banging a gavel on the bench and saying in a loud voice, 'Dismissed.'

Harry was hustled down the stairs and back to his cell. Halfway down, he glanced back to see Emily standing at the top. He still thought he was dreaming until, back in the cell, the warder bent to remove the shackles and said, 'You're a lucky young feller, having Bill Brent as well as a beautiful young lady to speak up for you.'

* * *

Emily paced the corridor, shooting anxious glances at the closed door. It seemed like hours before the door opened, and Bill joined her. To her relief, he was grinning. 'He's got to finish his sentence – four more years – in Botany Bay, I'm afraid.'

'Four years though,' Emily said. 'It's a long time.'

'But he won't have to go back to the hulks. They'll keep him here until there's a ship.'

'Can I see him before they take him away?' she asked.

'Not officially.' He pointed to the end of the corridor. 'Through that door there. If you hurry, you might get a glimpse, but don't tell anyone I said so.'

Emily rushed away and threw the door open. Harry, shackled between two policemen, was halfway down the stairs. He looked up at the sound of the door opening. A smile lit his face as he realised who was there.

Her heart pounded and she tried to smile back. 'Good luck,' she whispered.

One of the policemen tugged at his arm but Harry managed to say, 'Thank you,' before they dragged him away.

Emily stood at the top of the stairs, tears rolling down her face, only turning away when she heard the clang of the cell door echoing up the stairwell.

Bill was waiting for her and put his arm around her shoulders. 'Come along. Let's get you home.'

'Oh, Bill, you were right – four years in Botany Bay. Poor Harry, all for an apple.'

'But it could have been worse. At least he's away from that gang. Australia's a huge country. It's unlikely he'll run into them when he gets out there.'

Emily knew the policeman was trying to reassure her, but she wasn't convinced. She sighed. No use worrying about it. She knew she would probably never see Harry Jones again, but deep down she couldn't help hoping for a miracle. There was something about the skinny ginger-haired lad that had wormed his way into her heart.

* * *

Harry wouldn't say that it was exactly lucky not to be going back to the stinking hulks, but he couldn't complain. And not exactly lucky to be shipped off across the world to Australia. He just hoped that he wouldn't have to wait too long for a ship. Locked in his cell again he couldn't help feeling better. In court, the beautiful Emily had spoken on his behalf, and she had smiled at him and wished him luck. He knew he would never see her again but the memory would sustain him through the long years that remained of his sentence.

Chapter Six

Waking a few days after the court case, Emily realised It was nearly Christmas, their second in St Paul's Close. She was determined to make it special for her younger siblings. Last year, they had still been grieving for their mother, and none of them had the heart to celebrate. She had done her best to provide a special meal and had sewn a doll for Cissie. Joey, despite protesting that he was too old for toys, was delighted with the little sailing boat carved by their father. But any spare money had gone to make the cottage more homelike.

Now, a colourful curtain hung at the window, and she had stuffed an old pillowcase with rags to make a cushion for Dad's chair. He said it helped his aching back after a hard day at work. She had bought a pine table from the second-hand furniture dealer in the High Street, as well as a couple of rickety chairs so that the children could sit up at the table to eat instead of sitting on the floor.

She looked around with satisfaction at the cosy room, pleased with what she had achieved. The smile faded as she realised that, despite earning extra money, there was little chance of a happy Christmas for Joey and Cissie. She sighed and reached up to the shelf over the range, taking down the rusty tin where she kept her savings. She tipped the coins onto the table and counted them up – more than she'd thought. She would be able to buy some treats for the children. She scraped the money up and put it back in the tin. She would buy the Christmas goodies nearer the day. If Joey knew sweets were hidden away, he would be tempted to sneak a few. Besides, she had enough from Dad's last wages to buy flour and sultanas to make a cake and get something for their evening meal.

It had stopped raining, and she decided to go to the shops straight away, but it was still too bitter to take Cissie, who had developed another sniffy cold. She hated relying on Agnes too much, but she knew the older woman loved looking after the toddler.

She put her coat on and wrapped Cissie in her shawl. Agnes opened the door and welcomed them in, as usual offering a cup of tea.

'No thanks. I must get to the grocer's – I need some flour. I hope you're not too busy to keep an eye on Cissie for a while. I don't want to take her out while she has this cold.'

Agnes laughed. 'Never too busy to take care of this little angel. She brightens my days, so she does.'

'Thank you, Agnes. Can I get you anything from the shops?'

'Could you get me some tea – only an ounce mind. It's so expensive, but I use the leaves more than once to make it last.' She thrust a couple of coppers into Emily's hand.

Hunching her shoulders against the cold wind, Emily hurried round the corner into the High Street. As she passed the court house she shuddered, remembering her ordeal a few weeks ago. Not as bad as what Harry went through, she thought. Was he still in the cells, or was he even now on a ship sailing towards that unknown land?

Maybe she would ask Bill if he had any news. She knew she should put Harry out of her mind, but he'd impressed her with his manners and a genuine wish to shun a life of crime – not that his crime had been that awful, she thought. Most of those imprisoned on the hulks - murderers and thieves - thoroughly deserved their fate.

She sighed, knowing she might never see Harry again but she could think of him in Australia – a country she knew little about, except that it had weird animals and plants, was hot most of the time, and was vastly bigger than England.

She shook the thought away and entered the grocers, returning Mrs Collins's greeting and assuring her that Cissie was well. 'Just a cold,' she said.

She bought flour, sultanas, a few other items, and, after counting her change, two ounces of tea for Agnes. Her friend would protest, of course, and try to insist on paying for the extra, but Emily would be firm. It was little enough thanks for the times she had looked after Cissie.

She still had a little money left and she popped into the chemist next door for some cough syrup for Cissie. It would help her sister to sleep better.

As she came out, she bumped into Mark Thompson, the school master.

She apologised and made to push past him but he said, 'Do you have a moment, Miss Williams?'

She hesitated, hoping that he wasn't about to complain about Joey. 'I'm sorry, I can't stop. I've left Cissie with my neighbour.'

'It won't take long. I was going to call on you, but as we've met...

'What is it?' Emily shuffled her feet, anxious to get out of the wind

'I was wondering if you'd thought any more about coming to work at the school.'

'I'm not sure. I don't have a lot of time with looking after the house and Cissie and helping Agnes with the laundry.'

'If you worked for me, you wouldn't have to do laundry.' He seized one of her hands. 'It's not right that you have to work so hard, especially in this bitter cold weather. Look at you – hands so red and sore.'

Emily snatched her hand away. What business was it of his?

Before she could protest, he said, 'I'm sorry. It's just that I see a bright, intelligent girl, trying to do her best for her family. I want to help.'

Emily found her voice. 'It's very kind of you, sir. I'll think about it. Now, I must get home – lots to do.'

'Yes, I should get back too. I've left Miss Cook in charge. I had to collect my wife's medicine. She's been very poorly.'

'I'm sorry, sir. I hope she's better soon.' With that she hurried away, turning back at the corner to see him standing there, gazing after her.

On her way to Agnes's house, she was still pondering the school master's job offer. She remembered that when Joey had first started at the school, Mrs Thompson had been her husband's helper. She hadn't realised she was ill and for a moment she felt sorry that she had not agreed. It must be hard for him, looking after a sick wife and running the school.

When she got back, Agnes was sitting by the fire with Cissie on her lap, and Emily thought she looked tired.

'I've got the tea,' she said cheerily. 'Shall I put it in the caddy for you? I can put the kettle on if you like.'

'That would be lovely, dear,' Agnes said.

Emily made a pot of tea, being sparing with the tea leaves despite the extra she had bought. She set the pot and a cup down on the table and bent to lift Cissie from her friend's lap.

'Enjoy your tea,' she said. 'Sorry, I can't stop – so much to do, and Joey will be home soon.'

Before Agnes could protest, she wrapped the shawl around her little sister and opened the door, hurrying across the yard and into the warmth of home.

Thank goodness I banked the fire up before going out, she thought, picking up the poker. She rattled it against the bars, stirring up a blaze.

Cissie stood transfixed by the flames, holding her hands out to the warmth.

Now that she had plenty of flour, Emily set about making a suet roll with chopped onions and bacon pieces, a filling dish to keep out the cold. She would make the cake later.

As she rolled out the suet pastry, she looked down at her hands and thought about what Mr Thompson had said. She had been very annoyed. What a cheek, making such personal remarks. How dare he. But her annoyance faded as she realised he was right. Constant immersion in hot water and washing soda was already having an effect. She had always worked hard and it was impossible to keep her hands and nails as pretty as they had once been, despite applications of goose grease when it was available, but they were getting worse.

Seeing how Agnes suffered had brought home to her that it wasn't just looks. Her friend had been doing laundry for years, and her fingers were gnarled and twisted with rheumatism, making it hard to do manual tasks. Added to that was the constant pain. I don't want to end up like that, Emily thought. It wasn't a selfish thought. She had to be fit to look after her family.

Perhaps she should think again about Mr Thompson's offer. But she didn't want to let Agnes down.

* * *

The next day was bright and sunny but still cold and Emily dressed Cissie warmly in the coat she had bought from the second-hand shop on the High Street. She decided to take her sister with her today. It would do both of them good to get out in the fresh air. Tomorrow it would probably be damp and misty again, as it was so often near the marshes. Besides, she couldn't expect Agnes to look after Cissie all the time.

The little girl was growing fast and walking well now, and she kept tugging on Emily's hand, trying to run. She chattered away, pointing to everything they passed – not that it was a very interesting walk with the tall brooding wall of the dockyard on one side and the shabby shops and naval businesses on the other. Emily had always preferred to walk down to the water to look at the ships, but she hated seeing the hulks and picturing the prisoners held there. She prayed that Harry was now on a ship and sailing far away.

Lost in thought, she pushed open the grocer's door, as someone pulled from the other side and she almost tumbled into the shop.

'I'm so sorry. Are you all right?'

Emily looked up into the concerned face of Mark Thompson.

She nodded and bent to make sure Cissie hadn't fallen.

'I'm glad I've seen you again,' the school master said. 'I still need an assistant. Have you decided whether to come and work at the school?'

'I thought your wife would be back to work by now,' Emily said.

Mark shook his head, a frown creasing his forehead. 'I'm afraid she's no better. The doctor said it will be some time until she is fit again.'

'I'm so sorry.' Emily thought quickly. 'I don't have time to discuss it at the moment, but could I call at the school later this afternoon?'

'You mean you will take the job?'

'I haven't decided. But perhaps we can work something out. I can't let Agnes down but...'

He grasped her hand. 'Thank you. It would be such a help.'

Emily pulled her hand away and said, 'I must get on.'

'Sorry. I didn't mean to detain you.' He pushed open the shop door and held it for her. 'Until later then.'

She nodded and ushered Cissie into the shop, wondering if she really should take the job. She had little enough time to herself as it was.

Mrs Collins, the grocer's wife greeted her with a smile and came round the counter to make a fuss of Cissie.

'My, she's growing into a little beauty,' she said, stroking Cissie's blonde curls.

The little girl smiled up at her, and Mrs Collins produced a toffee from her apron pocket.

'Say thank you, lovey,' Emily said.

Cissie was too busy unwrapping the sweet and Emily thanked the grocer's wife and said, 'I'd like some cheese, and a pat of butter, please.'

Mrs Collins weighed the goods and wrapped them. 'Anything else, dear?'

Emily glanced across at Mr Collins, who was presiding over the bacon slicer, wishing she could afford a couple of thick rashers. The grocer grinned as if reading her thoughts. 'I've got some nice bacon scraps,' he said.

'Thank you, I'll have some please.' She would make a suet roll again. It was cheap and filling and both Joey and her father enjoyed it.

'Tuppence worth?'

'Yes please.'

She put the shopping in her string bag, paid and said goodbye to the couple.

As she made her way home, she wished she could afford to buy more from the little shop. The Collinses were so kind and generous. It occurred to her that if she took up Mr Thompson's offer, she would be able to do just that.

The prospect of earning more money made her mind up for her. She would take the job. The extra money would ensure they had a good Christmas. She was sure she'd manage to fit it in with the laundry and looking after the family.

That afternoon, she left Cissie with Agnes and walked to the school. On the walk, she imagined cooking thick rashers for their tea with eggs and baked beans instead of making stodgy suet rolls with barely a taste of bacon.

As she neared the building, she could hear chanting and she smiled, remembering how her mother had taught her the times tables. She hoped Joey was paying attention.

She walked to the side entrance and knocked on the door. There was no reply, and she wondered if she ought to come back after school had finished. Mr Thompson must be busy in the classroom. Just as she went to turn away, the chanting stopped, and a few minutes later, the door opened.

'Come in, Miss Williams. I was beginning to think you'd changed your mind.' Mark Thompson beckoned her into his office and offered her a chair.

She sat down, perching on the edge and clasping her hands in front of her.

It suddenly occurred to her that she had no idea what sort of work he was offering. Perhaps he only wanted a cleaner, she thought. But no, surely he wouldn't have mentioned her workworn hands if that was so. She was so nervous she hardly took in the head master's next words. She looked up in surprise when he said, 'I know you have no experience of teaching, but you are intelligent, and I'm sure you would be fine helping the little ones with their letters.'

She swallowed and said, 'I'm not sure, sir.'

'Joseph has told me how you continued your mother's teaching with him after she died. He is coming along well – thanks to the good grounding he had with you.'

'Thank you, sir. I will give it a try.'

Mark nodded. 'Good. And then perhaps you could keep the register and collect the dinner money. That would be a great help.'

Emily frowned. 'But I couldn't work for the whole school day, sir. I can't expect Agnes to look after Cissie for such a long time.'

'Perhaps just the mornings then.' He stood up and leaned across the desk to shake her hand. 'We'll work something out. Start after the Christmas break.'

'Yes, sir. Thank you, sir.' As he ushered her out, Emily's head whirled. Was she doing the right thing? Well, she had time to talk it over with Dad. If he approved, she would go ahead and see how she got on. She couldn't deny it would be good to have a bit of extra money.

Chapter Seven

Harry woke to the sound of shouting and rattling chains. The door to his cell flew open and he cringed. He had got used to the peace and quiet of the court house cells. As the only prisoner, he was well treated and it had been a shock to be told he was returning to the hulks.

'Only for a few days, son. A ship's on its way from Gravesend and will call in to pick you and a few others up,' one of the warders had told him.

The few days had turned to weeks, and Harry began to think they had forgotten him. Life in Australia couldn't be worse than being shut up in this stinking hole, he thought. The only consolation was the absence of Toothless's gang, but the warders were still bullies, and the food was sparse and almost inedible. He tried to tell himself things must be better in the penal colony, but he didn't really believe it.

He huddled in the corner, watching as the warders fitted ankle chains to his cell mates. One of them loomed over Harry, pulling him to his feet.

'You too, lad. Come along.' He fastened the heavy chains around Harry's ankles and hustled him out into the gangway. 'Hurry along there. Tide's on the turn.'

Up on deck, Harry looked about him, gasping at the sight of the tall ship moored alongside the hulk. Sailors swarmed in the rigging, getting the ship ready to set sail.

So this was it, he thought. They were on their way.

He shivered in his thin clothes, and the warder pushed him forward, laughing. 'Don't worry, lad. It'll be hot enough where you're going – hotter than hell.'

As the prisoners were hustled towards the hatch that led down into the bowels of the ship, he glanced back at the shore, picturing the cosy little cottage and the family who had been so kind to him. His heart raced as he caught a glimpse of someone standing on the dockside, golden locks gleaming in the sunshine. It was her - Emily. She raised her hand, and he was sure she was smiling.

His last thought as the hatch closed over him, plunging the hold into darkness, was that, come what may, he would find his way back to the island – and Emily. Four years wasn't so long, he told himself.

* * *

There were many times over the next weeks and months when Harry's optimism waned, and he almost sank into the depths of despair – almost but not quite. Crouched in the dark of the hold, only seeing daylight when the hatch was opened and food was handed down to the men, he listened to the groans of the surrounding prisoners and vowed not to give in. Many of them succumbed to sea sickness, much to the amusement of the sailors and marines.

'Hardly at sea yet,' Harry heard one of them scoff.

He thanked God that the motion of the ship didn't seem to affect him too much. The smell was the hardest to bear.

He had lost count of how many days they'd been at sea when the hatch was opened and bright sunlight streamed in.

At the head of the gangway stood a marine, his rifle pointed menacingly at the men below. 'Right lads, stand up,' he shouted. He gestured to a warder. 'Get those chains off. No chance of escape now we're in the middle of the ocean unless they want to try swimming home.' He gave a raucous laugh.

When the chains were off, the prisoners were ushered up on deck in batches. 'Thirty minutes exercise – keep moving,' they were ordered.

Stumbling a little, his legs weak from days of inactivity, Harry made his way up on deck, blinking in the strong sunlight. He looked up at the sails billowing in the breeze, smelled the fresh salty air and felt the sun on his skin. For a few moments, he was almost happy. He had heard that the voyage was dangerous but it hadn't been too bad so far and now, here he was, breathing in fresh air.

The thirty minutes was soon up, the men were hustled below once more and another group allowed on deck. When they were all back in the hold, thankfully minus the ankle chains, the hatch was slammed shut and they were in darkness once again.

The periods of exercise lasted for three days, and the wind rose on the fourth day. Huge waves broke over the decks, and the prisoners were locked below. Harry lost track of how long the storm lasted. Now he, too, succumbed to sea sickness. He'd never felt so ill and like many of his fellow prisoners, he prayed for death.

Would he ever reach Australia, let alone ever see Emily again? A lurch of the ship as it breasted a huge wave threw him against the bulkhead and he lost consciousness. His last thought was of Emily, her sweet smile and those incredible blue eyes.

Chapter Eight

Emily enjoyed working at the school, although she didn't have a lot to do with the pupils unless one of them was unwell or fell over in the playground and needed a bandage for a grazed knee. Mark Thompson seemed to have forgotten that she was to help teaching the infants. Not that she minded. The office work was interesting and didn't take up too much of her time. After doing the laundry with Agnes in the morning, it was good to have a change of scene in the afternoon. At least now she did not have to deliver the clean washing to the big houses near the Dockyard Church. Instead, she gave Joey and Bobby the job to keep them out of mischief. They were pleased to earn a few pennies after school. Dad had made a cart for them out of scrap wood and fixed some old pram wheels to it.

Emily's school job mainly consisted of tidying the paperwork which littered Mark's desk, helping with dishing up the school dinners and setting out the books for each lesson. She also marked the register and collected the dinner money.

The week leading up to the Christmas break was hectic and she had little time for cooking and making preparations for the big day. Never mind, she thought, I'll have my pay and I can have a real shopping spree.

She preferred working alone and only ventured into Mark's office when he was teaching in the classroom. She couldn't really put her finger on why that should be as she really admired him, especially his dedication to the children in his care.

He was always polite and respectful, always addressing her as Miss Williams except when there was no one else around. Then it was 'Emily' and he had asked her to call him 'Mark.'

'Education is so important,' he often said, and Emily agreed with him.

She enjoyed their occasional conversations. It was good to talk to someone about subjects other than housekeeping, shopping and the price of bread. But after she had been at the school for a few months, she felt he was becoming a bit too friendly. He made no secret of his admiration for her and how she cared for her family.

'You work so hard,' he said. 'And you are a proper little mother to Joseph and Cissie.'

Perhaps she was reading too much into it but she was wary of becoming involved with a married man, especially one with a sick wife. She had met Jemima Thompson several times when she had first started work at the school and they had got on well. Then she fell ill and Emily took on more of her work. She had been ill for some weeks now and Emily wasn't sure what was wrong with her.

The last time she asked after her, Mark frowned and said in a low voice, 'I don't think she'll ever get better.'

'I'm so sorry,' Emily had said, laying her hand on his arm in sympathy.

He had seized her hand. 'I know you understand. It's so good to have someone to talk to.'

She had pulled away and murmured a non-committal response.

He apologised at once and started to shuffle some papers on his desk. Sensing his embarrassment, Emily excused herself and hurried away.

Since then, she had tried to avoid being alone with him. If she had to talk to him, she would always ask after Jemima as if reminding him of his obligations and married status.

The problem was, she did find him attractive, although in the back of her mind, she always carried a memory of a skinny ginger-haired lad with green eyes and a wide smile. Harry Jones had stolen a piece of her heart, and she prayed nightly for his safety, although she knew there was no chance of them ever meeting again.

* * *

That Christmas was the happiest the Williams family had spent since their mother's death. Emily was proud of the way she had learned to deal with the complicated oven. She hadn't used it often because it used so much wood to keep it up to the right temperature. Now that she had a little more money, she didn't worry about how much she used and had even splashed out on a bag of coal.

She'd baked a rich fruit cake that had turned out well. Pity she couldn't afford to ice it but she managed to decorate it with a few sprigs of holly, kindly donated by the greengrocer.

She had shown Cissie and Joey how to make paperchains from pages torn from a couple of old magazines given to her by Mark Thompson. Everyone was so generous, she thought. On the last day of term, when he handed her the envelope with her wages, he also thrust a small package into her hand.

'Something for the children,' he said.

She wanted to protest but he insisted she accept it. 'Have a good Christmas, Emily, my dear,' he said.

She thanked him although she was reluctant to take gifts from a married man and she was embarrassed by his familiarity.

As she hurried home to complete her Christmas preparations, she told herself he didn't mean anything by it. But she still felt uncomfortable. Perhaps she would think again about resuming her work at the school after the holidays.

* * *

On Christmas Day the little cottage rang with laughter. Emily had invited Agnes to spend the day with them and she surprised them all by standing up after the meal and singing an old music hall song.

Loud applause greeted her, and she curtsied, almost falling over with the effort. 'Oh, it's me knees,' she said, but her voice was filled with laughter.

'Dad's turn now,' Joey shouted.

He didn't take much persuading, and they all joined in with the sea shanties he had learned working on the boats.

Emily looked around at her little family, and her heart was filled with love. There was one person missing, and she whispered a little prayer that Harry was safe and well.

She noticed that Cissie's eyes were drooping and she said, 'Time this little one was in bed.'

'Me too,' said Agnes. 'It's been a lovely day but I'm worn out.'

Dad stood up and stretched. 'I'll see you across the yard. It's a bit frosty out there. Don't want you slipping on the cobbles.'

'Thank you, kind sir,' Agnes said with a smile.

There was a flurry of thanks and goodbyes and Emily carried Cissie up to bed.

104

To her surprise, Joey followed without the usual protests.

By the time Dad returned, the children were asleep, and Emily had tidied the room.

'I was going to do that,' Dad said. 'You must be worn out.'

'I am a bit tired,' Emily admitted. 'But it was a good day.'

'It surely was. You're a good girl, Em,' he said. 'Now, off you go to bed. I'll see to the range.'

She yawned and stretched and without protest she mounted the stairs and, within minutes she was curled up alongside Cissie and fast asleep.

Chapter Nine

Despite her reservations about working at the school, Emily had changed her mind and returned after the Christmas holiday. She had so loved being able to treat the family to a special Christmas and she had got used to having extra money to spend on them. Cissie was growing so quickly and it was good to be able to buy her nice dresses, albeit second-hand.

To her relief, she hadn't seen much of Mark lately. His wife had taken a turn for the worse and he spent as much time with her as he could, leaving most of the teaching to Miss Cook.

Emily found herself dealing with more of the administrative work and she enjoyed it. She still helped Agnes with the laundry but she sometimes felt guilty for preferring to be in the warm office rather than fighting with wet sheets against a freezing wind.

Today, however, there was a feeling of spring in the air and Emily breathed deeply as she crossed the yard to Agnes's cottage. It was laundry day and she smiled, looking up into the blue sky.

A good drying day, she thought, after those days of blustery rain and cold wind,

She would help her friend to get the sheets out on the line and then hurry around to the school in time to help with the pupils' dinners.

Cissie laughed and paused to splash in the puddles that still lay in the shady part of the yard.

Emily called out to her to hurry up. To distract her, she said, 'Come and say hello to kitty.' Agnes had recently given a home to a scrawny tabby cat, and her new friend enchanted Cissie.

The little girl's face lit up, and she abandoned the puddles, running across to Agnes's house.

The door opened, and Cissie rushed inside, calling, 'Here, kitty, kitty.'

Agnes laughed. 'She don't bother to say hello to me these days,' she said.

Emily joined in the laughter. 'It's good to see her so lively. I was quite worried about her over the winter, but the fine weather seems to have perked her up.'

Agnes nodded. 'Let's hope it lasts.' She looked up at the sky. 'At least till we get the washing dry today.'

Emily followed her into the cottage, noting that her friend had made a start with filling the copper with buckets of water. She had also lit the fire under the copper and steam was already rising from the water.

Cissie was chasing the cat, and Emily made her go to the living room and sit down in the corner. 'We don't want you getting scalded with the hot water. Stay over there.' She reached into her bag and brought out a rolled-up scrap of material attached to a piece of string. 'Here, play with Kitty,' she said.

The little girl was soon involved in a game with the cat, and Emily set to, pummelling the sheets on the washboard and then rinsing them in cold water. Then, it was time to take everything outside to the mangle. Agnes turned the handle while Emily fed the heavy, wet sheets through the rollers. When it was done, Emily sighed and stretched, her hands on her aching back.

Before they started hanging the washing out, Emily went indoors to check on Cissie. Her sister was still playing with the cat and seemed happy enough. The little girl felt just as at home in Agnes's house as her own.

When she went outside again, Agnes struggled to hang the sheets on the line that stretched across the courtyard. 'You're not supposed to do that. It's my job,' Emily said, lifting one end of the heavy material that almost dragged on the ground.

'Oh, I hate feeling so useless,' Agnes fretted.

'You're not useless. You've done your share of the work. Now, do me a favour and go inside to keep Cissie company. And while you're in there, put the kettle on. I'm dying for a cuppa.'

'If you insist,' Agnes said, but with a smile.

'I do. Now go on. I'll finish off here.'

Soon, the washing was blowing in the breeze and, with any luck, would be dry by the time Emily returned from school.

Agnes had made a pot of tea and Emily sat down for a few minutes to enjoy it. 'I'll have to go soon,' she said. 'I'm helping with the children's dinners today.' She delved into her bag and brought out a tin of corned beef and half a loaf. 'This is for yours and Cissie's dinners,' she said. 'I can't thank you enough for looking after her while I'm at work.'

'No need to thank me. I've said before, she's a joy to look after. She brightens up my day.'

Emily finished her tea and put the cup on the draining board. 'Better be off.' She paused at the door. 'Be a good girl, Cissie, and,' - turning to Agnes with a smile, 'Don't you dare bring that washing in. I'll do it when I get back.'

To her relief, she didn't see Mark when she arrived at the school, and she was kept busy helping Miss Clark. Mrs Brown, the woman who usually came in to serve the school meals, was unwell, but Emily liked Miss Clark and enjoyed working with her.

When she looked up to see Joey holding out his plate she smiled and was about to speak. But he ducked his head and moved along the queue. She realised he was embarrassed having his sister working at the school and he scarcely acknowledged her when their paths crossed. But he could have at least acknowledged her, she thought.

The children soon finished eating and went out into the playground for a few minutes exercise before starting afternoon lessons. Emily started to clear the dishes and Miss Cook said, 'I must get the children into the classroom. I hope you don't mind doing all this washing up on your own.'

'Of course not.'

'Let's hope Mrs Brown will be back tomorrow.' Before she left, Miss Cook handed Emily an envelope. 'Could you take this to Mr Thompson? It's the dinner money.'

Emily nodded and tucked the envelope in her pocket. She hoped the head master's office would be empty. She would just leave it on his desk.

She opened the office door quietly and peeped in. She scurried across to Mark's desk and put the money on his blotter. Perhaps she should leave a note. No. He would know what it was.

As she turned away, she noticed a large book lying open on a table by the door. The map spread across both pages, and there was one word at the top in large letters. 'Australia'. Her heart leapt, and she breathed, 'Harry.'

Was he there yet? Constable Brent had told her that the voyage took four months, sometimes longer. He must have surely arrived by now. What was life like for the convicts? If only it were possible to exchange letters. She leaned over the map, reading the words around the edge. Sydney, Botany Bay, Port McQuarrie. There were very few words in the centre of the map. The word 'Desert' covered a large part of the middle.

Lost in thought, curious about this strange country, she didn't hear someone come in until he spoke.

'Ah, Miss Williams - Emily, I see you are interested in geography.'

She gasped. 'Oh, Mr Thompson, I'm sorry.' She gestured towards his desk. 'I brought the dinner money.'

'And was waylaid by the atlas.' He smiled. 'Well, given your adventures with the convict last year, I can understand your interest in Australia.'

She sensed a slightly sarcastic edge to his voice and shook her head. 'Not just that,' she protested. 'I was curious as to what the country is like.'

'A most inhospitable place, I hear. Mostly forest or desert except for around the coast. The convicts are kept hard at work building settlements and roads.' He paused and looked intently at her. 'I take it your interest is in the young convict you spoke up for in court.'

'Not at all,' Emily said firmly. She didn't know why she denied it except that she had a feeling Mark didn't approve. She moved towards the door, but he stopped her, and she was proved right when he said, 'I would not advise you to show your interest. You spoke up for him in court, and that was understandable. However, respectable people would not understand. Besides, he won't be back - that is, if he has survived the voyage.'

Emily nodded and hurried away, swallowing the lump in her throat. That last remark had hit home, but she had to admit he was right. She had accepted she would not see Harry again and she should get on with her life. She had so much to be thankful for - a home, a loving family and a respectable job.

* * *

Emily did not see Mark for several days after their encounter, and she tried to put their conversation out of her mind. What business was it of his anyway? She was just an employee, and so long as she did her work to his satisfaction, her private life had nothing to do with him. He was right of course. In time people would forget her connection with the escaped convicts. Working at the school was a respectable occupation and in time people would accept that. She must try to forget Harry and get on with her life.

When she got back to St Paul's Close after a busy afternoon at the school, Agnes greeted her at the door, and Emily could see at once that something was wrong.

'Cissie?' she gasped, her hand to her mouth.

Agnes shook her head. 'She's fine. But...' she jerked her head in the direction of Emily's house. 'Your dad's home. His mate Lenny and another bloke brought him.'

'What's happened?'

'I think he's had a fall or something. Lenny and another bloke were helping him along.'

'I must see him'. Emily pushed her way past Agnes and reached for Cissie, who was playing on the floor with the kitten.

'No, love. Leave her with me. Go and see to your dad.'

Emily bent and gave Cissie a quick kiss, then rushed out of the door.

Joseph was slumped in the armchair, his face grey, his breath coming in quick gasps. She recognised Lenny Lomax, her father's workmate, from when they had lived on the hulks. He was standing near Joseph, running his hands through his hair, his face etched with concern. The other man had returned to work.

'What happened, Lenny?' Without waiting for an answer, she turned to her father. 'Dad, are you all right?'

Her father looked up at her, his eyes clouded, a look of confusion on his face. He mumbled something, and Emily bent to try to catch his words, but nothing made sense. She turned to Lenny. 'What happened?'

'I'm sorry, love. It was an accident. We were working down in the hold and he tripped, banged his head on the bulkhead. He seemed fine at first. The overseer took a look at him, got the naval surgeon. But he said there was no real damage. He'll be OK with a bit of rest.'

Emily looked at her father and turned back to Lenny. 'He doesn't look all right to me. Don't tell me they tried to make him go back to work.'

'Joe told them he was OK. He wanted to carry on but...' He paused and shrugged. 'I don't know. He started shaking, and he passed out. Then he came round after a few minutes, but he was all confused like.'

Emily sunk to her knees beside her father, stroking his hair. 'Oh, Dad, please talk to me.'

He mumbled something but she couldn't make out the words. She ran her fingers over his hair and felt a raised bump just above his right temple. She parted his hair and saw a livid bruise with a darker line bisecting it. He must have hit his head on something sharper than the wooden beam. She thought it might have been a nail or something sharp protruding from the bulkhead. 'Didn't the doctor see this?' she demanded.

Lenny shrugged. 'I'm not sure. They thought he wasn't badly hurt, but they told me and my mate to help him home. Sam's gone back to work, but I thought I'd better stay with him.'

'Thank you, Lenny. That was kind.'

'I think the boss thought he'd be back at work tomorrow. Just a little bump on the head.'

'I don't think so, do you?'

'You're right. He doesn't look too good, does he.'

'Thanks for bringing him home anyway.' Emily smiled at him. 'Would you mind stopping with him for a few minutes. I must go over and fetch my little sister. She's with a neighbour.'

'A pleasure. Can I do anything for you while I'm here.'

'No thanks. My brother will be home soon. He'll help.'

Agnes was waiting by the door, anxious to hear what had happened. Emily hurriedly explained and said she must get back to her father. 'Thanks for looking after Cissie. I'll pop back tomorrow and let you know how Dad is. Hopefully, a good night's sleep will see him right.'

But as she took Cissie's hand and entered her own home, she knew deep down she was being unduly optimistic.

Chapter Ten

Joe Williams did not recover. It wasn't just a bump on the head. Whatever had caused the gash had probably penetrated far deeper into the brain, causing the tremors and confusion.

Spring turned to summer, and Joe became increasingly confused and less able to do anything for himself. Emily did her best to care for him, but now, without his wages, the need to earn enough to keep the family from destitution meant she had to leave her father alone for hours.

The dockyard authorities refused to take responsibility for Joe's condition, saying he should have been more careful. No one was at fault. Lenny, who called around often to see how Joe was doing, explained that if he had been killed, there might have been some compensation.

Joey was a tower of strength and helped as much as he could. He was growing up fast and, at the end of the summer term insisted on leaving school.

One evening Mark turned up at the cottage saying he needed to speak to Emily's father. He knew about the accident and appreciated that Emily sometimes had to take time off to care for Joe.

She invited him in and offered to make tea. He accepted and drew up a chair near to Joe's armchair. Emily could see that he was shocked at the older man's condition. Joe had been a well-built man, his face and arms tanned from working outdoors. Now, he was a shadow of his former self, his skin grey and lined, his hair once dark, now white.

'Well, Mr Williams, how are you today?' Mark said in a falsely cheerful voice.

Joe's reply was an unintelligible mumble accompanied by a trickle of spittle running down his chin.

Mark turned to Emily. 'Why didn't you tell me how bad he was?' he demanded.

'It's hard to talk about,' Emily said. 'At first I hoped he'd get better but...'

'I'm so sorry.' He stood up and came towards her, grasping her hands. 'You poor child. I wish there were something I could do.'

She snatched her hands away. 'There's nothing anyone can do,' she snapped. 'You shouldn't have come.'

'I thought I'd be able to talk to Mr Williams. I didn't realise...'

'What is there to talk about?'

'Your brother. I wanted to persuade your father to allow him to stay on at school. He's a bright lad, so much potential.'

'And now you see why that's impossible. Joey needs to find work.'

'Let me help. I hate to see you struggling.'

Emily bit back an angry retort. How could she let a man – any man, let alone a married man with a sick wife – help her financially? Maybe that's not what he meant, but it was what other people would think. She took a deep breath. Perhaps he meant well and she could not afford to upset him. She needed the school job, little as it paid. She forced a smile. 'I know you mean to be kind but we are managing. Now, I have to see to our meal so perhaps you'd better leave.'

'Very well.' He stood and fastened his jacket. He turned to Joseph and said, 'It was good to see you, Mr Williams. I will try to call again.'

Emily could see that he was struggling to act as if this was a normal social call and she appreciated his tact. She saw him out, and as he hurried away, she spotted Lenny Lomax approaching through the archway. Mark stopped and said something to him, and then he was gone.

Lenny had been a frequent visitor since Joe's accident, chatting to him about the goings-on in the dockyard and gossiping about his workmates. It didn't seem to bother him that he got no response.

He often brought wood for the fire as Joe had always done and would also pump a pail of water for Emily to save her from having to do it.

Lenny had no family, and he had told Emily he lived in lodgings with a slatternly landlady who didn't feed him well. 'I pay her enough, but she makes excuses when I complain,' he said with a sigh. 'If only I could find somewhere else, but lodgings in Marine Town are too dear, not to mention too far from work, and there's nothing round here.'

Emily felt sorry for him and sometimes asked him to join them for a meal if she had enough to go round. He always thanked her and complimented her on her cooking and she soon found that she looked forward to his visits. It helped to take some of the pressure off caring for her father. None of his old workmates bothered now.

* * *

The summer term was drawing to a close and Emily was worried that work at the school would come to an end. How would she manage with only the small amount Agnes paid her for helping with the laundry?

Her father had developed a cough that wouldn't go away despite the summer weather. Much of her wages went on medicine to try to help him. But his health was failing, and she dreaded the winter months. She prayed that Joey would find work soon, although she wished it wasn't necessary. Was it only a year ago that they had been making such plans for his future?

She felt a little apprehensive when Mark called her in on the last day of term. Was she about to be dismissed? But he greeted her with a smile and hastened to put her mind at rest.

'Obviously there isn't as much to do in the holidays but I still have enough to keep you busy for a few hours a week.'

'That's good news, Mark,' she said. 'What will I be doing?'

'I'd like you to sort out my bookshelves. Many of the books are old and dilapidated. The children sometimes treat them a bit carelessly - pages get pulled loose and the covers bent. The school can't afford to replace them, but I'm sure you can repair them and give them a bit more use.' He smiled at her. 'Would you be willing to try that?'

I'm sure I could cope with that, Emily thought. After all, I'm very good at mending and making use of old household stuff. She nodded. 'I'll certainly try,' she said.

'You realise I can't pay as much as you've been earning,' Mark said.

'It will be a help – and I've still got the laundry work,' she said.

He pursed his lips. 'I hope your brother gets work soon – then you won't have to do that,' he said.

Emily bit her lip, stifling a retort. So, it was all right for her to work for him but not to help out her friend. He was such a snob. What did it matter? Both were honest jobs.

* * *

During the first week of the summer break Joey was such a help, chopping wood for the range – even in the warm summer weather it had to be kept alight to heat water and cook their meals. Sometimes he would go down to the dockyard gate and beg scraps of wood from the workers as their father had done.

Emily never had to pump water now - Joey always made sure the buckets were full. And he never minded looking after Cissie when she went to the shops.

'I'm so proud of you, Joey,' she told him. 'I don't know how I'd have managed without you.'

Joey squirmed, and his face reddened. 'I like helping.' He glanced across at his father asleep in the chair. 'I'm the man of the house now.'

Emily grinned. 'You certainly are.'

Joey frowned. 'I must get work soon though.'

He was right. She was finding it a struggle managing on her reduced income from the school. She hadn't realised how comparatively well-off they'd been with her father's regular wage.

'I'll get by. Lenny's a great help,' she said with a brave smile.

'Good old Lenny,' Joey said, a bitter tone to his voice.

Emily wished she hadn't mentioned her father's friend, especially given Joey's proud voice when he'd boasted of being the man of the house. But surely he wasn't jealous.

She resolved that in future she would not accept Lenny's help so readily and she would make sure Joey knew how much his help was appreciated.

* * *

A couple of weeks later, Lenny called in on his way home from work. He had brought some offcuts of wood for the stove, which Emily accepted gratefully.

'Go and sit with Dad while I make a cup of tea,' she said.

'I'll just pump some water for you,' he said, lifting one of the buckets. 'Oh, it's full. Your Joey's been busy then.'

Emily smiled. 'He's being such a help. He's just taken Cissie down to the shops.'

Lenny pulled up a chair next to Joe and said, 'He's a good lad.'

'He is. I don't know how I'll manage when he starts work.'

Lenny grinned. 'Well, I've got good news. I know you'll miss having him around, but I had a word with my foreman, told him about Joey, and he's found him a job.'

'Oh, that is good news,' Emily said. 'Where – and when does he start?'

'In two days' time. In the dockyard.' He stretched his legs out and leaned back in the

122

chair. 'It's not bad pay, but it's hard work and long hours.'

'Joey won't mind that,' Emily said. 'It's very good of you to speak up for him.'

'Least I could do. I know you've been struggling.'

'I can't deny the money is welcome but...' She sighed. 'You're right. I will miss having him around.'

'I'm sure you will. One good thing though – you won't have to work so hard yourself. You shouldn't be doing two jobs as well as looking after your family.' He turned to Joe and said, 'I'm right, aren't I, mate? She needs looking after.'

Joe nodded and grinned but it was obvious to Emily that her father hadn't taken in what his friend had said.

She swallowed an indignant retort. What a cheek. She did not need looking after. Instead, she said quietly, 'Lenny, you know it's no good expecting a response. Dad is in another world. He's getting worse.'

'I'm sorry, Emily. I know that, but sometimes I wonder if he takes anything in, and if we talk to him as if he's normal, it might help.'

His words somewhat placated Emily. She had often thought the same and when they were alone, she would chat to him herself.

She made the tea and passed a cup to Lenny, changing the subject. 'Thank you for getting the job for Joey. He'll be back soon, and you can tell him yourself.'

Emily bustled around preparing their evening meal while Lenny finished his tea. 'You'll stay for tea, won't you, Lenny?' she asked.

'I don't want to impose,' he said.

'You're not. Besides, you want to speak to Joey.'

Lenny nodded and turned to Joe. 'I like watching your girl working. She's a good little housekeeper; make someone a good wife one day.'

Emily felt herself blushing but she pretended she hadn't heard. She felt uncomfortable when Lenny complimented her but she couldn't protest, not wanting to upset him. He'd been a good friend to Dad, and she was grateful, but she couldn't help feeling that if her father was fit and well, he would have something to say. I'm not yet seventeen, too young to be thinking of marriage, especially with a family to care for. She glanced over at Lenny, wondering what he'd meant by his remark, but he wasn't looking her way and appeared to be engrossed in talking to her father.

He was much too old, she thought, about the same age as Dad and not bad looking she supposed with his thick black hair and brown eyes, his skin tanned like her father's from working outside.

He glanced up and saw her looking his way. 'Where's that lad of yours got to?' he said.

At that moment the door opened and Cissie tumbled over the step, laughing. 'Daddy, Uncle Lenny. Look what I've got,' she said.

She thrust a bunch of wilting daisies into her father's unresponsive hand. Lenny reached across and took them. 'Let's put them in water, lovie,' he said.

Emily took down a mug from the shelf above the range and filled it. 'Where did you find them?' she asked.

'By the churchyard. They were growing out of the wall.'

Emily handed the mug to Lenny, who put the flowers in it and set it on the table.

'There, lovie, aren't they pretty – just like you,' he said, ruffling her hair.

Joey had come in behind his sister, hauling a heavy bag. 'Got the potatoes, Em, and a cabbage,' he said, ignoring Lenny.

'Thanks, Joey,' Emily said. 'Say hello to Lenny. He's got some news for you.'

'News?'

'A job, son – in the dockyard. Just labouring, fetching and carrying for the men building the new dry dock. Not much to start with but it could lead to better things.'

Joey shuffled his feet. 'Dad promised me an apprenticeship. I was going to be a shipwright.'

'Can't be helped, son. You're lucky to get anything.'

'Joey! It's not Lenny's fault. Say thank you, you ungrateful boy.' Emily rarely spoke sharply to her brother, but she was embarrassed by Joey's lack of enthusiasm, especially since he had always said he would do anything to earn money to help Emily.

'Sorry. Thanks, Lenny,' Joey mumbled.

'Pleasure, my boy,' said Lenny, but Emily could see he wasn't too pleased by her brother's reaction.

She dished up the meal and sat beside her father, trying to persuade him to eat a little. Most of it went down the front of his shirt and she ended up fetching a spoon and feeding the rest of it to him. It was becoming a regular ritual as Joe became more incapacitated.

In the early days after the accident, she had nursed the hope that her father would get better, but as time went on, she had been forced to accept that, in fact, he was worse. He spent day and night slumped in the armchair, sleeping most of the time. Even with Lenny's help, they could not get him up the narrow stairs to bed. It was all getting too much. Many a night, Emily cried herself to sleep, stuffing the corner of the blanket in her mouth to stifle the sobs so as not to disturb her brother and sister.

How long could she carry on, she asked herself. She took a deep breath and tried to concentrate on the conversation at the table. She was pleased Joey seemed to be taking an interest as Lenny talked to him about the job.

It was one less thing for her to worry about.

Chapter Eleven

Joey had been working at the dockyard for over a year, and he seemed to have settled down. He even confessed that he enjoyed the work.

Cissie had started school and Emily was working longer hours as well as helping Agnes with the washing when she had time. But even with Joey's wages she still struggled to make ends meet.

Lenny had called one day with the news that he could no longer keep her supplied with wood. The dockyard authorities had found there was too much pilfering going on and had stopped the, until now legitimate, practice of allowing the workers to take scrap wood home. Now she had to buy coal for the stove and, with winter approaching, Emily wondered how they would get through the cold, dark days.

Her main worry though was her father, whose condition seemed to deteriorate day by day. She'd spent precious pennies on calling the doctor out, hoping there was something he could do to improve Joe's condition. But the man had shaken his head, advising her to carry on as she had been.

She begrudged the hours spent at work when she would have preferred being at home to look after Dad, making nourishing broth and making sure he was warm enough as the doctor had advised.

Agnes was proving to be a real friend, calling in when Emily was at work to check on him and making sure he was drinking enough.

Lenny, too was proving a true friend to his old workmate, spending hours on his off days reading to Joe from the daily paper.

'I know he don't take it in,' he said one day, folding the paper and sighing.

Emily stirred the soup on the range and turned to him. 'It doesn't matter, Lenny. I'm sure he knows you're there. It's good of you to give up your free time.' She went back to stirring the pot, stifling a sigh.

She appreciated Lenny's help but it seemed he was always there these days. She knew he wasn't happy in his lodgings and she had to admit she enjoyed his company. It was good to talk to another adult, to have the sort of conversations she had enjoyed with her father. The problem was, Joey didn't get on with him and she was getting tired of trying to cope with the tension between them.

The door burst open and Cissie entered, running over to Lenny with a smile. 'Hello Uncle Lenny.'

He ruffled her hair and grinned. 'Good day at school, lovey?'

'I learned my two times table,' she boasted. She leaned across and patted her father's knee. 'Daddy, I can say my two times table.'

There was no response as usual and Cissie pouted.

Lenny pulled her to him and said, 'Poor Daddy's not well. Let him rest.'

'Come and sit at the table. Joey will be home soon and we can eat.' Emily turned to Lenny. 'You will stay, won't you?'

'Not today, thanks. I've promised to meet some of me mates for a drink.'

Emily tried to hide her relief. There wasn't much to share. 'Oh, I forgot it was payday - your weekly treat.'

Lenny patted Joe on the shoulder. 'Goodbye, mate. See you tomorrow.' He tucked his scarf inside his jacket and made for the door which flew open as he reached for the doorknob. 'Joey, mate – finished early have you?' he said with laugh.

'Not as early as you,' Joey said.

He laughed, seeming not to notice the edge in the lad's voice. 'Different shift, son.' He said goodbye to Cissie and Emily and hurried across the yard.

Joey stared after him, kicked his boots off in the doorway and gave Emily a kiss on the cheek. 'How is he today?' he asked nodding towards his sleeping father.

'Same as usual - worse if anything.'

'Worse?' Joey groaned.

Emily stopped stirring the soup and pulled the pot away from the heat. She wiped her hand across her face and pushed a strand of hair off her forehead. 'Oh, Joey – I don't know how I can keep going. It's all getting so hard.'

'I know, Sis. I wish I could do more.'

'You're doing enough already – working all the hours God sends. Your wages help us to keep afloat – just.'

'I worry about you.'

'No need. I get a bit down sometimes but I manage. And Lenny's a great help.'

'I wish you didn't have to rely on him.'

'He's good to us, Joey – and he seems to care for your dad. He spends hours reading the paper to him even though he knows Dad can't take it in.'

'I know, Em.' Joey frowned. 'It's just that he's here every day.'

'Well, I like him - and he's very kind to Cissie.'

'Yeah, right.'

Emily ignored him. He was always grumpy these days, no longer the cheerful, funny lad he had been. Perhaps the hard work and long hours were taking a toll. She sighed. If only their circumstances hadn't changed so drastically a year ago. Joey would now be enjoying his apprenticeship, well on the way to becoming a qualified shipwright. She glanced across at her father, staring vacantly into space. Poor Dad. It wasn't his fault.

* * *

Emily was on her way home from school holding Cissie's hand. Mark had agreed to her finishing work at the same time as school finished for the day. She didn't like her sister walking home on her own now that it was dark by teatime.

As she reached St Paul's Close, she heard wheels rumbling over the cobbles. She pulled Cissie closer to her and waited for the cart to pass. It stopped and a voice hailed her out of the gloom.

'Emily – look what I've got.'

It was Lenny. Emily stepped closer and saw that the cart held a flock mattress. 'What on earth...?'

'It's for Joe,' Lenny said with a grin. 'I hate seeing him stuck in that chair. He must be so uncomfortable.'

'That's kind of you, Lenny.' Emily felt bad that she hadn't thought of it herself. Not that there was really room for it in their small living room. The rest of the family slept in the small upstairs room. Besides, even if they had room for another bed, they'd never get Dad up the narrow stairs.

Cissie was excited. 'Can I help, Uncle Lenny?' she asked.

'No, love. You'll just get in the way. Why don't you go over and say hello to Agnes,' Emily suggested. 'You can play with Kitty for a while.'

Cissie nodded and ran across the yard.

Emily helped Lenny to manoeuvre the mattress through the door and leaned it against the wall. 'We'll have to shift things around,' she said.

There was just room to put the table and two chairs which had been in the middle of the room between the sink and the door.

Emily looked around the room thinking for a moment. 'We'll have to move Dad's chair near the range.'

'Let's put the mattress down and make up the bed, then move him,' Lenny suggested. 'We'll put the mattress over against the wall.'

'That should work but it'll be a squeeze to get past and up the stairs. Still, we'll manage.' Emily tried to sound cheerful but she wasn't too sure about all the upheaval. Joe was still slumped in his chair and she had to agree that he would sleep better on the mattress.

'We're going to try and make you more comfortable, Dad.' She gently removed the blanket tucked round him. He looked at her blankly but did not resist when she and Lenny helped him up.

They lowered him on to the mattress and Emily retrieved his cushions from the chair, propping him up in a sitting position. 'There, Dad. That feels better, doesn't it?'

As usual, there was no response and Emily sighed. She wasn't sure if the effort had been worth it. She turned to Lenny, forcing a smile. She didn't want to sound ungracious after his kind gesture. He meant well.

'Thanks, Lenny. One problem though.'

'Problem?'

'Well, I don't think he ought to stop in bed all day.'

'You're right but I thought your brother could help get him up and settled in the chair before he goes to work and then I'll come round to help get him to bed.'

'You don't have to do that. You've done enough for us already. Joey can help in the evenings.'

'It's no bother, Emily, love. Joe's my mate, I'll do anything for him.' He leaned over to clap Joe on the shoulder. 'All right, mate? I've got to be off now - take the cart back.'

Emily thanked him again and saw him out. She stood for a moment deep in thought. She knew she should be grateful for Lenny's friendship but he had been getting a bit too familiar lately, acting like one of the family. She wasn't happy with him calling her 'love' either, although it was a common term among friends. Even Mr Burston, the butcher called her love as did his wife. As for Cissie calling Lenny 'uncle', she knew Joey didn't like it, but what could she say?

I'm just being silly she told herself and with a shake of her head she went across to fetch Cissie from Agnes's house.

Joey got home from work a bit later than usual and at first, he didn't notice the changes. He only felt relief that for once Lenny Lomax wasn't there.

Only one lamp was lit and he peered through the gloom to where Emily was standing by the stove, mashing potatoes.

Cissie ran towards him and grabbed his hand. 'Look what Lenny brought,' she said excitedly.

Joey's hackles rose. So, he'd been here again. Good job he's not still around, he thought. I'd have something to say.

He stooped to take his boots off, trying to ignore Cissie pulling him into the room. 'Wait a mo,' he said. He looked up and spotted the bed in the corner of the room, his father propped up on cushions.

'What's all this?' He turned to Emily with a frown.

'Lenny brought it. He said he didn't like to see Dad stuck in that chair all the time.' She put down the fork she was using and went over to her father, tucking the blanket around him. 'He does look more comfortable, doesn't he.'

Joey nodded. He had to agree, although he was cursing inwardly for not having thought of this himself ages ago. He hadn't given a thought to his poor father confined to that armchair all these months. Why did it have to be Lenny, poking his nose in, acting like one of the family? He supposed he should be grateful to him. It was hard for Emily, coping with Dad and doing two jobs, as well as all the household chores. Joey wished he could do more to help but, although he liked his job, after a long day run off his feet doing the bidding of the more senior dockyard men he came home exhausted.

It wouldn't be so bad if the pay was better and he could contribute more to the household finances.

Joey shook off his bad thoughts and concentrated on listening to Cissie's chatter. Usually, she talked about her day at school and how sweet Agnes's little cat was. But today it was all about 'Uncle' Lenny and his gift. When had she started calling him 'Uncle'? Joey's resentment burned.

Emily turned from the stove. 'Would you mind fetching a bucket of water, please?'

'I thought that was Lenny's job,' Joey snapped.

'No, Joey. It's my job but as you can see, I'm busy getting our tea ready.'

Joey flinched. He wasn't used to harsh words from his sister. He picked up the bucket and said, 'Sorry, Sis.'

When he got back indoors with the full pail, Emily said, 'What's got into you lately, Joey?'

He shrugged. 'Just tired.'

'The food's ready. Come to the table, you too Cissie.'

Emily dished up and took Dad's plate over to him. 'Eat your own food before it gets cold,' Joey said, suddenly feeling ashamed of his bad mood. 'I'll help Dad with his.' He knelt down beside the mattress and took the plate from Emily.

'Wait a minute. I'll prop him up a bit,' Emily said.

Joey tried to get his father to eat but Joe didn't seem interested in food, turning his head away. In the end Joey fed him, trying to stop the gravy from running down his father's chin.

He scrambled to his feet with a sigh and went to the table to eat his own meal. He ate in silence, wishing he hadn't been so grumpy. When he'd cleared his plate, he looked at Emily and summoned a smile. 'That was good, Sis. Thanks.'

He took his and Cissie's plates to the sink. 'I'll wash up.'

'No need. I don't mind doing it. Read a story to Cissie. I'll just get Dad settled and then I'll get her ready for bed.'

'You don't have to do everything. I'm happy to help.'

She just smiled.

He watched her tidying Dad's bed and settling him down for the night. When she'd done that, she lifted Cissie down from the table and said, 'Say goodnight to Joey and Dad.'

Cissie knelt down beside Joe's bed, leaned over and kissed him, 'Night night, Daddy,' she whispered.

While she was upstairs, Joey poured water from the kettle on to the crockery and started to wash the dishes. He'd almost finished when Emily came downstairs.

'You didn't have to do that,' she said.

'I know, but it's done now.' He dried the last plate and put it in the rack over the sink. He glanced across at his father. 'Dad's asleep. Let's sit by the fire for a while. We don't often have time for a chat.' (without Lenny here, he added in his mind.)

He moved one of the kitchen chairs nearer to the stove and sat down. 'You have Dad's chair – more comfortable for you.'

'I'm sure he'll sleep better on the mattress but I don't want him to stay in bed in the daytime.'

'Don't worry, Em. I've thought of that. I'll help you get him into his chair before I go to work.'

'Thank you. I didn't like to ask. You work hard so I don't want to put any extra burden on you.'

'Looking after Dad the way you do is a burden.' He reached over and took Emily's hand. 'I'm sorry I've been so bad-tempered lately. It's just...' He paused and couldn't go on. How could he explain his feelings about Lenny without upsetting his sister?

Emily squeezed his hand and said, 'I understand. Life hasn't worked out the way we hoped for either of us. We just have to make the best of things.'

'I suppose so.' He shifted in his seat. 'Well, I have to be up early as usual so I'll say goodnight.'

Upstairs, he slipped behind the curtain that separated his bed from his sisters' sleeping quarters,

Before he drifted off to sleep, he faced up to his real reason for disliking Lenny. He had to admit that the man had been a good friend to his father and he appreciated the help he'd been to the family. No – not the family, he thought. Emily. He was worming his way into her affections with his little gifts, his eagerness to fetch coal or water. Cissie too.

His constant references to doing everything he could for his 'old mate' didn't ring true. Joey wondered how friendly the two men had been before the accident. Not very, he thought. Since he'd started work at the dockyard he'd begun to realise that Lenny was not very popular among the men. I'm not the only one, he thought.

His friend of the family act was all to impress Emily and she was falling for it.

If only there was someone he could talk to about his concerns. Joey sighed and turned over, finally falling into an uneasy doze.

Chapter Twelve

There was no shade anywhere. The sun beat down on Harry's head and, despite his hat, he felt the beginnings of a headache. Sweat soaked his shirt and he was tempted to take it off, but he had learned the hard way that this wasn't a good idea. He'd tried it once and ended up with blisters and red raw patches across his shoulders.

His red hair and fair skin were the worst combination in this harsh climate. 'Ginger' his mates called him but the nickname no longer suited him. His once flaming hair was now almost white, bleached by the sun, and his face was lined and leatherlike so that he looked much older than his twenty years.

He had served a year of his sentence on a chain gang, building roads between Sydney and Port Macquarrie. Hard work but he had survived, despite the harsh conditions.

With three more years to serve, he was mightily relieved to be given his ticket of leave which meant he could seek work elsewhere in the Colony and, what's more be paid for his efforts. He would not be able to leave the Colony without permission. Being able to return to England at the end of his sentence would depend on his good behaviour as a convict, as well as having the means to pay for the voyage and support himself afterwards.

It was a stroke of luck when he met Bruce Kennedy, the owner of a sheep station who was in town looking to hire hands. Harry had eagerly shown him the document permitting him to work and had been taken on at once.

He had settled down to the job and, in some ways, had been almost happy away from the brutal warders and restrictions of the penal colony. He had learned to ride a horse and to tell a ram from a ewe. He grinned, recalling his first encounter with a sheep out on the Sheppey marshes. Then he had been terrified of the strange animal, not even sure what it was.

No sheep in sight today. He was engaged in putting up fencing to protect the grazing from kangaroos and other invasive animals before letting the flock loose.

He glanced around at his fellow worker, shirtless and seemingly unaffected by the searing heat. After more than four years in Australia, he, too, should be used to the climate, but since leaving Sydney for the outback, he had learned that life in the city was totally different from this part of New South Wales.

Now, almost three years later, his sentence was coming to an end he would no longer be a convict but free to seek work and make a life here in this so-called land of opportunity.

But he had always clung to the dream of returning to England and seeking out the girl who had stood up for him in court. And if he wanted to return to England, he had to get permission and, more importantly raise enough money to pay for the voyage.

And he would – one day. He had to go back to find the girl who had helped him all those years ago. She wouldn't remember him, of course. Besides, she was probably married by now, maybe with children. But he had never forgotten her and his dreams of sweet Emily had kept him sane during those years of hard labour.

In the meantime, he would work and save until he could afford to go back. Life on the sheep station was hard but nothing to compare with his earlier life. He wasn't afraid of hard work. Life as a convict had toughened him up. He was no longer that frightened lad who would do anything to escape a beating – or worse.

'Hey, Ginge. Time for a break mate.'

It wasn't long since their last break but Ernie was always ready to down tools and lounge in the shade if the foreman wasn't around.

Harry shrugged and threw down the mallet he'd been using to drive in the fence posts. They sat down in the meagre shade of a stunted tree where the horses were tethered, their tails in constant movement, swishing the flies away.

Ernie produced a bottle of water. 'Here, 'ave a swig of that, mate.'

'Thanks, Ernie.' Harry took a small swig and coughed. It wasn't water.

'Hey, where did you get this?' he asked, glad he'd only taken a small sip.

Ernie grinned and tapped the side of his nose. 'Ask no questions, mate…'

'I think I'll stick to water for now. Maybe have a drop of that later if you want to share.' Harry tried to keep his tone friendly. He hated the way the other man always addressed him as 'mate'. They weren't mates and never would be, although Ernie was friendly enough on the surface. But he had a temper which could flare up at the slightest thing.

After his experiences on the hulks in Sheerness and during the long sea journey Harry had learned not to trust anyone. Best to keep on the right side of Ernie, he thought.

He gazed round at the barren landscape, the dry red soil broken up by clumps of spiky spinifex grass, the sparse trees with their glaring white trunks and grey green leaves – so different to England. How he longed to be back. Home, he thought, although he had never really had a home. He had grown up on the streets of London, sleeping in doorways or abandoned warehouses, begging for food – that is, until he met Sid, a scrawny lad like himself who had offered him friendship as well as food and a place to stay. Who could blame him for accepting? But how could he have been so naïve as to not see there would be strings attached?

He'd soon realised that Sid survived by picking pockets and, in return for his friendship, he had expected Harry to help him. In a way, stealing that apple and getting caught had saved him. Sid had got away, leaving Harry to face the copper. His relief was short-lived when he had been convicted and fallen into the clutches of Tony and his gang.

He sighed and pushed himself to his feet. 'Better get back to work,' he said. 'Foreman'll soon be on 'is way.'

Ernie shrugged and stood up. 'Right slave driver he is. How do they expect us to work in this heat?'

'Well, we're better off than we were on the chain gang. At least we're being paid.'

'Suppose so.' Ernie grinned. 'And we can get a drink when we get back to town, have a game of two-up and try to make more dough.'

Harry nodded. 'Too right.' He wasn't going to let on to his mate that drinking and gambling were the last things on his mind. He was saving every penny. When he had enough to prove to the authorities that he could support himself, he would be on the first ship back to England. Labouring on a sheep station wouldn't be forever.

He reached for the mallet and pounded on the stake he'd been fixing. There were still miles of fencing to do. He looked around, staring out at the acres of seemingly barren land. Amazing to think that all of this belonged to one man. The homestead and its outbuildings were miles away.

Ernie gave him a nudge. 'Hey, stop daydreaming. We've got to finish this stretch by grub time and it's a long ride back to the station.'

Harry summoned a grin and set to with his mallet. 'Don't worry – we'll get it done.'

'Stringing the wire tomorrow,' Ernie said. 'I 'ate that job.'

'Me too. Still, it's better than road-building with those overseers cracking their whips.'

'S'pose you're right. At least we're left to get on with it and can take a break now and then.'

They worked on in silence. It was too hot to talk and the job took all their energy.

Harry paused to wipe the sweat from his eyes and looked back along the line of fence posts. They disappeared into the distance, those furthest away shimmering in the heat.

A moving dot on the horizon caught his eye. A kangaroo? As it came nearer, Harry recognised a figure on horseback. He called to Ernie who was taking another break, leaning back on his elbows and looking up at the sky.

'Foreman's coming, mate. Better get on your feet.'

Ernie scrambled up and grabbed his mallet. 'Thanks for the warning, mate.'

Harry shrugged. 'You'd do the same for me.' Truthfully, he was annoyed. Ernie was a lazy bugger and did as little work as he could get away with. Harry put up with it, reluctant to cause any trouble.

They would both be punished if either of them were seen to be malingering. Covering for Ernie had become second nature.

By the time the horseman was in hailing distance the two men had hammered in three more fence posts. They didn't look up as the foreman called out, 'Good job, lads.'

They turned and Ernie grinned. 'Never stopped, did we, Ginge?'

'Yeah, pull the other one,' the foreman said with a dry laugh. 'Still, I didn't expect you to get so far, given this heat. So, come on, get packed up. Time we was back at the homestead.'

They picked up their tools and tied them to the horses' saddles, mounted and followed the foreman back along the trail.

It was a long ride and Harry could hardly keep upright in the saddle. Ernie seemed all right though. But then, he'd only erected two fence posts to Harry's three. No wonder he wasn't quite as exhausted.

Back at the homestead, the stockmen and other workers were already queuing up at the cookhouse for their grub. There was a lot of good-natured banter as they settled down to eat.

'Coming to the pub, Ginge?' one of the men asked.

The small town of Burston Creek was several miles away but the men had the use of a wagon which held six or eight men. Others rode their own horses. Payday was for drinking and carousing.

Harry shook his head and Ernie laughed. 'Going to write to your sweetheart?' he jeered. He turned to his mates. 'Always writing he is. She never writes back though.'

The men joined in the laughter.

Will, the foreman cut in. 'Leave him alone, lads.' He turned to Harry. 'Why don't you come with us?'

'Nah. My poor old nag's worn out, the miles we've done today. I'll give him a rest.'

'You could come in the wagon – there's room,' Will said.

'P'raps I will, for a change,' he said.

Amid much teasing and jostling, he joined the men in the wagon. 'Fed up with writing to her then? Don't blame you if she don't write back,' Sid said.

The others laughed and Harry gave a sheepish grin. 'Spect she's given up on me.'

The wagon pulled up in front of the pub in the small town of Burston Creek and the men tumbled out, pushing their way through the swing doors.

Soon the drink was flowing but Harry managed to make his pint last most of the evening. He begrudged dipping into his precious savings and ignored the jeers of his fellow workers.

Several of them gathered round a table where a couple of men were playing two-up. Harry didn't join in. He couldn't see the sense in losing his money. The gamblers were strangers, not the usual station hands who frequented the pub. They looked a bit shifty and Harry watched them carefully. After a while he became convinced they were cheating and was glad he hadn't joined in.

As the evening drew on, the men from the Kennedy station lost interest, mainly because they were losing. Ernie beckoned Harry over to where he sat with a stranger.

'Here, listen to this,' he said. He nudged the man. 'Show him, mate.'

Reluctantly, he drew a small leather pouch out of his pocket. He looked round furtively before pouring a few stones on to the table.

Harry gasped as the myriad colours glowed and twinkled in the lamplight. He had never seen anything like them, even in the windows of the posh jewellers in London.

'Opals,' Ernie breathed, picking one up and holding it up to the light.

The man snatched it away from him. 'Look, don't touch, unless you're going to buy.'

'You really found these mining in the outback?' Ernie asked.

'Well, you have to know where to look. I could show you – for a price.'

Ernie grinned. 'What do you say, Ginge? Shall we join the opal hunters?'

Harry hesitated. It was tempting. But he shook his head. 'I can't leave the station until I get my documents. If I skive off I could end up back in the Colony on the chain gang. No thanks.'

The miner began to scoop the jewels up but Harry put out a hand to stop him. One of the stones had caught his eye. It was very small, tinier than his little fingernail. But the colour made him gasp. He'd only seen that shade of blue once before in his life.

He reached out for the stone. 'How much?' he asked.

'More than you can afford, mate.'

Undaunted, Harry repeated, 'How much?'

The sum quoted made Harry's eyes water. It was almost half the amount he had already saved towards his passage home. He swallowed, took a deep breath and said, 'I'll have it - that one.'

'Some of these are worth more,' the man said.

'I don't care. I want that one.'

Ernie laughed. 'You're mad, mate.'

Harry didn't care. He took the coins from his money belt and handed them over, picked up the stone and stowed it away. The blue matched Emily's eyes exactly. He would

have it set into a ring for her when he got
back to England.

He was silent on the journey back to the
Kennedy station, oblivious to the raucous
singing of his mates. He was dreaming of the
day he would give Emily the ring. Ernie
clapped him on the back, bringing him back
to reality. No use dreaming – would he ever
find her again?

* * *

Joey dragged his feet, reluctant to get
home from work. The hundreds of dockyard
workers had poured out of the gate ages ago.
At one time, he would have been among
them, eager to get home and be with his
family. He loved playing with Cissie, telling
her stories, as well as helping his sister with
her chores.

But Lenny Lomax always seemed to
arrive before him, fawning around his sister.
Joey guessed he managed to skive off early
and be at the dock gate before anyone else.

Joey was beginning to hate the man, and
he didn't know how much longer he could
put up with it. If only there was someone he
could talk to. But what could he say? He
couldn't deny that Lenny had been a great
help to the family. He'd thought about
confiding his feelings to Bill Brent, but he
had no evidence that Lenny had done
anything wrong—just the opposite, in fact.

Bill sometimes called to see how Joe was but since his promotion to sergeant he didn't have so much time. Joey understood. Fewer of Dad's mates called in now either. Dad had deteriorated so much over the past few months. He didn't recognise people, and could not hold a conversation.

Joey kicked a stone in the road, muttering curses. He started as a hand fell on his shoulder. 'You all right, Joseph?'

Joey knew it was the school master. No one else called him Joseph. 'Mr Thompson. Good evening.'

'How is your father?' Mark Thompson asked.

'Just the same. He doesn't get any better – or any worse.'

'I'm so sorry. I wish there were something I could do for him – for your family.'

'There's nothing anyone can do. We manage. Emily works too hard, though.'

'I know. She is a great help to me in the school. It is such a shame she has to do two jobs. Sometimes she looks so tired.'

Joey felt a flicker of annoyance. Was the man criticising him? 'I do what I can to help,' he protested.

'I know, Joseph. You are the best of brothers.' He shook hands and said, 'It's good to talk to you. Will you tell Emily - Miss Williams – that I will call in and see your father after church on Sunday.'

'Yes, sir. Of course.'

'Now, I must hurry home. My wife has been too long alone.'

He hurried away.

Joey stared after him. It was obvious how much Mark admired Emily. If only he weren't married. Daft thought, Joey told himself as he entered the close, hoping that Lenny would not be there.

Talking to Mark had made him think. Emily liked the teacher, but it couldn't be anything but liking. Still, his sister deserved to have someone in her life. She couldn't remain a drudge for the family forever. He shuddered as realisation dawned. That's what Lenny was after – a wife to clean and cook for him. Yes, and someone to earn money to pay for his beer. He was always moaning about his landlady and his drab lodgings. He'd already made himself at home, taking over Dad's chair and making a fuss of Cissie.

Over my dead body, Joey thought, kicking open the door and stomping indoors.

Emily was tending to her father and she straightened up, staring at him.

'What's wrong, Joey? What's all the noise about?'

Joey was almost disappointed that Lenny wasn't there. 'Nothing's wrong. Em. Just a bad day at work. Sorry.' He crossed the room and looked down at his father. 'How are you, Dad?' He always spoke to Joe as if he could hear and understand. Of course, there was no reply, just the usual blank stare.

Emily reached for his hand. 'He's been a bit restless today.'

Joey turned away, swallowing the lump in his throat. Would he ever get used to seeing his father, once so strong and vibrant, lying there like a log? He might as well be dead. Shocked that he'd almost uttered the words aloud, he shook his head and plonked himself down in the old armchair. He took his boots off and threw them in the corner.

'No Lenny today?'

'He's working late. Said he might pop in later.'

Might? Of course, he would. Joey bit the words back, tried to speak calmly. 'And where's our Cissie got to?'

'She's over at Agnes's playing with the cat.' Emily smiled. 'She can't keep away.'

'She's good company for the old lady.' Joey started to relax. It was good to spend time with his sister without the ever-present Lomax.

'Can I do anything to help, Em?' he asked.

'No thanks. I'll just finish the spuds, and then we can have a chat.'

Joey felt a little frisson of alarm. Emily sounded serious. What was there to chat about? Lenny, he thought. Had the bastard asked her to marry him – or had he done something worse? Joey's fists clenched. He forced himself to relax. Surely Emily was too sensible to fall for him.

He moistened his lips and said, 'Em – is everything all right? You're not worried about anything?'

Emily turned from the sink, the saucepan of potatoes in her hand. She put it down on the hotplate. 'Not more than usual,' she said, nodding towards the bed where her father lay.

'Oh, Em. Poor Dad.'

'I had hoped he would get better but it's been so long and no change. How long can he…?' She broke off with a sob.

'Don't get upset. You're doing all you can for him.'

'It's Cissie I feel for. She chats away to him, and sometimes she looks so sad when he doesn't answer. If only he'd just blink or something, give some sign that he recognises her.'

Joey shifted in the chair, suddenly feeling uncomfortable that he'd taken his father's place. He glanced down at the mattress. 'Has he been lying there all day? I thought Lenny was going to get him up.'

'He didn't have time before work.'

Bloody Lenny. Joey hoped he was getting fed up with helping Dad and wouldn't be around here so often. Some hopes. Helping Dad was just an excuse to sit in Dad's chair, eat their food - and make up to Emily.

Emily opened a tin of corned beef and tipped it out onto a plate. 'Spuds'll soon be done,' she said. She turned one of the kitchen chairs round and sat down opposite Joey.

'I'm worried about Dad,' she said in a low voice. 'I think he's getting worse. He hardly eats anything. It's a real struggle to get anything down him. He's so thin, too. You don't realise when he's all wrapped up in blankets, but when I was washing him the other day...'

Joey ran his hand through his hair. 'I wish I could do more. One good thing – I'm due a raise. If I'm earning more, you could give up one of your jobs. You won't get so tired.'

'That's good news. I could give up the school. If I'm working with Agnes, I'd be close to home, keep an eye on Dad.'

'I don't think Mr Thompson would be very happy if you gave up. I saw him earlier on, and he was singing your praises.' Joey grinned. 'He really likes you.'

Emily blushed. 'You mustn't say that. He's a married man.'

'Just teasing, Em.' Once again Joey wished that Mark Thompson was single. He wouldn't have to worry about Lenny Lomax then.

* * *

Emily got up and checked the potatoes, drained them into the sink and mashed them, wishing she had a little bit of butter or milk to make them tastier. She sliced the corned beef and set it out on the plates. She glanced across to Joey, meaning to ask him to fetch Cissie from Agnes's, but he was fast asleep.

Poor lad. He worked so hard. She wiped her hands on her apron and ran across the yard. 'Cissie, tea's ready,' she called, opening the cottage door. Agnes was sitting in her armchair, the cat on her lap, and Cissie was stroking the animal and chatting with it in her usual way.

Agnes looked up with a smile. 'I think she comes to see Kitty, not me,' she said.

Emily laughed. 'Both of you, I'm sure,' she said.

'No Lenny today?' the old lady asked.

'He's busy. Might pop in later.'

'He's a great help, isn't he?'

'So's Joey. He's home early today for a change.' Emily was defensive. She had detected a slightly sarcastic tone in her friend's voice. She hoped Agnes wasn't reading too much into Lenny's frequent visits. He was her father's friend – not hers.

'Come along, Cissie. Say goodbye to Kitty.'

Joey had woken up when they got indoors and was piling wood onto the range. Emily thanked him and they sat down at the table to eat.

They had just finished their meal when the door opened, and Lenny came in without knocking. He glanced at their empty plates and went across to say hello to Joe. He threw himself down in Joe's chair and rubbed his hands together. 'Cold out there,' he said.

'Cup of tea, Lenny?' Emily asked.' No milk though – sorry.'

He nodded and Emily's lips tightened. Not even a please or thank you. And why was she apologising? He seemed to take it for granted that he was welcome to share whatever they had to spare. She made the tea and summoned a smile as she handed the cup to him. I'm just tired, she thought. It's not Lenny's fault. After all, he had proved to be a good friend to her and the family. How would she have managed to care for Dad without his help?

Chapter Thirteen

Emily fought the wind as she dragged the washing off the line, and Agnes helped her fold it into the laundry basket. Thank goodness the wind had dried it today. There were too few sunny days due to the constant mist coming off the nearby marshes. Emily hated having damp laundry cluttering up the small living room. She was sure it didn't help her father's health.

'Sorry, Agnes. I'll have to leave you to sort this lot out. I must go and see to Dad. I've neglected him a bit today.'

'You go on, love. You've done enough.'

'I want to get a few jobs done before Cissie comes home from school.'

'Send her in to me then. That will give you more time to get on.'

'Oh, Agnes. I don't like to put on you too much.'

'It's no bother, love. She's good company. And she can help me fold the washing.'

Emily smiled her gratitude and crossed the cobbled yard to her own cottage.

She glanced across to her father, who was still lying on the mattress. Joey hadn't had time to help him get into his chair before going to work, and Lenny hadn't called that morning. She should at least make an effort to sit him up, she thought. But he was fast asleep, and she didn't like to disturb him.

She lifted the lid on the water bucket, relieved that it was half full. She filled the kettle and set it on the hob. She could do with a cup of tea, but she'd better wash up the breakfast things and prepare their evening meal before sitting down to rest.

She went upstairs, tidied the beds, and put Joey's clean shirt in the drawer. Downstairs the kettle had boiled and she poured water on to the plates, then re-filled the kettle.

Dad was still asleep, and Emily decided to leave him. She'd give him a drink when she'd finished the washing up. As she worked, she recalled Joey's teasing about Mark Thompson. Such nonsense, she thought. Still, she had to admit she liked him and knew he liked her. But there was no way she would get involved with a married man.

Suddenly, a picture of a skinny ginger-haired lad with startling green eyes flashed into her mind. Harry Jones might have been an escaped convict, but something about him had invited her trust. Her dad and Sergeant Brent must have seen it, too. Why else would they have helped him?

She shook her head as she dried the last plate. What was the point of thinking about him now? She prayed he had made a new life in Australia now that he had probably finished his sentence.

She sighed and wiped the draining board down. Time to see to Dad now. He was still sleeping so she bent over the mattress and gently shook his shoulder. 'Wake up, Dad,' she murmured.

As usual, there was no response, so she shook him harder. She pulled the blanket away and tried to turn him to face her. 'Dad, come on. I've made you a drink.'

His eyes were open, and there was a blue tinge around his mouth. Her heart began to thump, and she shook him again. 'Dad, wake up – please.'

It was no use and she sank back on her heels, breathing heavily. No tears. She had been expecting this for some time. Yet it was still a shock.

Joey, where are you? she thought. She needed her brother. But he wasn't due home for ages. Cissie! She'd be home from school soon. She mustn't see Dad like this. She hurried outside, under the arch and looked up and down the street. A group of children streamed past, laughing and chattering. Emily sighed with relief when she spotted her sister.

'Cissie, come here. I'm busy, so I want you to stay with Agnes for a bit.'

Cissie's eyes lit up. 'I can play with Kitty,' she said.

They knocked on Agnes's door and opened it before she could reply. 'Here she is,' Emily said, forcing a cheerful note into her voice. She ushered Cissie into the room. 'Go and play with Kitty and be a good girl. I'll come and fetch you later.'

Agnes put a hand on her arm. 'Everything all right, love?'

Emily shook her head, choked back a sob. 'It's Dad. He's...' She couldn't say the word.

'Worse? Shall I fetch the doctor?'

'No. Too late for that.'

Agnes clapped a hand to her mouth, then, glancing at Cissie, she said quietly, 'I'm so sorry. Can I do anything?'

'Just look after Cissie for me till Joey gets home. We'll tell her together.'

'I'll give her some tea. She can stay as long as needed.' Agnes raised her voice. 'Cissie, love. How would you like to stay for tea and keep your old Auntie Agnes company?'

Cissie clapped her hands. 'Ooh, yes, please.'

'Be good now,' Emily said. Crossing the yard, she wondered when she would next see that happy smile on her little sister's face.

* * *

Joey knew something was wrong the minute he walked under the arch and saw his sister standing at their door on the far side of the yard. Usually, Cissie was waiting for him, rushing into his arms as soon as she spotted him.

His first thought was that something had happened to her, but as he passed Agnes's cottage, he heard her high, excited voice calling the cat. Relief flooded him as he crossed to where Emily waited.

As he drew near, he could see that she was very upset. His fists tightened. Bloody Lenny. If he...

Emily fell into his arms, sobbing. 'Oh, Joey. It's Dad.'

'Dad? What's happened?'

She drew him inside and pointed to the bed. 'I thought he was asleep,' she sobbed.

Joey strode over to the bed and looked down at his father. He had known deep down that this had to happen someday, but not yet, he thought. Poor Emily, finding him like this. He wasn't sure what to do next. He couldn't leave his sister to deal with everything.

He took Emily's hand. 'I'll go and talk to Bill Brent. He'll know who we have to report this to.'

Emily nodded. 'Cissie?'

'I'll get Agnes to look after her a bit longer. I won't be long. You'll be all right on your own?'

Joey hurried round the corner to the policeman's house, hoping he'd be in. He'd seen plenty of death in his short life. Living on the hulks was not the healthiest place. He remembered his mother dying. He'd been not much older than Cissie, and it had taken him a long time to cope with the loss. Now, he resolved to take on the responsibility of arranging the funeral. He couldn't leave everything to Emily. Perhaps they'd give him time off from work to sort things out.

Bill was at home and invited him in, making him sit down before asking him what had happened.

'I know it's a shock, lad. But you must have been expecting it,' Bill said.

'Yes, in a way. But...'

'I understand. How is Emily taking it?'

'Devastated. I don't think she's really taken it in.' Joey explained that his sister had found him when she got home from work. 'She thought he was asleep at first.'

Bill's wife offered him a cup of tea, but he shook his head. 'I must get back to Emily.'

'Well, don't worry about a thing. I'll get someone to call about the arrangements. Do you have enough for a funeral?'

Joey nodded. 'We have a bit put by for emergencies.'

He said goodbye and hurried back to St Paul's Close.

* * *

Emily was sitting by her father's bed, holding his hand and smoothing his hair back from his forehead. While Joey was gone, she washed him and changed the sheets. He looked so small and frail, and she tried to remember him how he had been before the accident.

She missed the man he had been, but she would equally miss the invalid she had cared for since his accident. She had done her best for him as he had done for his family after their mother died.

Lost in thought, she didn't hear anyone come in until the door swung shut with a bang.

'Joey,' she cried, jumping up. When she saw who it was, her face fell. 'Lenny.'

'Sorry I wasn't here earlier. I've been working late,' he said, glancing towards the bed. 'How is me old mate today?'

Fury rose in Emily's breast. 'Can't you see? He's dead,' she screamed.

'Dead? How...?'

Emily's shoulders slumped. 'I thought he was sleeping.' She burst into sobs.

Lenny's arms came round her, and he hugged her tightly. 'There, love. You have a good cry.' He patted her back.

At that moment, the door flew open, and Joey strode in. 'What do you think you're doing? Leave my sister alone.' He raised his fists.

'Hang about,' Lenny protested, taking a step away from Emily. 'I'm just comforting her, seeing as you weren't here to do it. She's upset.'

'Of course she's upset. But it's not your place to...'

'Stop it. Both of you.' Emily's harsh voice stopped them in their tracks. She turned to her brother. 'Now then. What did Bill Brent say?'

'He's going to help with the arrangements.'

'Good.' She faced Lenny. 'You do understand why Joey was annoyed?'

'Yes – and I'm sorry if I upset both of you.' He hung his head. 'It's just – I can't bear to see a woman cry.'

He sounded sincere, and Emily accepted his apology. She looked at her brother and he relaxed.

'I accept that you're sorry, but don't let it happen again. No one takes advantage of my sister,' he said.

Lenny began to mumble something, looking at the floor, but Emily said, 'Perhaps you'd better go. '

'All right. You'll let me know when the funeral is?'

'Of course.'

When he'd gone, she said, 'What was all that about? I can look after myself, you know, and he didn't mean any harm.'

'You're so young, Emily. You don't understand men like that. He's always smarming around you. I don't like it.'

'You're being silly. I might be young, but I'm not stupid. Anyway, you're younger than me, so don't tell me what to do.' She sighed. 'I don't know what you've got against Lenny.

He was just being helpful, and he's been a good friend to Dad.'

* * *

Joey sat in the chair he always thought of as Dad's and covered his face with his hands. He was sorry for upsetting his sister but not sorry for his reaction. Emily always saw the best in people and nothing he said could persuade her that Lenny Lomax was bad news. Not wishing to upset her more, he resolved to try and hide his dislike of the man. But he would keep an eye on him. Just let him take one step out of line and...

He sighed and straightened. 'We must tell Cissie what's happened. Shall we do it together?'

'She'll have to be told. Poor little thing.' Emily stood up. 'Come on then. Let's get it over with.'

As they crossed the yard, Emily said, 'Perhaps she can stay with Agnes tonight.'

'We'll see,' Joey said.

Cissie was sitting up at the table eating a jam sandwich when they entered the cottage. When she saw them, she squealed and jumped down, rushing over to Joey. 'Have you come to see Kitty?' she asked.

Agnes looked up from her knitting. 'She's been a very good girl,' she said, shaking her head and frowning. 'I haven't said anything to her.'

Joey glanced at Emily, not sure what to say. He picked Cissie up and set her on his lap. 'We've got something to tell you,' he said. 'It's about Dad.'

'He's very sick, isn't he? He sleeps all the time.'

'Yes, love. Very sick.' Joey swallowed a lump in his throat, struggling to get the words out.

Before he could speak, Cissie said, 'A boy at school said he's going to die. Is that true?'

Joey nodded and reached for Emily's hand as tears rolled down her cheeks.

Cissie looked from one to the other. 'Has it happened?'

When they both nodded, she began to cry, and they both put their arms around her.

Agnes left them to grieve, bustling around making a pot of tea. When their sobs subsided, she said, 'Would you like her to stay with me?'

'That's very kind.' Emily turned to Cissie. 'Would you like to sleep here tonight?'

The little girl shook her head forcefully. 'No. I want to see Dad.'

Seeing Emily was about to protest, Joey said, 'Come on then. Let's go.' He took her hand and went to the door.

Emily followed after thanking Agnes for looking after her.

'I'm always here,' Agnes said.

                    * * *

Joey was surprised that after seeing their father, Cissie had seemed to accept his death. She was sad, but she didn't cry. He supposed that months of seeing Joe lying there, unable to speak or acknowledge their presence, had prepared her in some way.

She was at school when the body was taken away, and when she came home and saw he was gone, she said, 'He's gone to live with the angels, Miss Cook told me. They'll look after him.'

Joey would have sneered if Emily had said anything like that but he couldn't hurt his little sister. He was glad she had something to believe in.

The funeral was held while Cissie was at school. Another damp grey day, tendrils of mist swirling around the graveyard as the mourners stood shivering. Joey was surprised how many of Joe's former workmates, the local tradespeople and neighbours crowded into the little church.

Emily and Agnes had helped the landlady of the Red Lion to prepare food for the mourners. Lenny was there, of course, shaking hands with everyone and generally acting like chief mourner. Joey swallowed his fury, but if Lenny mentioned 'me old mate, Joe' one more time, he'd have a job to stop himself from smashing his fist into Lomax's face.

Chapter Fourteen

For a change, it was a bright and sunny day. 'Looks like spring's on the way,' Emily said, smiling at the sight of clean sheets fluttering in the breeze.

'Can't come too soon for me,' Agnes said, flexing her arthritic fingers.

'Time for some spring cleaning,' Emily said. 'I've been neglecting my chores since...'

'I understand, love. I know life must be easier for you now, but you must miss him.'

'I do. It was hard work looking after Dad, but it was a labour of love. I never resented him. It's strange. Now I don't have much to do, I feel less like doing anything.' She sighed. 'I must pull myself together for Cissie and Joey's sakes.'

'And for yourself too,' Agnes said.

'If you say so.' Emily accompanied her words with a laugh. 'No time like the present. I'll make a start now.'

She said goodbye to her friend, went into her own cottage and stood for a moment looking around. Where to start? That mattress would have to go. It would make more room in here. Shame to chuck it out though. Perhaps it could go upstairs. She'd ask Joey to help her move it when he came home. He'd be more comfortable sleeping on it rather than the thin straw pallet he'd slept on since moving here.

Decision made, she set about cleaning the bedroom to make room for it. She pulled cobwebs down from the ceiling, cleaned the little window and scrubbed the floor.

All done, she looked around with a glow of satisfaction. In the years she had lived in St Paul's Close, she had never stopped feeling thankful for their good fortune in having this little cottage – a real home, she thought. Her life on the hulks was a dim memory overlaid by the shadow of the convicts housed there now.

The thought of the hulks recalled her meeting with Harry Jones, the escaped prisoner, the lad she was convinced should never have been there in the first place. She often thought of him, wondering if he had managed to find a new life in Australia now that the remaining years of his sentence were surely up.

Her thoughts were interrupted by the sound of the downstairs door opening and Cissie's voice calling up the stairs.

'I'm coming down, Cissie.' Emily hurried downstairs and gave her little sister a hug. 'It's all nice and clean up there now,' she said.

'Have the spiders all gone?'

Emily laughed. 'Every one of them.'

'I'm going to see.' Cissie ran up the stairs.

It was good to see her little sister so lively, Emily thought. She no longer stared at the mattress where their father had spent the last months of his life, tears glistening on her cheeks.

Now that the weather had improved, she often played outside after school and Emily was pleased that the sunshine and fresh air was helping her to grow up into a sturdy, healthy child. She sighed. She didn't want to admit that this was due in part to Lenny.

Since their father's death, he had become an almost daily visitor, always turning up with a pocketful of treats for Cissie. On a Sunday, he would insist that he take both of them for a walk along the sea wall, saying that it was good for Emily to have a rest from housework and for Cissie to get out in the fresh sea air.

Joey didn't like it, but he tried to hide his animosity. There wasn't anything he could take exception to. Lenny always treated his sisters with respect – at least when he was around.

'Why don't you come with us, mate?' Lenny asked one warm Sunday afternoon.

'Too much to do. I've got a load of wood to chop up. Need to make sure there's a good store for when winter comes.'

'Plenty of time for that,' Lenny said.

'I'd rather get on with it.'

'Suit yourself.' Lenny shrugged and called to the girls who were upstairs getting ready. 'Come along, ladies. Let's make the most of this sunshine.'

They ran down, laughing and Lenny took Cissie's hand.

* * *

It was hot in the enclosed courtyard and Joey paused to wipe the sweat from his forehead. He had attacked the woodpile in a fury, imagining with each blow of the axe that it was Lenny's head. He hated the man more with each day that passed. But he couldn't get Emily to share his feelings. If he tried to warn her that Lenny was no good, she leapt to his defence, reminding Joey how he had been such a good friend to their father. And how kind he was to Cissie.

Yes, he was – and where did he get the money for those treats? He earned more money than Joey, but not that much more, and he was always moaning about the extortionate rent he had to pay for his lodgings. He must be up to something – but how to prove it?

Joey sighed and grasped the axe again. He chopped the remaining wood into manageable lengths and then began to stack them in the shed. As he picked up another armful, Agnes opened her door and called to him.

''Have a rest, lad. Here, I've made you a drink.' She held out a mug and said, 'I'll bring out a chair.'

'I'll do that,' Joey said. He dropped the wood and went into Agnes's cottage. Bringing out two chairs, he grinned. 'You deserve a sit down too. I bet you've been busy.'

He sipped the cool drink and licked his lips. 'Lovely – what is it?'

'Elderberry cordial. The last of it. I make it every year.'

'You'll have to show Emily how to make it,' he said.

'The berries should be ripe in a few weeks.'

'Where do you get them?' Joey asked.

'The trees grow along the bank of the ditch, on the edge of the marshes.' Agnes frowned. 'I'm not sure if I can do it this year.' She held out her hands, trying to flex her arthritic fingers. 'It was hard enough picking the berries last time.'

Joey laughed. 'Don't worry about that. You've got three pairs of hands to help now.'

Agnes shook her head. 'Emily's much too busy, and you're working.'

'You'll see. She'll be happy to help.' He finished his drink and handed the mug back to her. 'Better get on. The girls will be back soon.'

'I see they've gone out with that Lenny Lomax again.' Agnes pursed her lips. 'He's really getting his feet under the table.'

'I had noticed.' Joey groaned. 'What can I do about it, Agnes? Emily won't hear a word against him.'

'Pity.' She paused. 'Joey, lad. I don't want to speak out of turn, but I've heard things.'

'What things?'

Agnes shook her head. 'You ask Gladys and the other neighbours. They've known him for years.'

Although Joey pressed her, the old lady refused to say more. He nodded. So, his instincts were right. Lomax was bad news. Now, he had to get Emily to see it, too.

'Thanks, Agnes – for the drink and the chat.'

He went back to stacking the logs, his mind a whirl. What did Agnes know? She had seemed reluctant to tell him anything more.

He'd have a word with some of his workmates tomorrow. Everyone in the dockyard knew Lenny. He'd just have to be careful to talk to the right people. It wouldn't do for him to get wind of Joey's suspicions.

He had just finished and shut the shed door when he heard Cissie's high excited voice. The three of them entered the yard, laughing. Joey tensed when he saw that Lenny was holding hands with both his sisters.

Cissie pulled away and ran up to Joey. 'We had such fun,' she said. 'We watched some men fishing off the jetty, and one of them caught an enormous crab. He pretended to make it bite me and they all laughed.' She frowned. 'I wasn't frightened, though. Uncle Lenny told him off.'

Joey swallowed his annoyance and schooled his face into a smile. 'Glad you had fun, Cissie.' He hated his little sister calling that man 'uncle.'

Emily smiled. 'It was nice down by the water. You should have come with us.'

'I told you - I had jobs to do. The shed's full of wood for the winter now.'

'I hope you didn't work too hard.'

'Agnes gave me a drink and we sat down for a chat.' He followed them indoors and told them about the elderberry cordial.

When Lenny sat down in Dad's chair, Joey almost lost his temper. Any other visitor would be welcome to sit there, but it was Lenny's assumption that he could make himself at home that rankled. I suppose the bastard will want to stay for tea now, he thought.

He made up his mind to speak up this time but before he could say anything, Lenny pulled a package from his pocket. 'There was a man on the seafront selling hot pies from a cart, so I bought some. I thought it would save Emily cooking for us.'

Emily smiled. 'That's kind of you, Lenny,' she said. She turned to Joey. 'I expect you're hungry after all that wood chopping.'

He nodded. 'My back's killing me.'

'Oh, Joey, why didn't you say. Lenny, let Joey sit in Dad's chair for a bit.' She laughed. 'We still call it Dad's chair.'

Lenny got up slowly and plonked himself down on one of the kitchen chairs. Joey could tell he was annoyed, and he suppressed a grin. That will show you who's master here, he thought.

Chapter Fifteen

It was the first day of the autumn term, and Emily was busy in the office making a new register for the children who had just started school. She hadn't seen Mark today, although he was usually there very early, especially at the start of a new term.

Miss Cook had given her the list of new children and then left her to get on with it. Emily hadn't asked where Mark was. Since Joey had teased her about the head master's interest in her, she had tried to avoid him. Although she had laughed off her brother's comments, she was fully aware that Mark didn't want just friendship. And she wasn't prepared to get involved. She knew how sick his wife was and felt sorry for him but that was all.

She finished writing the names in the register and threw her pen down, leaning back and stretching, easing the ache from bending over the desk for so long.

The door opened, and Mark entered, going over to his own desk and sitting with his head in his hands. Not even a good morning, Emily thought. There must be something wrong. Dare she ask?

She cleared her throat and said, 'Is everything all right, Mr Thompson?'

He looked up, his face haggard, his eyes red-rimmed. 'I've just been talking to the doctor. He said...' He broke off and covered his face with his hands.

Emily waited. Jemima must be worse. 'Can't he do anything for her?' she asked tentatively.

'He's done his best but – it's hopeless.' He looked up at her. 'Oh, Emily, I'm losing her.' His voice broke.

Emily's heart went out to him, and she went over to put her arm round his shoulder. 'I'm so sorry, Mr Thompson,' she whispered.

He caught her hand and pulled her to him, clutching at her as he sobbed. 'It's been so hard, all these months, watching her slowly fading away.'

'I understand.' She gently stroked his hair, thinking of her father and the strain of looking after him. At least she had been fortunate to have her brother's support - and Lenny's, she thought.

Poor Mark had no one. How could she help him?

Lost in thought, she suddenly became aware that his arms had tightened around her. She gently tried to ease away, worried that Miss Cook or one of the children would come in.

'Emily, sweet Emily. How would I have got through without you?' he murmured.

Horrified, she pulled away. 'Please Mr Thompson...'

'Mark – I've asked you before to call me Mark. No need for formality when we're alone.'

'It's not right, Mr Thompson. You know it's not. I know you're upset now, so I'll just...' She stepped away from him and opened the office door.

'Please don't go.'

She pretended she hadn't heard him and hurried into the playground where Miss Cook supervised the children. The teacher spotted her and called out, but Emily couldn't face her.

She raised a hand and called, 'Sorry, I have to go.'

She ran all the way home and threw herself into Dad's chair before bursting into tears.

After a few moments she sat up, running her hands down her face. Why was life so complicated? She couldn't go back to the school after today. Now, she was forced to admit that she did find Mark attractive. Maybe if things were different... But no, it wouldn't do.

She smoothed her hair, went over to the sink, picked up the face flannel, and wiped the tears away. Keeping busy, that was the answer. She looked in the pantry under the stairs, but there wasn't much there. She'd have to go to the shops. Good thing Joey got paid tomorrow. She sighed. How would she manage if she gave up her school job?

She only had a few coppers in her purse – just enough to buy some carrots and onions to make soup. And there was a little bread left over from breakfast. It would have to do.

She took her jacket off the hook behind the door, jumping back as it opened from the other side.

She gasped. 'Lenny what are you doing here? Why aren't you at work?'

'I took the day off,' he said abruptly.

'Is everything all right? You haven't lost your job, have you?'

'No, no. I had to sort things out at home.'

Emily knew Lenny didn't get on with his landlady and often complained about his lodgings. 'What's happened?'

'She's chucked me out, the old cow.'

'Can she do that? You've always paid your rent on time, haven't you.'

Lenny nodded. He sank into Dad's chair. 'Her son's come home. She needs my room.' He sighed and looked up at Emily. 'What am I going to do, Em?' He dropped his gaze to the mattress, which was still in the corner.

She guessed he was hinting at being asked to stay here, but it was impossible. They were cramped already. No one had slept in Dad's bed since his death, and she had been planning to change things around so that Joey had his own space.

'I'm so sorry, Lenny. I hope you find somewhere soon.'

Lenny spread his hands. 'I've been looking all morning. There's nothing.'

Emily filled the kettle from the bucket on the draining board and set it on the hob. 'I'll make some tea,' she said. All thoughts of her encounter with Mark Thompson faded as she pondered how to cope with this new problem. Her instinct was to offer Lenny a bed for the night, just for tonight of course. Joey wouldn't like it, but he could hardly turn his father's old mate away.

Lenny's relief when she offered was overwhelming. He stood up and grasped her hands. 'Thank you, Emily. I hardly dared ask – but you offered. So kind, but then you're a very kind girl. I can't thank you enough.'

He went towards the door. 'I'll just get my stuff. I left it outside.'

Emily was a bit taken aback when he returned carrying two bags and a paper-wrapped parcel.

'Sorry,' he said. 'The old cow made me pack up all my things and take them with me.'

'That's all right, Lenny. But it's just for one night, mind. And only if Joey agrees.'

Lenny nodded and stowed his bags behind Dad's chair, then sat down again.

Emily handed him a cup of tea and then got on with making the soup, wondering how she could stretch it between the four of them. She reached up to a shelf over the sink, took down a box, and shook it. Only a little left but enough pearl barley to thicken the soup, she thought with relief.

As she worked, she noticed that Lenny kept glancing at the door. He was probably as nervous as she was about the coming confrontation with her brother. He must be aware of Joey's animosity. She just hoped there wouldn't be a row.

* * *

A week later Lenny was still staying at the cottage in St Paul's Close. Joey wasn't happy about it and had begun to dread getting home from work to find the other man ensconced in what had been his father's chair. Sleeping on his dad's mattress, too. He'd have to say something soon and risk upsetting his sister.

How does he always manage to get home before me, Joey wondered. He must skive off early. And how does he manage to get away with it?

Emily had persuaded him to let Lenny stay 'for just one night', but the swine was still there.

Joey couldn't let this situation go on; he'd have to have another go at persuading Emily to send him packing. He sighed. She'd only get upset and plead with him to let Lenny stay. 'He's got no one,' she said the last time he mentioned it. 'And he was such a good friend to Dad. He deserves our help.'

182

'He's taking advantage of your kindness, Em,' Joey had said. But he was unable to resist her pleading. He just hoped she wasn't getting too fond of the bastard. He was old enough to be her father. If only she could find a decent man – someone like Mark Thompson, he thought. Pity he wasn't available.

Joey was convinced there was something dodgy about Lenny Lomax. He had listened to gossip in the dockyard and had learned that Lomax was not popular with most of the men. He only seemed to be matey with a few blokes who Joey had noticed skulking in corners, doing as little work as possible. They were up to something, probably stealing from the stores. There was plenty of stuff they could sell on. If only he could find out for sure. Then he'd have a reason to warn Emily off. No wonder he was so generous to the girls. He obviously had another source of income. Joey knew his sister would not want anything to do with a criminal. She would be horrified to think she was benefitting from ill-gotten gains.

Cissie was playing in the yard with the cat when he got home from work. She ran up to him with a smile. 'Come and say hello to Kitty,' she said. His bad mood melted away at the sight of her, and he swung her up on his shoulder.

'How's my best girl today?' he asked.

'I got all the answers right in the spelling test,' she said with a broad grin.

Joey gave her a smacking kiss on her cheek. 'Such a clever girl.'

She held out her arm. 'Look what Uncle Lenny gave me,' she said, spinning the bracelet of blue beads around her wrist.

'He's not your uncle,' Joey snapped. He regretted speaking so sharply as his little sister's face crumpled and tears welled up.

'I know – but Em'ly said it's not polite to call grownups by their name,' she sniffled. 'She said Lenny could be my pretend uncle.'

Joey took a deep breath and controlled his annoyance. 'That's all right then – if Emily said so. Sorry.'

He hated upsetting Cissie. One more black mark against Lomax, he thought. Now the swine was coming between him and his adored little sister, as well as Emily.

As he was about to go into his home, Agnes came out of her cottage. 'Hello, lad. You look tired.'

'Busy as usual,' Joey said. He set Cissie down, and she ran indoors.

'So how come his lordship manages to get home early?' Agnes asked, nodding towards the Williams's front door.

Joey shrugged. He didn't want to get into a discussion with her. She had let him know how she felt about their new lodger more than once.

'He's still here then?' she persisted. 'You should send him packing before he really settles in.'

'I can't. Emily gets upset if I say anything. And he does pay his way. Besides, she says we shouldn't begrudge helping an old friend of Dad's.'

'Old friend?' Agnes scoffed. 'Did you know him before he brought your father home after the accident?'

Joey shook his head. 'Not really.'

'I thought not.' Agnes pursed her lips. 'I bet he was trying to impress his mates – playing the good Samaritan.'

'But they were workmates, good friends, I thought. And to be fair, he was a great help during Dad's illness.'

'Maybe.' She touched Joey's arm. 'If I were you, I'd ask around at work. You need to find out more about him before Emily gets too fond of him.'

It was what Joey had been afraid of. 'I'll have a word,' he said, 'make her listen.'

As he went to walk away, Agnes seized his hand. 'There's another thing. Don't know if it's true, but Gladys over the way told me he'd been chucked out of his lodgings for not paying the rent.'

'That's not what he told Emily.' So, the bastard had been lying. Seething, he opened the cottage door, ready to confront him. Bile rose in his throat at the sight of Lomax sprawled in what he still thought of as his father's chair.

Emily turned from the stove, a spoon in her hand. 'Had a good day, Joey?' she asked with a smile.

He nodded, managing to swallow his anger, although he longed to fly at Lomax, order him out of the house. So, Lomax had lied, but Joey had no proof that he'd done anything else wrong. No sense in worrying Emily until he could prove his suspicions. He decided that for the time being, he would try to be pleasant to the man.

The next day, he went about his work with his ears open. Usually, he took no notice of the other men's chat. They were always playing tricks and teasing the younger lads. The place was rife with gossip too – who was playing around with someone's wife, who was cheating at cards. He needed to find out if Lomax was being talked about.

Several days passed, and he began to despair about finding anything. He'd have to speak to Gladys and the other neighbours in St Paul's Close without alerting Emily to his suspicions.

A few days later, before he had a chance to do that, the foreman gathered the men in the boat house together and told them that there would be an inspection before they were allowed home at the end of their shift.

'There's been too much pilfering lately,' he said. 'I'm sorry to tell you that you'll all be searched at the end of shift today. Anyone found with something they shouldn't have on their person will be sacked on the spot.'

There were a few disgruntled murmurs and a couple of the men laughed nervously. 'Bit daft telling us beforehand,' one of them said.

Joey agreed. He had convinced himself that Lenny and his mates were among the guilty. Now forewarned, they could get rid of anything incriminating.

One of the older men grabbed Joey's arm. 'They're not that daft, son. They know stuff goes missing and, as long as it doesn't get out of hand, they turn a blind eye.'

'So why the search then?'

'I reckon they have an idea who they're after. They'll be watching to see where they hide the stuff.'

Joey nodded. That made sense. He wasn't sure why he was so convinced that Lomax was a thief. But he always seemed to have plenty of money to spend on those little treats for his sisters, more than he could afford on what he earned in the dockyard. Joey told himself his suspicions were because he hated the man and wanted a reason to get him out of his sister's life. Well, after the search, he would know for sure.

Chapter Sixteen

Joey's team had been among the first to be searched and, despite knowing he had done nothing wrong, he felt a bit nervous as he emptied his pockets and handed over his tool bag.

'Sorry about this, mate,' his overseer said, handing back the bag.

Joey grinned and nodded. For one dreadful moment, he'd been afraid that Lomax might have tried to incriminate him by slipping something into his bag. He wouldn't have been surprised if Lomax had tried to get him arrested. He knew the man hated him, despite his efforts to be pleasant in front of Emily. If he was arrested, it would leave the way open for him to worm his way further into the lives of the two Williams girls.

He was desperate to hear the outcome of the search and was tempted to hang around but he decided to wait until he got home and heard what Lomax had to say.

Emily greeted him with a smile. 'Nice to see you home early for a change,' she said, glancing behind him. 'Where's Lenny?'

Joey bit back a retort and said, 'Some of them had to stay behind.' He didn't mention the stealing and subsequent searches.

Cissie sat at the table, drawing with her crayons on an old paper bag. He went over and sat beside her. "What are you up to then, princess?'

She showed him a barely recognisable picture. 'It's Kitty,' she said.

'Very good,' he said, ruffling her hair. He turned to Emily. 'Been busy today?'

'Not really. I've given up my job at the school.'

'Why? I thought you liked working there.'

'It's too much.' Her voice rose. '– doing two jobs and looking after the family as well as a lodger.'

'Why don't we get rid of the lodger then? That would make your life easier.'

'I can't. He has nowhere to go.'

'That's his problem, not yours.'

Emily's lips tightened. 'Why are you so hard on him?'

Joey was saved from answering when the door opened and Lenny came in, a big grin on his face. So, he'd got away with it then – that's if he actually was guilty of anything. Maybe it's just my suspicious mind, Joey thought. And the fact that I can't stand the man.

'How did it go then?' he asked, trying to sound pleasant.

Lenny laughed. 'They didn't find anything. Bit daft warning us about the search, don't you think?' He sat down in the armchair.

Joey nodded, unable to speak, the sight of the other man's smug smile told him his suspicions were correct. His hatred of Lomax taking over his father's chair as if he had a right to it, caused his temper to rise. One day he knew he would not be able to control himself.

'What's all this?' Emily asked.

Lenny told her about the stealing and how everyone was under suspicion. 'It's caused a lot of unrest among the men. Not very nice being suspected of pilfering,' he said.

'Well, nothing to worry about if you haven't done anything wrong,' Emily said.

'Well, I didn't like being treated like a criminal,' Lenny snapped. 'Don't you agree, Joey?'

'They were just doing their job.'

'Don't have to like it though, do we?'

'Now, then, you two, calm down. Tea's nearly ready. Joey, could you please get some wood in for the stove? And Lenny, could you set the table while I mash the potatoes?' Emily smiled at each in turn, and they hastened to do her bidding.

Joey grabbed an armful of logs and slammed the shed door. Why couldn't she ask Lomax to get the wood? He took the fuel indoors and, as he stacked it by the stove, he glanced at Lomax and was sure he caught a smirk on the man's face.

He stood up and grabbed his jacket off the back of the door. 'Sorry, Em. Just remembered I promised to meet Bill in the Red Lion. I'll have mine when I get back.'

He rushed out without giving Emily a chance to answer.

At the entrance to the Red Lion, he paused and took a deep breath. He didn't know how he had stopped himself from ramming his fist into Lomax's smirking face. He'd just had to get out of the house. He pushed open the door to the public bar, hoping that Bill Brent would be there. The policeman wasn't a regular drinker, but he sometimes popped in for a pint after work. He'd try and bring Lomax into the conversation. Perhaps Bill would know something about the man.

* * *

'Put your crayons away and eat your tea,' Emily said, plonking a plate of sausage and mash in front of Cissie.

Lenny leaned across the table. 'You can do your drawing after tea. I'll help you,' he said.

Cissie pouted. 'I wanted Joey to help.'

'Well, he's gone out, so you'll have to make do with me.' He softened his words with a laugh.

Emily smiled. 'Joey won't be long.'

Cissie didn't reply, just dug her fork into the creamy mash.

The three ate in silence for a few moments, then Emily said, 'I wonder why Joey had to go out in such a hurry.'

'Might be something to do with what went on at work today. Perhaps he has some information for your policeman friend.'

'I don't think so, Lenny. He would have said. Bill's a friend. They often have a pint together.'

Lenny didn't reply and carried on eating. Emily wished Joey would come home. She hated it when he was in a mood, which seemed to be more often lately. He'd always been such a cheerful willing lad, and such a help during their father's illness. Since going to work in the dockyard he had changed. He never complained, but she sometimes wondered whether he resented not being able to take up his apprenticeship.

Joey had still not returned by the time they finished their meal, and Lenny helped her wash up. She got Cissie ready for bed and went up with her, waiting until she had settled down to sleep before going down and joining Lenny.

As usual, he was sitting in Dad's chair. She didn't mind as long as he gave it up to Joey when he got home. It was the only comfortable chair they had and he had been hard at work all day as well.

She sat at the table with her sewing basket and started to mend one of Cissie's dresses which she had torn while running around the playground at school.

Lenny looked across at her and smiled. 'What a lovely picture you make in the candlelight. Still, you shouldn't spend too long sewing. It's not good for your eyes.'

She felt her face flushing, not being used to compliments. 'It's all right, Lenny. I must get this done so Cissie can wear it to school tomorrow.'

'It's nice just the two of us, isn't it,' he said. 'Why don't you come and sit near me? I've got something to say to you.'

Emily's heart beat a little faster. She had an idea of what was in his mind. She wasn't sure how she would respond. It wasn't like it had been with Mark, a married man. She looked across at him, smiling.

'What it is?' she asked.

He sat up straighter in the chair, leaning forward with his hands clasped in front of him. 'I've been thinking. In fact, I've been a bit worried.'

'Worried? What about?'

'Well – me living here. You know – these old gossips around here, talking about you – a single woman – living with an older man.'

Emily shifted in her seat. It had not occurred to her that there was anything wrong in their arrangement. 'But Joey's here as well,' she protested.

'He won't always be here. He said something the other day about joining the navy.'

'No. I don't believe you. He would have mentioned it to me.'

'He's afraid of upsetting you.'

Emily was shocked. She didn't want to believe that Joey would abandon his family. But then, he hadn't been himself lately. That must be what was on his mind. She took a deep breath. 'I can't stop him, if that's what he wants...'

'Of course. You can understand he doesn't want to be a dockyard labourer for ever, smart young man like him.' Lenny leaned back in the chair. 'If he goes away, I wouldn't want me being here to cause you any bother.'

Did he mean he would leave, too? Suddenly, Emily felt cold. The thought of being left to fend for herself with only Cissie for company was frightening. She suddenly realised how much easier her life had been recently with two men bringing in a wage. It was why she'd felt she could give up her school job.

She threw her sewing down. 'Lenny, please, you wouldn't have to leave.'

'I don't want to, but – your reputation...' He sighed. 'I can think of a way out if you...'

'If I what?'

'If you married me. That would make things right, wouldn't it?' Before Emily could speak, he went on, 'Oh, I know you're going to refuse me. I'm too old, I couldn't give you a nice home...'

'No, no – you're not too old,' Emily protested.

He stood up and seized her hands. 'You mean...?' He gazed into her eyes. 'Emily, sweetheart, you don't know how I've longed to ask you. I didn't dare hope...'

How had she not realised before? He had been so gentlemanly, never a look or word out of place. Her thoughts flew to Mark and the way he had behaved,

Emily didn't stop to think. She smiled up at him and said, 'Yes, I will marry you.'

He pulled her towards him. 'Now, at last, I can kiss you.' She raised her face to his and his lips met hers. After a moment, she pulled away, whispering, 'Joey might come in.'

'Don't you worry about him, my love. He'll be pleased for us, I'm sure.'

Emily wasn't so sure.

* * *

It was getting late, and Joey still hadn't come home. Emily said goodnight to Lenny, allowing him another kiss before going upstairs and snuggling down beside Cissie. Usually, she was asleep in minutes, but tonight, she couldn't settle. The events of the evening went round and round in her head. That first kiss had been nothing like she had imagined, pleasant enough, but it hadn't roused in her the romantic feelings she had dreamt of.

Living in such close conditions on the hulks, she had been well aware since she was a child of what went on between men and women. She had not thought much about being married and had never thought she would meet anyone who'd be willing to take on her sick father and younger sister.

But Lenny – had she really agreed to marry him? She had no doubt he would be a good husband, kind and generous to both her and Cissie as he had been since the day he brought her father home after the accident. And look at how he'd cared for her father ever since. Yes, she was doing the right thing.

As she turned over in bed and began to drift off to sleep, she heard voices. She sat up. Oh good, Joey's home, she thought, and lay down again. Her eyes closed, only to fly open at the sound of a slammed door.

Who had gone out at this time of night? Joey or Lenny? Whoever it was, hadn't just gone across to the privy in the yard. The slamming of the door told her something was wrong.

She sat up, stroking Cissie's hair as the little girl whimpered softly in her sleep. 'It's all right, lovie,' she whispered.

Careful not to disturb Cissie, she got out of bed, halting at the top of the stairs as the door at the bottom opened.

'Sorry, love. Didn't mean to wake you,' Lenny said quietly.

'Where's Joey gone?

'I don't know – think he had a bit too much to drink. Don't worry, he'll be back. Go back to bed, love. We'll talk in the morning.'

'Goodnight then.' Emily crept back to bed, but she couldn't sleep. Joey never drank to excess. Something must have upset him. She thrust away the thought that it might have anything to do with Lenny. She knew Joey didn't like him, but surely he would want her to be happy.

As she drifted off to sleep, a picture of a lad with bright red hair and startling green eyes invaded her memory. Harry Jones had never been far from her thoughts in all these years. She always remembered him in her prayers and hoped that he had found a good life in Australia. She'd kept count as the years passed and knew he would have finished his sentence a year ago. What was he doing now, she wondered. She sighed and turned over in bed. Harry was miles away, on the other side of the world. Besides, he had probably forgotten her.

Marriage to Lenny was her only option. She and Cissie would be secure, even if Joey did decide to join the navy.

Chapter Seventeen

The wedding was a very simple affair in St Paul's Church with just her family there, as well as Sergeant Brent and a few neighbours, including Agnes and Gladys.

Lenny had no family, and one of his workmates was the best man, someone Emily had never met.

At one point Emily had feared that her brother wouldn't attend. He had spent the past few weeks trying to persuade her not to marry. But she had refused to give in.

'I don't know why you're so against it,' she'd cried. 'You don't have to like him, just accept him.'

'I think you could do better for yourself,' he said.

'If you could give me one good reason...'

'He's too old,' was all he could say.

Joey finally gave in to Emily's tearful pleas and agreed to give her away, only after she told him she would ask Sergeant Brent to stand in for their father. 'It should be one of my family,' she'd sobbed.

As she walked up the aisle on his arm, with Cissie as a bridesmaid, she wished with all her heart that her father was still here. He should have been the one holding her arm today.

She bit back a sob and forced a smile as she approached Lenny, looking very smart in his Sunday best, his wiry dark curls slicked down with water which had made the grey streaks less prominent. She thought he looked almost handsome.

He took her hand and whispered, 'You look lovely. I'm a very lucky man.'

He had wanted to buy her and Cissie new dresses for the wedding but she had refused. She had cut down one of her old dresses for Cissie and sewed pink ribbons and lace onto it. Cissie had been delighted with it. Emily was wearing one of her late mother's dresses which she had been keeping for just this sort of occasion. It was pale green with white lace trimmings, bought when the family had been better off. She still had the silk dress her mother had been married in, but something had made her choose this one. She was pleased Lenny seemed to like what she was wearing.

The service passed in a blur, and before she knew it, Emily was standing in the church porch, Lenny's hand gripping her arm. The vicar shook their hands, and the neighbours showered them with congratulations.

Emily just wanted to get home, but Lenny raised his voice. 'Come on, everyone. Drinks on me at the Red Lion.'

'They're not open,' Emily protested. 'Besides, we can't take Cissie in.'

'Landlord's a mate of mine, opening up specially so it's all right for Cissie to come in. His wife has laid on some food.'

They all followed him to the nearby pub, where he ordered drinks for everyone. They raised their glasses in a toast to the happy couple, and Lenny bowed and grinned, basking in the attention.

'Come on, Joey, drink up,' Lenny urged. 'Have another.'

Joey scowled but drained his glass and held it out for a refill. Emily glanced across at him, wishing he would try to look happy for her. She sipped her drink and chatted to her friends, smiling as Cissie danced around the room. At least she was enjoying the occasion.

And so was Lenny from the sound of laughter from the other end of the bar. She'd lost count of how many drinks he'd had. Joey, leaning on the bar, also seemed to have re-filled his glass a bit too often for her liking.

Perhaps it was time to make a move for home.

Cissie was showing off and getting a bit too excited. It was time she was taken home, too. She called out to her, but Cissie ignored her, tugging on Joey's hand. 'I've just told Agnes – Lenny's not my uncle any more, he's my brother, so I can call him just Lenny.'

Joey scowled. 'Not your real brother. He's your brother-in-law.'

'Is he your brother too now?' she asked.

'I suppose so.' He slammed his glass down on the counter. 'Well, I'm off,' he announced.

It was the signal to break up the party, and Emily was relieved when Lenny finished his drink and thanked everyone for coming. The landlord looked relieved, too, as it was nearly time to open up for the evening session.

As they neared St Paul's Close, everyone drifted away until only Agnes remained. She spoke to Emily in a low voice. 'Would you like Cissie to stay with me tonight?' She nodded meaningfully. 'Give you two some privacy.'

'Good idea,' Lenny said.

Emily shook her head. 'That's kind, but Joey will be back soon.'

Agnes tightened her lips. 'I doubt it.'

Lenny bent down and took Cissie's hand. 'You'd like to stay with Agnes, wouldn't you?'

Cissie nodded. 'I can play with Kitty.' She followed Agnes into her cottage, turning to wave to Emily.

Lenny seized Emily's arm and almost dragged her into the house. Inside, he put his arms around her and pulled her close. 'At last. I've been longing for this moment all day.'

He looked around the room, his eyes gleaming, a smile playing around his lips. 'I see you've been busy.' He looked towards the stair door. 'I take it the room's all ready for us.'

She nodded, a warm flush stealing over her face.

He laughed. 'No need to be shy, my love. I bet you're not as innocent as you look.'

Emily wanted to protest. She knew what to expect, but that didn't mean she'd ever done anything she shouldn't. She hoped that wasn't what he had meant.

He urged her towards the stairs, looking around with approval at the changes she had made up here. Joey's narrow bed had been moved downstairs, and the mattress he and their father had slept on was now under the window, which was made up with clean sheets and a paisley-patterned eiderdown.

* * *

Emily lay with her eyes wide open, staring at the outline of the window and praying for dawn. This wasn't how she'd imagined her married life would be. And this wasn't the Lenny she thought she'd known.

She'd expected some tenderness, gentleness but he had shown another side of himself. She was sure she'd have bruises from his frenzied attack. Just as she had started to drift off to sleep, he had grabbed her again.

'I didn't hurt you, did I, love? I didn't mean to - I just couldn't stop myself. I've waited so long...' He ran his hands down her body. 'It will be better this time.'

But it wasn't. Emily was thankful that Cissie wasn't in the room. Tears squeezed between her eyelids. What have I done, she asked herself. She couldn't understand how someone who had been so generous, so kind to her and her little sister, could turn into a monster overnight.

She didn't love Lenny, didn't even like him sometimes, but she had been willing to overlook his drinking and nastiness to her brother. It was worth it for the sake of security for her and her little sister. I must make the best of things and try to be a good wife to him, she vowed, if only for Cissie's sake. She sighed and turned over in bed, hoping she would manage to sleep at last.

Memories of life on the hulks and the awful things she had heard through the thin partitions between the living quarters crept into her mind. Her mother had explained that not all men were like that. 'I'm so lucky to have a husband like your father,' she'd said. 'I hope that you'll find one like him one day.'

The next morning, Emily crept downstairs, trying not to wake Lenny. He lay on his back, snoring, and she looked at him with contempt. It was going to be hard to act the loving wife, especially in front of her brother. She dreaded what would happen if Joey ever got an inkling of her husband's true character.

Joey was still asleep too, sprawled out on the narrow bed in the corner of the living room. His mouth was open, and she grinned. Too much beer. I bet he'll have a blinder of a headache when he wakes, Lenny too. Serve them both right.

I suppose I'll have to fetch water before we can have a cup of tea, she thought, but as she went to pick up the bucket, she was surprised to find it full. She knew Lenny hadn't done it, and she hadn't heard Joey come home last night. He must have come in really late, and he couldn't have been as drunk as she'd thought.

She filled the kettle, riddled the embers in the range and added kindling. The fire soon flared up, and in minutes, the kettle was starting to boil. She made a lot of noise preparing breakfast, not caring if she woke the two men.

She was sitting at the table sipping her tea and nibbling toast when Lenny stumbled downstairs, rubbing his eyes and yawning.

'Why didn't you wake me?' he asked.

'I thought you needed your sleep,' she said. 'Anyway, breakfast is ready. Help yourself. I'm going over to fetch Cissie.'

'You can pour my tea first – and make more toast,' he said.

She didn't answer and stood up.

'Good girl,' Lenny said. 'What a good little wifey you are.'

Emily swallowed and moved towards the door. 'I said I'm going to fetch Cissie.'

He stepped towards her and grabbed her wrist. 'I want my breakfast,' he snapped.

'As I said, it's there on the table. I won't be a minute.'

At that moment, Joey sat up. 'Ooh, my head,' he mumbled.

Lenny dropped Emily's hand and leaned towards her, brushing her cheek with his lips. 'Go and fetch Cissie, sweetheart. We'll all have breakfast together – a real family.'

Joey laughed. 'None of that lovey-dovey stuff just because you're married now.'

Emily rushed out of the door, her cheeks burning. So that was how it was going to be – putting on an act for her brother and showing her his real character in private.

She knocked on Agnes's door and pushed it open, forcing a smile for her friend and little sister.

Cissie ran up to her and threw her arms around her. 'I slept in Agnes's bed. She said it was nice to have someone to keep her warm.'

Agnes laughed. 'It was, too. Kitty joined us too, so we were really cosy.'

'Can we go home now? I want to see my two brothers.'

'Lenny's not your real brother,' Emily said. 'He's my husband now, so as I explained, he's your brother-in-law.'

Cissie thought for a moment. 'Joey's still my brother, though?'

'Of course he is.'

'That's all right then.' She tugged Emily's hand. 'Come on then.'

'I'll pop over later, Agnes, help you to fold that laundry. Don't you dare try to do it yourself.'

* * *

Emily had been married for three weeks and she was proud of the way she was coping. Her days had really not changed much, except that she seemed to be tired all the time. Not surprising considering Lenny's nightly assaults on her body. She longed to confide in somebody, but there was only Agnes, and she couldn't burden the older woman with her problems. She was in constant pain from her arthritis and never complained. Emily helped her all she could, and the hours spent working together were all she had to look forward to now.

When anyone was around, Lenny was the old, kind, helpful man he had been before their marriage. But alone, he constantly criticised her cooking, her household skills and her care for Cissie.

'That child is getting out of hand, thinks the sun shines out of her arse. She's spending too much time with that old woman across the way. Spoilt, she is.'

'You were the one who spoilt her,' Emily protested.

'All very well when she was a little tot, but she's growing up. She's got to learn she can't always have her own way.'

Emily knew better than to argue further. Lenny would get angry and end up breaking something. Never in front of Joey, though. Emily had lost count of the number of times she had owned up to dropping a plate or a cup. Anything to avoid a row.

Sometimes Emily thought about confiding in Joey. He would believe her. After all, he was the one who had warned her against marrying Lenny. But remembering how she had fought his concerns and insisted on going her own way, she didn't expect any sympathy.

On this bright but chilly autumn afternoon, Emily had finished her chores and decided to go down to the grocer's before Cissie got home from school.

Mrs Collins greeted her with a smile. 'How are you liking married life then, Em?' she said with a twinkle in her eye.

Emily blushed and said, 'It's fine.'

'You're looking very well on it.'

Emily didn't answer but consulted her shopping list.

As she piled the goods onto the counter, Mrs Collins continued to chat, asking how Cissie was getting on at school and how Agnes was. Emily answered briefly, then when she'd paid for her shopping, she said, 'Sorry, Mrs Collins. I must go. Cissie will be home from school soon. Goodbye.'

Outside the shop, she paused, hoping she hadn't appeared rude to the shopkeeper.

But it was hard to keep up the fiction that she was a happy newlywed.

As she turned the corner, she saw Cissie playing hopscotch with a couple of children from the next close.

'I'm sorry I wasn't home when you finished school,' she said. 'I don't like you coming home to an empty house. Better come along now.'

'Can't I finish the game? Lenny said I could play for a while. He said he wants to talk to you.'

'Lenny's home?' Emily caught her breath. Why so early? She nodded to Cissie. 'Yes, but don't stay out too long.'

She hurried across the yard, not stopping when Agnes called to her. The door flew open and she was dragged inside. 'Where have you been?' Lenny hissed.

'Shopping,' she stammered.

He grabbed her shopping bag and looked inside., then threw himself down in the armchair. His face changed and he looked sad. 'I was worried about you. I got home to find the house empty and Cissie playing out in the street. I thought...' He covered his face with his hands.

She almost felt sorry for him but she realised what he had been thinking when he asked, 'Who served you then? Was It that Mr Collins?'

Not concern for her welfare then or worried she might have had an accident, but jealousy. She could have laughed if she hadn't been so angry. Poor Mr Collins, sixty if he was a day and devoted to his wife.

'I had a chat with Mrs Collins,' she said, 'and then came home.'

'A chat! You women spend too much time gossiping when you should be home looking after your menfolk.'

Emily did not deign to reply, just got on with preparing the meal.

* * *

A few days later Cissie came home from school bursting with news. Before Emily could ask why she was home early, she said, 'Miss Cook told us we must all be very quiet as she had something sad to tell us.'

Emily held her breath. It was news she'd been expecting for some time.

'Mr Thompson's wife has died,' Cissie said. 'The poor lady has been ill a long time, Miss Cook told us.'

'That is sad news,' Emily said. 'I knew she was ill but...'

'Anyway, no school tomorrow – to show respect Miss Cook said.' Cissie's sorrowful face was replaced with a smile, and she tugged on Emily's hand. 'So, can I help you and Agnes with the laundry? I like turning the handle on the mangle.'

It would be good to have help, Emily thought. Perhaps they'd get the laundry finished before Lenny came home from work. He was always bad-tempered when she wasn't at home to greet him.

Joey was late, and Lenny refused to wait for him. 'If he wants to eat, he should get home on time,' Lenny snapped. 'I'm hungry, so get on with dishing it up.'

Emily complied, anxious to keep the peace in front of Cissie.

They sat at the table eating their meal when Cissie broke the silence, 'No school tomorrow. I'm helping Emily with the laundry.'

'No, you're not.' Lenny's fork clattered onto the table. 'You're too young to start work.' He turned to Emily. 'What's the idea? And why didn't you discuss it with me?'

'It's only for tomorrow. The school is closed because of the headmaster's bereavement.' Before she could say more, he laughed.

'So, his wife's kicked the bucket. He's free at last.' His voice changed, and he banged his fist on the table. 'Free to come sniffing round you again. Pity you didn't wait a bit longer.'

Emily swallowed the tears that threatened. 'How can you say such a thing? There was never...'

'So you say, but I've heard things.'

Emily pushed her plate away and stood up. She had saved Joey's tea and put it in the oven to keep warm.

As she began to clear away, Lenny said, 'Don't bother keeping it hot. He's probably in the pub.'

* * *

When Joey got home, he sensed an atmosphere. Emily looked near tears and Lenny, tight-lipped, was tapping his fingers on the table.

'Sorry I'm late – overtime,' he said, attempting to sound cheerful. 'I hope you've saved me some grub.'

'Of course, I have.'

'Thanks.' Joey sat at the table and looked at Emily. 'What's up?'

Cissie spoke up. 'We're sad because Mr Thompson's wife died.'

'Sorry to hear that. Still, not unexpected, is it? She'd been ill a long time.'

Emily got his plate out of the oven and placed it on the table. Joey nodded his thanks, and she sat down opposite him. 'I expect you'll go to the funeral,' he said.

'I don't think so,' Lenny said quickly. 'Emily didn't know the woman.'

Joey didn't like the other man's tone, but he didn't comment. Emily had a mind of her own. She would go if she wanted to. He remembered how he had wished Mark Thompson was a free man. Pity it was too late now, he thought.

He tried to hide his dislike of his sister's husband and instead asked Cissie how she was doing at school, laughing when she told him she was going to help with the laundry. 'You're a bit little to be turning that big mangle,' he said.

'I'm little, but I'm strong,' she said. 'And when I'm old enough to leave school, I'm going to work with Em and Agnes.' She gazed at him earnestly. 'Poor Agnes is very old, and she can't work as hard as she used to. They need my help.'

Before Joey could reply, Lenny butted in. 'Cissie love. You can get a better job than that. Besides, Agnes can't pay much. You could earn a lot more working in the ropery at the dockyard.'

'She won't be working there,' Joey snapped.

Cissie looked from one to the other, bewildered. 'Em – I don't have to leave school now, do I?'

'Of course not. You've another two years yet. Plenty of time to talk about work.'

'Don't worry, Cissie, love,' Joey said. 'I know you meant you were only helping Agnes tomorrow, and it's kind of you to lend a hand.' He turned to Lenny. 'We're not so hard up we have to send a child out to work.'

'You got me wrong, Joey, mate.' He turned to Cissie and stroked her hair. 'I only want what's best for you, love.'

'I'm sure you do, Lenny,' Emily said.

Joey finished eating and took his plate over to the sink. 'Shall I wash up for you, Em?'

'No thanks. You and Lenny have both been at work all day so...'

'I thought of popping down to the Red Lion for a pint. You coming, Lenny?' He didn't really want his brother-in-law's company, but he hated leaving the girls alone with him, although, now that he and Emily were married, he couldn't do much about it.

Lenny heaved himself out of the armchair and grabbed his jacket. He kissed Emily on the cheek and followed Joey out of the door.

The pub was full, and Joey sighed with relief when Lenny joined one of his mates, leaving him to lean on the bar and sip his beer.

He nodded greetings to a couple of acquaintances but wasn't in the mood to join in a game of darts or crib. He didn't recognise the man Lenny was talking to but they seemed very friendly. He wondered what they were talking about, especially when Lenny looked up at him and then turned his back. Both men lowered their voices, too, and Joey was suddenly reminded of the recent trouble at the dockyard. The thieves hadn't been caught, but Joey still suspected that Lenny was involved. No proof, though, and suspicions weren't enough.

Poor Emily was stuck with that nasty piece of work. Lenny could be as caring and loving as he liked in public, but deep inside,

Joey knew it was a different story when Emily was home alone with him.

Lomax was very careful, but sometimes the mask slipped. Joey couldn't wait to catch him out. He was so worried about his sister. In the past few weeks, she had become pale and listless, and she'd lost weight. She would never admit it but he knew she was bitterly regretting her hasty marriage. At least there were no signs that Lomax was violent towards her – so far.

Joey clenched his fingers around his glass. If he ever saw signs of bruises on his sister, he would make the bastard pay, whatever the consequences.

Chapter Eighteen

It was payday, and Harry's mates had gone off to the pub, but this time, he would not be persuaded to join them. He went back to the bunkhouse and lit a lamp, retrieving his writing materials from the box under his bunk.

He lifted the false bottom and took out the leather pouch containing his savings. Before adding his week's pay, he counted what was in the pouch and sighed. The carefully hoarded coins still didn't quite add up to enough to gain his freedom.

He picked up the opal he had bought from the miner, almost regretting that impulse to spend such a big portion of his savings. He would have had enough by now to make his way to Sydney and book his passage. He held the stone up to the lamplight, twisting it round to catch the play of colours. That blue! It reminded him so much of Emily. He pictured her face when he handed it to her and smiled. Despite the teasing from his mates, he would not give up his dream of seeing her again, and he wouldn't give up writing to her.

He sat for several minutes, chewing the end of his pencil and telling himself that, one day, his dream of receiving a letter from her would come true. But tonight, he couldn't hold on to the dream. Common sense told him she wouldn't know where to write. And how could he even be sure Emily had received his letters - and if she did, would she bother to read them? He wished he'd had more schooling. The pencilled scrawl was badly spelt and almost illegible. Why bother?

He threw his pencil down and leaned back in his chair. But he couldn't give up. He'd have one more try. He'd tell her his sentence was up, and it wouldn't be too long before he'd be on his way home. He always thought of Blue Town as home. He pictured himself knocking on the cottage door, her delight as she recognised him and welcomed him in. Or was that just a dream, too?

He picked up the pencil again and started to write. When he'd finished, he signed his name and wrote the address he thought he'd remembered from all those years ago. Why did he bother when he didn't even know if she'd received his letters?

He almost screwed up the sheet of paper, but after a moment, he folded it and put it in his pocket. He wasn't sure whether he would post this one.

He pulled his box from under the bunk, the one that held all his worldly possessions – not much, just a change of clothes, a couple of tattered books given to him by Jack Kennedy, his boss,

He added this week's wages and counted the coins again, although he knew how much he had. Surely it would be enough to return to Sydney and book passage on an England-bound ship. Now that the dream had become a possibility, he wasn't sure he would go. After all, what was there for him in England? Nothing really.

But then an image of Emily crept into his mind. Emily as he'd last seen her – beautiful, her blue eyes sparkling, that lovely smile as she waved to him and whispered, 'Good Luck.' She would have changed for sure, as he had. But he couldn't get that picture out of his head – it had kept him sane through those years of hard labour on the chain gang, followed by his so-called freedom on the sheep station.

He had just tipped the coins back into the bag when he heard raucous singing and laughter. The station hands were back from the pub. He should have gone with them, not stayed behind brooding. Ernie's voice was the loudest of all as he stumbled into the bunkhouse,

'Ginger, me old mate, you missed a good night out.' He slapped Harry on the back, his eyes widening as he heard the clink of coins.

'What ch'er got there, mate?' He turned to his mates. 'Ginger's been holding out on us. He's got plenty of moolah.'

'Not enough for a stake though, I bet, eh Ginge?' Chalky said.

'What do you mean?' Harry hastily tucked the bag into the box and folded his clothes over it.

'We've been talking about giving up here and going opal hunting,' Steve said. 'We met that bloke again, the one you bought the stone from.'

The men all began talking at once, and Harry waved at them to stop. 'Opal hunting? Are you mad?' He knew those dazzlingly beautiful blue and green stones were worth more than gold. He'd heard stories of amazing finds and realised he'd been lucky to get that small opal at such a reasonable price.

But to go into the outback digging for them, hoping to make their fortune. They must be mad. Harry could understand anyone being tempted. But he had also heard tales of those who had ventured into the outback and lost everything, sometimes even their lives.

'It's worth a gamble,' Ernie said. 'Better than breaking our backs and risking a whipping from that bastard of a foreman.'

Harry could understand the appeal of maybe striking it rich, but he wasn't a gambler. 'You mean to give up a paying job with good grub and a roof over your head, not to mention a regular wage?'

'Yeah. We only have to find a good spot, and we'll be quids in.' Ernie slapped Harry on the back again. 'Why don't you join us? You could make enough in a few weeks to

take you back to England and plenty left over
to start afresh.'

'No thanks. I've already made up my
mind.' He grinned at the men surrounding
him. 'Good luck fellas. You'll need it.'

Tom, who'd been quiet so far, said
hesitantly, 'We can't go yet though, we
need...'

Ernie seized his arm, and Tom yelped.

Harry looked from one to the other.
'What...?'

'We've been trying to raise a stake – you
know, a down payment on supplies, tents,
food, tools.'

Harry guessed what Ernie was hinting at
but he shook his head. If they needed money
so badly, why spend it in the pub? 'Sorry,
fellas. Can't help you.'

'You've got plenty. I know you've been
squirreling it away every payday.'

'Only enough to get me back to England.'

'What's the rush? Come in with us and
you'll go back to the old country a rich man,
have something to offer that sweetheart
you've been writing to.' Ernie grinned. 'Come
on, you can't lose.'

'I'll think about it,' Harry said. He
pushed his box under the bunk and climbed
into bed.

Ernie shrugged. 'OK, fellas. Looks like
we'll have to stick it out here for another
couple of paydays, and then – Lightning
Ridge here we come.'

After a bit of grumbling, the men settled into their bunks, and Ernie turned out the oil lamp.

Chalky leaned down from the top bunk. 'We hoped you'd help with the stake. Ernie reckons you've got plenty.' His voice rose. 'We would have paid you back once we struck lucky.'

'Sorry. I'm going back to England.'

Chalky sighed. 'It's your loss.' He turned over, and soon, only the sound of snoring filled the bunkhouse.

Harry didn't sleep, though. Chalky and Tom were decent blokes, but he didn't trust Ernie or Steve, who were both former convicts. They knew he'd been saving to get back to England, and they must have a pretty good idea of what he had in that box. They must have known he'd refuse to go in with them – all he ever talked about was getting back to the old country. They were forever teasing him about it. He was convinced they planned to steal his stash.

He'd have to make his move before they had a chance to rob him. He'd already spoken to Mr Kennedy, who'd given him his letter of discharge and would take him into town next time he took the wagon in. Harry couldn't wait that long now. He'd just have to chance that he had enough for his passage. As a last resort, he could sell the opal.

He slid out of the bunk, quietly pulled on trousers and shirt, then slipped his feet into his boots. He fumbled in the dark for the leather bag, wrapping it in a spare shirt to hide the clink of coins. He'd have to leave the rest of his belongings behind.

He froze for a moment at the sound of a grunt and muttered exclamation from the bunk above him. Then Chalky turned over and, in seconds, was snoring again.

Outside, the full moon lit up the surrounding landscape, and Harry raced across to the stables, stopping in the shadows to catch his breath.

He opened the door of the end stall and whispered, 'It's only me, Bluey.' The horse gave a soft whicker, and Harry stroked the animal's nose, whispering soothing words. He knew horse stealing was a capital offence, but he had no qualms about taking the animal. After all, Bluey was 'his' horse, the one he'd ridden since coming to work here. And he didn't intend to keep him. He would ride Bluey into town and leave him at the pub with some money and a note. If he rode hard, he would be there before he was missed. The mail coach to Sydney went through once a week. He just hoped he'd got the right day. If not, he'd just have to start hitching.

He wasn't worried about being caught. Mr Kennedy was a fair man and Harry was sure he would not pursue him. Hadn't he wished him luck when he'd given notice and offered any help?

So Harry salved his conscience as he rode Bluey through the night, leaving the

Kennedy station behind without a backward glance.

* * *

The small settlement was just coming awake as Harry rode along the main street. He passed the forge where the blacksmith was already hard at work shoeing a horse and the store which sold everything imaginable from flour and sugar to tools and pots and pans. The storekeeper standing on the veranda raised a hand in greeting. Harry responded and rode on towards the pub.

A woman was sweeping the dusty veranda, and Harry called out to her. 'Boss around?'

'Round the back,' she replied.

Harry dismounted and tied Bluey to the rail. 'Good boy,' he murmured, patting the horse's neck and then walking round the side of the building.

Ned, the publican, straightened when he heard Harry's footsteps. 'What you doing here so early? Pub's not open yet.'

'I'm not after a drink. Need a favour.'

'Oh, yeah? What then?'

Harry explained that he was on his way to Sydney and had hired one of the Kennedy horses. 'Can you look after him until someone picks him up?' He handed Ned the note and money. 'Just a few bob to pay for the hire and a bit for yourself of course,' he said.

'No worries.' Ned pocketed the coins and the note.

'It is today the mail coach comes through?' Harry asked.

Ned nodded. 'You've got a long wait, though. He won't be here till late afternoon.' He scratched his head, and after a moment's thought, he said, 'I'm expecting a beer delivery soon. If you don't want to hang about, I'll get the drayman to take you.'

Thank goodness for Ned's offer, Harry thought as he thanked him. The mail coach, despite being drawn by four horses, would take days to reach Sydney, stopping off at every town and hamlet on the way, as well as the outlying homesteads. More chance for one of the station hands or Kennedy himself to catch up with him. He'd told himself over and over that if he was pursued, they were sure to accept that he hadn't meant to steal the horse. Still, the sooner he was on his way, the better.

He didn't have to wait long. Soon, a wagon loaded with barrels trundled into town and was driven round to the back of the pub. Harry gave Ned time to explain about the unexpected passenger before making his presence known.

'No worries,' the man said. 'I'll be a while – need to unload this lot first.'

'I'll give you a hand,' Harry said.

With three working, it took no time to unload the full barrels and roll them into the cellar. Then they piled the empty ones onto the wagon. Harry thanked Ned and climbed up beside the wagon driver, who whipped up the horses and they were away.

They stopped briefly at a wayside store cum pub for refreshments, and then they were off again. Dusk was falling as they approached the city, and Harry's spirits rose. He could hardly believe that his years in this inhospitable country would soon be over.

He gazed around at the bustling city, noting the changes since he'd last been here. The place had grown, new buildings springing up everywhere, especially around the harbour.

The drayman dropped him near the dock. 'Plenty of lodging houses round here,' he said. 'Careful not to get ripped off though. Don't let them know you've got dosh.'

'I'll be all right,' he said. 'Thanks, mate.'

Harry had already taken the precaution of transferring a small amount of money into his pocket. The leather bag was now firmly attached to the lining of his trousers.

After a sleepless night in a filthy lodging house, he went out into the street and looked around. He could see the masts of several ships towering above the harbour buildings.

He made his way towards the docks just as a ship was tying up at the wharf. He stood and watched, waiting for the passengers to unload. More convicts, he thought, turning away, not wanting to be reminded of his own arrival here.

To his surprise, the people who disembarked looked reasonably happy, relieved that the long journey was over. There was an air of excitement as they looked around, taking in the new sights and sounds.

An old man leaning on a bollard, smoking a pipe, turned to Harry. 'More settlers,' he said, pointing his pipe.

'What about the convicts?' Harry asked.

'Haven't you heard? They stopped the transportations a couple of years ago. Now the government is encouraging people to come out and settle.'

Harry pictured the hulks he had been imprisoned on. They'd already been in a bad state. Probably rotted away altogether by now, he thought. What did they do with criminals now, he wondered.

He asked for directions to the shipping office, anxious to be on his way. If it weren't for the hope of seeing Emily again, he would never have dreamed of setting foot on the Isle of Sheppey again. The memories of the hulks and the hours stumbling around those treacherous marshes were too painful. But he had to try and find her. If he wasn't lucky, he would just have to go back to London and try to make a life there.

He learned that a ship was sailing for England the next day, and he happily handed over the passage money, pleased that he didn't have to sell the opal after all. Perhaps the ship would call in at Sheerness as it sailed up the Thames, and he thought with a little thrill of excitement that at last he was on his way.

Chapter Nineteen

Emily was exhausted, but she couldn't let Agnes down. The old lady's arthritis had got worse over the winter, and she was becoming more dependent on Emily's help. She leaned on the mangle to catch her breath after the last sheet had passed through the rollers.

'You all right, love?' Agnes asked as she folded the wet laundry into the basket.

'Fine Agnes, just a bit tired. Didn't sleep too well.' She hoped her friend didn't guess the reason for her lack of sleep. She couldn't tell anyone, least of all her dearest friend, what she suffered every night at Lenny Lomax's hands. She straightened and rubbed her back, then picked up the basket. 'Come on, let's get this lot on the line, make the most of this fine weather.'

It was still quite cold but dry and bright, with just a tiny feeling that spring was on the way. The close didn't get much sun at this time of year, but today, there was a patch of sunshine in the corner of the yard, just lighting up Agnes's doorway.

They finished the job and went indoors to make a pot of tea, then brought two chairs outside. 'Let's enjoy the sun,' Emily said. 'I'll have to run down to the shops when I've finished my drink.'

'It's quite warm here out of the wind, 'Agnes said.

'Why not sit here for a bit, make the most of the fine weather.' Emily took the empty cups indoors and came out carrying her purse and a shopping bag. The cat followed her outside and jumped up on Agnes's lap. 'There, Kitty will keep you company,' she said, bending down to stroke the cat.

Agnes gripped her hand, 'Before you go, there's something I need to talk about. Have you got time?'

'Of course.'

'I want you to take over my customers. You're doing most of the work anyway, and I can't do it anymore.'

'I don't know, Agnes. How are you going to manage with no money coming in?'

'My sons send me some now and then, and I've got a little bit put by.'

'I'm not sure. I'll have to think about it.'

'I didn't like to ask. I'm a bit worried about you.'

'No need. I'm fine.'

'Well, you're looking a bit pale and tired these days. Is there something you want to tell me?'

Emily's stomach flipped. Had Agnes guessed what was going on in her married life? She summoned a smile. 'Nothing I can think of.'

'Oh, I wondered...' Agnes paused as if embarrassed. 'Well, you've been married a while now, and I thought maybe...'

Emily relaxed as she realised what Agnes was getting at. She gave a self-conscious laugh. 'No. It's still early days.'

Agnes nodded. 'Yes, early days.'

'I must be off,' Emily said, hurrying away before Agnes could pursue the topic. Her friend might welcome the arrival of a little one, but as far as Emily was concerned, it was the last thing on her mind. She dreaded the thought of having a child with Lenny.

As she turned into the High Street and walked along in the shadow of the high dockyard wall, she shivered. The brief feeling of spring had vanished with the sun.

She pushed thoughts of Lenny and her marriage to the back of her mind. She was more concerned about poor Agnes. She had noticed how her friend's health had deteriorated over the winter. It was obvious she could not continue doing the heavy loads of laundry for much longer, even with her help.

But what would Lenny say if she took on Agnes's job? He had been against her working at the school, saying that he was quite capable of supporting a wife. But that wasn't the true reason. Emily knew he was jealous of Mark and didn't like the idea of her spending too much time in his company, especially now he was widowed.

He hadn't minded her just helping with the laundry, but recently, he had complained that Agnes didn't pay her enough. 'You're doing the heavy work already,' he'd said. 'You deserve more than coppers.'

Perhaps he would agree to her taking over, especially as it would mean more money for him to spend in the pub. She couldn't say that, of course. She bit her lip, a worried frown creasing her forehead. Lenny was so unpredictable. She would have to pick the right moment to broach the subject.

She reached the grocer's and greeted Mrs Collins with a cheerful smile, which she hoped would hide the worrying thoughts churning in her brain.

She paid for her goods and hurried away with the excuse that Cissie would soon be home from school, although her sister was quite old enough to be home alone and there was always Agnes to keep an eye on her.

As she turned the corner, she almost bumped into Mark Thompson. She hadn't seen him since his wife's funeral, and for a moment, she didn't know what to say.

'I'm glad I've seen you, Emily. I've been thinking of calling.'

Thank goodness you didn't, Emily thought, quailing at what Lenny's reaction would have been. She managed to smile and said, 'How are you, Mr Thompson?'

'I'm fine. And you?'

'I'm very well, keeping busy.'

'Not too busy to help me out, I hope,' he said

Emily's heart sank. Much as she had loved working at the school, she couldn't go back. Lenny would never allow her to spend time in the headmaster's company. He would prefer her to be slaving over a tub of hot water, ruining her hands with soda, and breaking her back turning the mangle.

'Help you how?' she asked.

'Come back to the school. I need you. I haven't been able to find anyone to replace you. My office is a mess.'

She took a deep breath. 'I'm so sorry, Mr Thompson,' she began.

'Mark. I've asked you to call me Mark,' he interrupted.

'Mark, then.' She sighed. 'I can't. My husband doesn't want me to work. He says my place is at home.'

Now it was Mark's turn to sigh. 'He's right, of course. My wife never had to work. And I appreciate you have your family to look after.'

Emily apologised once more and hurried away before he had a chance to say anything else.

What a fool she had been, she admonished herself, as she turned the corner into St Paul's Court. Rushing into marriage with Lenny had seemed the right thing to do at the time, especially as Joey had talked about joining the navy. Missing her father, having to care for Cissie, and worrying about money had all seemed too much. A husband with a secure and well-paid job had seemed the answer. And Lenny loved her, so she'd thought.

She recalled him holding her hand, stroking the red and swollen fingers and telling her she didn't have to ruin her hands doing other people's washing. 'Let me take care of you,' he'd said.

And she had fallen for it. That hadn't lasted long, though. He didn't mind 'borrowing' from her when he was short just before payday and wanted to go to the pub. He knew where she kept the few coppers Agnes paid her, and she knew he helped himself when she was out. Well, it was too late now. She must make the best of things.

The sun had disappeared, and a cold wind had sprung up. Agnes had gone indoors, and Emily popped in to tell her about Mark's offer.

'I can't accept, much as I would like to,' she said.

'Why not? You're not worrying that you won't have time to work for me as well?'

'It's not that.' Emily hesitated. 'I don't think Lenny will like it.'

Agnes nodded. 'But he's got nothing to be jealous about, has he.'

'Try convincing him of that, though.' Emily sighed. 'I've turned him down anyway.' She picked up her shopping bag. 'Better get this indoors.'

She crossed the courtyard, wondering why Cissie wasn't home yet. She had expected to see her with Agnes. But it was still light and much too soon to start worrying.

She threw open her own door and plonked her shopping bag on the table. Only then did she notice Lenny sitting in Dad's chair – it would always be Dad's chair. And Cissie was snuggled up on his lap.

Emily gasped. 'I thought you'd be at Agnes's,' she managed to say.

'No need for her to stay with the old lady,' Lenny said. 'I got off early, so I brought her home.'

Emily started unpacking her groceries. 'How come you got home early?' she asked.

'Oh, I thought I told you. Change of shifts. They've put me on a different gang. Starting earlier, finishing earlier.'

'Didn't Joey change too?' She wondered why her brother always seemed to work longer hours, but she didn't dare ask. Lenny didn't like being questioned, and Emily had learned to keep quiet. As for Joey, he was hardly ever at home these days anyway.

'He's still in the boat house,' Lenny said.

Emily nodded but didn't say anything. She started preparing the meal, glancing over to where Cissie was still cuddled up to Lenny. She was starting to resent her sister's fondness for her brother-in-law, who seemed to have supplanted Joey in her affections.

'Cissie, come and help me with these vegetables,' she said. 'And Lenny, could you please fetch some water.'

Without protest, Cissie scrambled down from Lenny's lap and came over to the sink. 'I like helping you, Em,' she said. 'I wanted to help Agnes too, but Lenny made me come home.'

Lenny sighed and reluctantly picked up the bucket.

Cissie glanced at the door as if to make sure Lenny had gone outside. She leaned closer to Emily and whispered, 'He wouldn't let me stay with Agnes.'

'Never mind, lovie. He's very fond of you and likes your company.'

Cissie seemed to accept Emily's explanation. But as she worked, Emily wondered if he really was fond of Cissie or if he was just putting on an act, trying to give the impression he was a devoted family man.

Lenny came back with the full bucket and plonked it down under the sink. 'You were gone a long time,' he said. 'Who've you been talking to?'

Her heart sank. She remembered when he'd accused her of flirting with Mr Collins, laughable as that was. She'd have to tell him about seeing Mark before someone else did. They were a tight-knit community. Anyone could hear about it, and the gossip would spread. She had declined his offer, but just the mere fact of her speaking to the school master would set Lenny off.

She swallowed and took a deep breath. 'I chatted to Mrs Collins for a few minutes, and then I bumped into Mr Thompson, the school master.'

'And I suppose you chatted to him as well.' There was a sneer in Lenny's voice as he said the word 'chatted'.

'No. I wanted to get home with the shopping, but he stopped me and asked me to go back and work at the school.' She put her hand on Lenny's arm. 'I said no, of course. Told him I didn't have to work now I'm married.'

He shook her hand off. 'Too right. The cheek of the man. He knows you're a married woman.'

He glanced at Cissie who was still peeling potatoes at the sink, her back to them. 'Cissie, love, you let me know if he bothers your sister again.'

'Yes, Lenny,' she whispered.

He grabbed Emily's arm, pinching it hard enough to leave a bruise. 'I don't want you speaking to that man again,' he hissed. He didn't give her a chance to answer, just let go of her arm and threw himself down in the chair.

She took the saucepan of potatoes from Cissie and set it on the hob, then opened a tin of corned beef and sliced it on to the plates. When the potatoes were cooked, Cissie mashed them with a splash of milk.

'It's ready,' she said.

Lenny grunted and came to the table. His face screwed up when he saw what was on offer, and Emily knew he would complain, but she ignored him and began to eat, forcing the food down.

She didn't think he would cause a row in front of Cissie but she would suffer for it later.

* * *

Emily was exhausted and longing for her bed, but she dreaded going upstairs and being alone with Lenny. She went about her tidying up mechanically, wishing that Joey was here. Lenny had gone up to read a bedtime story to Cissie despite the little girl protesting that she wanted to wait for Joey to come home. 'He always reads to me,' she'd whined.

'Well, he's not here, so it's me or no story,' Lenny said.

In the end, she had reluctantly gone upstairs with him leaving Emily annoyed with Joey. He had always taken care of his little sister when she was busy but lately, he was staying out later and later. Cissie missed him and life was easier for Emily when he was home.

Lenny was always nicer when her brother was around. He would offer to help with the chores, and his manner towards her was completely different from when they were alone. He would take her hand across the dinner table and say to Joey, 'Aren't I the lucky one, married to such a lovely girl.' The very picture of a kind, affectionate husband, Emily dreaded him finding out the truth. She always tried to smile and Joey would nod. It was getting harder to keep up the pretence in front of her brother.

She heard Lenny coming downstairs and felt a churning in her stomach.

'Chores all done - ready for bed?' he asked.

'I was waiting up for Joey.'

Lenny's lips tightened. 'He's a grown man. He doesn't need you to wait up for him.'

Emily knew he was right but he was still her little brother and she worried about him. There were a lot of rough types milling around outside the pubs when they closed.

But she couldn't argue with Lenny. She was already anticipating his punishment for daring to speak to Mark.

She was about to follow him upstairs when the door opened, and Joey stumbled inside.

'Em, Em, I've been celebrating,' he mumbled and flopped down in Dad's chair.

'Celebrating?' Emily asked.

'Never mind. He's drunk,' Lenny said. 'Come on. Leave him to sleep it off.'

Emily ignored him and shook Joey's shoulder. 'Joey - what are you celebrating?' She felt a cold finger of unease run down her spine. She knew what he was going to say.

'I've done it – I've finally done it.' He sat up and grinned at her. 'I've joined the Navy. I said I would, and I've done it.'

'Oh, Joey, how could you?'

'Em, love. I know you'll miss me but you'll be all right.' He waved his hand around the room. 'You've got a husband, a home. You don't need me.'

Emily couldn't speak, her voice choked with sobs.

Lenny spoke from the bottom of the stairs. 'He's right, Em. He's got to make his own way in life. You've got me. I'll look after you and Cissie. I love you both.'

He sounded so sincere. How could he change so quickly from a caring husband to a monster?

And as she followed him into the bedroom and began to undress, the monster emerged. He grabbed her and threw her down on the bed, tearing her clothes and muttering obscenities as he assaulted her body.

Chapter Twenty

The days leading up to Joey's departure were a torment for Emily. How could he abandon her, she fumed. She was almost tempted to confide in him what a mistake her marriage had been, tell him how badly Lenny treated her. But she was too ashamed. And, after all, what could Joey do? A husband's word was law. She had promised to obey, and that meant submitting to his every whim. She could cope during the day but at bedtime the nightmare would begin — every night. She tried not to cry out when the pain got too bad, conscious of her sister asleep behind the curtain. She prayed that Cissie never realised what went on.

Lenny didn't seem to care even with Joey downstairs, although he put his hand over her mouth to stifle her cries, threatening her with worse if she didn't keep quiet.

On the day of Joey's departure, Emily dragged herself downstairs and prepared breakfast for her brother. She had put clean clothes out for him and helped him pack his bag the night before.

She woke him when the food was ready, tears rolling down her cheeks. She watched him dress, thinking how grown-up, smart, and handsome he looked. She wished he was still that little boy, bringing home cockles for their supper and helping their father chop wood for the fire. Such happy days, despite having little money and being cramped together in their little cottage.

Even their life on the hulks hadn't been so bad, being part of a close loving family. And when her mother died, Dad had done his best for them, working hard, finding this house for them.

Joey sat at the table and began to eat. He looked up, noting the tears on her cheeks. 'Don't cry, Em, please,' he begged.

'I can't help it,' she sobbed. 'I'll miss you so.'

'I'm sorry, Em. I've got to do this.'

Emily swiped her hand across her cheeks and managed to smile. 'The next time I see you, you'll be in your uniform. I'll be so proud.' She tried not to think how long she might have to wait. Sailors didn't get much leave.

She glanced up, hearing movement from the bedroom. She took Joey's plate away and turned to the sink, wiping her face on her apron. She didn't want Lenny to see how upset she was.

But it was Cissie who appeared at the bottom of the stairs just as Joey picked up his bag, ready to go. She threw herself at him, wrapping her arms around his legs.

'You were going without saying goodbye,' she sobbed.

'Of course, I wasn't. I couldn't go without giving my little princess a goodbye kiss, could I.' He dropped his bag and lifted Cissie up, hugging her tight and kissing her on both cheeks. When he put her down, Emily could see he was struggling to hold back tears. It was as hard for him to leave as it was for them to say goodbye.

She was still angry with him for deserting them, but she understood. The animosity between him and Lenny was becoming more noticeable every day, and she knew it was inevitable that it would all blow up before long. She would never forgive herself if it came to violence, and Joey would be hurt.

'I'm sorry, Em. You do understand that I've got to go.' He hugged them both. 'Bill will keep an eye out for you. You can go to him if you need any help.'

Emily nodded and took Cissie's hand and they went to the door, giving Joey one last kiss. From behind her she heard a mocking laugh. 'So, you're off then. Maybe the navy will make a man of you.'

Joey ignored him, hefted his bag on to his shoulder and walked out of the door. Emily stood in the doorway holding Cissie's hand, the little girl waving until their brother disappeared through the archway.

'Well, woman, where's my breakfast? Do you want me to be late for work?' Lenny yelled, banging his hand on the table.

'It's all ready,' Emily said. 'Sit up to the table, Cissie.'

She dished up fried bread and bacon for Lenny and a bowl of porridge for Cissie and herself. Cissie pushed hers away, but Emily insisted that she eat. 'I know you're sad saying goodbye to Joey, but you'll be hungry soon. Besides, porridge is good for your brain. It will help you to learn your lessons.'

To encourage her sister, she took a mouthful of her own food, but she didn't feel like eating either.

Lenny shoved a forkful of bacon into his mouth and spoke before chewing it. 'Do as your sister says. I don't pay for good food to be wasted,' he snapped.

Cissie looked down at the bowl, tears glistening on her lashes. She wasn't used to Lenny speaking harshly to her. She picked up her spoon and began to eat.

They finished the meal in silence, broken only when Lenny threw down his knife and fork and scraped back his chair. 'Well, I'm off to work. I'll be back for dinner.'

When he'd gone, Emily sighed with relief, relishing the few hours of peace before he returned. With Joey gone, there was no need for Lenny to hide his true nature. Her life would be even harder from now on. As long as his nastiness didn't affect Cissie, she would cope. She would shield her sister as much as possible.

That night, he was more violent than usual, and her cries of pain woke Cissie.

When she tried to get up to comfort her sister, Lenny threw his arm across her, pinning her to the bed. 'Leave her. She'll be all right,' he hissed.

Somehow, she managed to throw him off and went to Cissie, whispering that she'd had a nightmare. 'All better now. Go back to sleep, love.'

When she got back in bed, Lenny was already snoring. But for Emily, there was no sleep that night.

Next morning, she could hardly move. The pain was worse than it had ever been. It suddenly occurred to her that Lenny's abuse had damaged her, and that was why she hadn't got pregnant. She didn't dare consult a doctor, though.

* * *

For a few weeks after Joey's departure, life carried on as usual. Emily missed him sorely. It felt like a big part of her was missing. Before Lenny came to live with them, she had been used to talking to him in the evenings, sharing stories of their day. Joey would often make her laugh with his tales of the things the other lads got up to. And they would sing and tell stories to Cissie. Even during the worst of their father's illness, they had managed to enjoy life. She couldn't believe she might not see Joey again for months or years.

Why hadn't she realised that Lenny was to blame for the change in their relationship? She had been totally taken in by him, by his care for their father, kindness to Cissie, and generosity to them all. He had seemed like a genuine friend, but Joey had seen through his act.

She had truly believed that he loved her and wanted to be part of a proper family. Now, with Joey's departure, her family had been torn apart.

It was the start of the summer break, and Cissie was helping Emily to clean the bedroom.

They had taken the sheets off both beds and thrown them to the bottom of the stairs, Cissie giggling as they landed in a heap. They would go in Agnes's copper when the next lot of laundry was due.

Emily stood and surveyed the room with her hands on her hips. Suddenly, she tore down the curtain that separated Cissie's bed from hers.

'What are you doing?' Cissie gasped. 'I don't want Lenny to see me in bed.'

'I've had an idea. You're getting too grown up to be sleeping in our room. I'm going to move your bed downstairs. We can put your mattress on top of Joey's so you'll be more comfortable.'

'What about when Joey comes home? Where will he sleep?' Cissie said, a worried frown creasing her brow.

'Cissie, love, he won't be home for a long time – and we can always change it back.'

'All right then.'

Together, they moved the mattress downstairs and made up the bed with fresh sheets. As they smoothed them out, Cissie patted the bed and said, 'It's nice having proper sheets, isn't it.' She sounded quite cheerful now.

'Thanks to the Admiral's wife,' Emily said. The lady was one of Agnes's customers, and Emily had done some mending for her. In return, she had given her some linen that was a little worn in places.

'You're good with your needle,' she'd said. 'You'll be able to patch them up.' Emily had accepted gratefully.

They finished tidying the upstairs room, and Cissie made a pot of tea while Emily took the soiled sheets over to Agnes.

'Can we put these in with the next lot of laundry,' she asked her friend.

'Of course. Looks like you've been busy. Time for a cuppa?'

'I can't stop. Cissie's making a pot. She's getting to be a real help.'

'How are you – still missing Joey?'

Emily nodded. She couldn't talk about her brother without getting upset. She hurried away, determined not to give in to tears. It would only start Cissie off.

* * *

Cissie carefully measured the tea into the pot and poured boiling water onto the leaves. She smiled proudly as she set the cups on the table. It was good to be trusted to do these little jobs. She loved helping her sister. Dear Emily worked so hard.

She went and sat on the bed – her bed now. Thank goodness she no longer had to share her sister's room. When she was little, she'd loved cuddling up to Emily, especially on cold winter nights. And with Joey snoring behind the curtain, she'd always felt safe. She tried not to think about Joey – he'd left them and she had to get used to it.

She knew Emily was missing him, too. She often woke in the night hearing noises. Sometimes, she thought Emily had been crying, but when she asked her in the morning what was wrong, she had always said she was fine. 'It must have been a bad dream,' she said.

Cissie, too, had bad dreams, but she never said anything to Emily. She couldn't explain why she felt so unsettled and didn't want to upset her.

Perhaps, now she had her own bed in a different room and couldn't hear the noises, the dreams would stop.

She jumped up from the bed as the door opened, and Emily came back. 'I've made the tea,' she said. 'How was Agnes?'

'She's in pain, but she doesn't complain,' Emily said.

Cissie poured the tea and they sat at the table together to drink. Cissie looked at her sister, noting the shadows under her eyes. She was getting thinner, too. Joey's leaving had affected them both.

She hoped Emily would come to accept his leaving. After all, they had Lenny now. She wanted to say so to Emily, try to cheer her up. But somehow, she didn't think it would help. He had changed lately. When she was little, she'd been fond of him, but just lately, he made her feel uncomfortable; she couldn't explain why. And she would catch him staring at her in a strange way which made her nervous. He was still generous, giving her little presents, calling her princess and little sister. He wasn't as kind to Emily though, as he had been before they got married.

Sighing, she got down from the table and cleared the tea things away, resolving to be a help to her sister as much as possible. She hoped it might help to stop her looking so tired and careworn.

* * *

Emily sat at the table, lost in thought, startled when Cissie got up and cleared away their cups. It was getting late and she must start to get their meal ready. Lenny would be home soon and he liked his tea on the table when he came in.

She did her best to keep him happy, but his moods were so unpredictable. It was hard when she never knew exactly what time he'd be home. He seemed to work such irregular shifts and he got irritable when she questioned him.

He must be earning good money, though. He always had plenty to spend down the pub, and he was generous with the housekeeping money and always paid the rent on time. She should be contented, she thought. Many women would envy her. She recalled the way some of the women had been treated when she lived on the hulks, the men constantly drunk and violent. She and her siblings had been fortunate having such loving parents, despite their poor living conditions.

Yes, on the surface, Lenny was a good husband and she would have been content were it not for his behaviour in the bedroom. She couldn't believe his treatment of her was normal, but she had no way of really knowing. It wasn't something she felt comfortable discussing with Agnes, her only friend.

She got up and began to prepare the meal. She would make shepherd's pie, Lenny's favourite. Perhaps that would put him in a good mood.

Cissie offered to help, but Emily said, 'You've worked hard today. Why don't you pop over and see Agnes and Kitty.'

'Thanks, Em. You sure I can't help?'

'Of course. Go on.'

She chopped an onion and added it to the mince, sniffing the appetising aroma. A tear rolled down her cheek - it was the onion making her cry, she insisted to herself, wiping her face on her apron. The worried frown had returned now that Cissie was out of the way. It was so hard to stay cheerful in front of her sister.

Why, oh why, had she married Lenny, she asked herself for the thousandth time.

The pie was in the oven, and she was tidying the utensils away when Lenny came home. He threw his jacket on the bed and sat in 'Dad's chair' to take off his boots.

'Something smells good,' he said.

Emily turned to him with a smile, thankful that he appeared in a good mood. 'Your favourite,' she said.

'Pity I won't be here to eat it,' he said.

'Oh, I was looking forward to an evening together,' she said, the lie coming easily.

'I did tell you – I'm meeting some mates at the Kings Head. Got a bit of business to see to.'

He hadn't told her, but she did not dare to argue or ask what business it was. 'The Kings Head?' she said. 'What's wrong with the Red Lion?'

'Nothing, just fancied a change.' He pushed past her and poured water from the kettle into the enamel bowl. He splashed his face and wet his hair, grabbed the scrap of cloth they used for a towel and dried himself, then combed his thick dark hair with his fingers.

'I'm off then. Save some of that pie for me,' he said with a grin.

When he'd gone, she slumped against the table. He must know she'd cooked it specially for him, but he didn't care. It would be spoilt by the time he got back, and then he would shout at her or, worse still, throw the plate at the wall.

She hoped Cissie would be in bed when he got home, then remembered she would be sleeping downstairs from now on. Perhaps that hadn't been such a good idea. She sighed, realising how hard it was to shield Cissie from Lenny's true character. Her sister was getting to the age where she noticed things and would soon start asking questions. Moving her out of their bedroom had to be for the best.

Chapter Twenty-One

When Lenny returned, it was almost bedtime. Emily had waited for him, and she looked up apprehensively as he stumbled through the door. But he was in a surprisingly good mood, a satisfied grin on his face as he came in, closing the door with exaggerated care. He pointed to the bed in the corner where Cissie lay fast asleep and put his finger to his lips.

'Mustn't wake the little princess,' he whispered.

Emily hated him calling her that – it had been Joey's pet name for her. But she summoned a smile. 'I've saved your pie,' she said. 'I hope it's not spoilt.'

'Been looking forward to this all evening,' he said. 'Work makes you hungry.'

What work, she wondered. He'd finished his dockyard shift ages ago and if he was hungry, he could have had his meal before going out. She got the dish out of the oven and transferred a good portion to his plate. There was plenty there. She and Cissie had eaten very little. Neither of them had much appetite these days.

She set the plate in front of him and would have stepped away, but he seized her hand. 'Good little wifey,' he said, his words slightly slurred. 'Lucky Lenny. Fallen on your feet – that's what one of my mates said.'

She tried not to pull away. He'd only grip tighter and leave another bruise. She recoiled at the smell of booze on his breath as he pulled her closer and landed a sloppy kiss on her cheek. Then, without warning, he pushed her away. 'Let me eat my meal in peace,' he snarled.

'All right. I'll go up to bed then.'

'No, you won't. You'll wash the dishes and clear up. You know I don't like to get up to a mess in the mornings.'

'Whatever you say, Lenny.' She filled the basin with water and added soda crystals. It had been a long day, and she was exhausted. She leaned against the sink, scrubbing the pie dish, making sure she got every scrap of burnt-on food off. By then, Lenny's plate was empty, and she reached across for it.

His hand shot out and grabbed her once more. 'Leave it,' he snapped, leering at her. 'You know what I want now, don't you?'

She nodded.

'Well, up you go.' He laughed as he followed her upstairs. 'Won't have to worry about waking little sister now,' he said. 'We can have some fun.'

Emily shuddered and stumbled a little as she reached the top of the stairs.

He pushed her into the room and threw her across the bed, falling down on top of her. She bit her lip, waiting for the inevitable assault. But he didn't move, and after a few moments, he started to snore.

She almost laughed aloud. He must have had more to drink than she'd thought. She carefully eased herself off the bed and crept downstairs. Crawling in beside Cissie, she closed her eyes, convinced she wouldn't sleep. But it was daylight when she woke, with just a dim light filtering through the small window.

It took a moment before she recalled getting into bed with Cissie last night. Was Lenny still asleep? And would he remember collapsing on top of her and passing out?

She glanced at Cissie, who was still asleep. Too early to wake her yet. She eased herself out of bed and went to the window to look out on a damp, drizzly morning, the houses across the way almost lost in the mist. She listened, an ear cocked towards the stairs, holding her breath. There was no sound. She hoped Lenny was still asleep, too.

It was getting late though and he would want breakfast before setting off to work. Should she wake him? He was bound to be hung over after the amount he'd drunk last night. Best to get breakfast started first.

She was quickly ready to dish up, but there was still no sound coming from above. Hesitantly, she crept up the stairs and went over to the bed. He was sprawled out, still fully dressed. His mouth was open, and he snorted as she gingerly touched his arm.

'Your breakfast's ready,' she said quietly.

'Eh, what?' He sat up, wincing as he clutched his head. 'Don't want no breakfast,' he muttered.

'You'll be late for work.'

'Ain't going to work today. Leave me alone.' He shook his head and groaned.

Emily knew better than to question him but she couldn't stop herself from saying, 'They'll dock your pay if you don't go in.'

'I said leave me alone, woman.' As she turned away, he groaned again and said, 'No, get me a drink. I'm parched.'

She went downstairs and filled a mug with water. It would have to do.

Cissie was at the table eating a slice of bread with a scraping of jam. 'Where's Lenny?' she asked.

'He's not feeling well, staying in bed.'

Cissie's eyes brightened. 'He's been drinking,' she said. 'Serve him right.'

'Cissie! You mustn't say such things. He's not well, so eat up and get off to school.' She took the drink up, expecting Lenny to complain, but he drank it down without a word, thrust the mug at her, then turned over and closed his eyes.

Emily covered him with the blanket. He must have a really bad head, she thought with satisfaction. As Cissie had said, serve him right.

She saw her sister off to school and set about her usual morning chores, trying to be quiet so as not to disturb Lenny. By dinnertime, he still hadn't come downstairs, so she decided to call in on Agnes, although it wasn't a laundry day.

Too bad if he got up expecting to be fed. She was a bit annoyed about him losing a day's pay although he always seemed to have plenty of money. So long as he paid the rent and gave her enough to feed them all, she wasn't really concerned. He would be back at work tomorrow anyway.

Agnes was sitting in her chair by the fire, a blanket over her knees. She tried to stand when Emily knocked and opened the door.

'Don't get up, Agnes. I can see you're not having a good day. Shall I make a drink?'

'If you would, love. These old knees of mine are playing up. It's the damp.'

'You just rest then.' Emily set about filling the kettle and setting it on the hob.

'Good job it's not a laundry day,' Agnes said.

'Too right. The mist has lifted a bit, but it would never dry in this weather.'

She made the tea and handed a cup to her friend. 'I can't stay long. Lenny's not well, still in bed.'

'Oh, what's wrong with him then?' She nodded, grinning as understanding dawned. 'I can guess. He was out late last night, wasn't he? He must've been really drunk. I heard him stumbling about in the woodshed – couldn't find his own front door.' She gave a cynical laugh.

Emily couldn't help smiling, too. 'Well, he's got a really bad head this morning.'

Agnes sighed. 'Why do you put up with him, love?'

'What else can I do? I've got Cissie to worry about.'

'Pity your Joey's gone off to sea. He'd look after you.'

Emily sighed. 'I must admit he's got worse since Joey left.' She stood up, took the cups to the sink and said, 'I must go to the shops, but I'll pop in later.'

Lenny had come downstairs while she'd been visiting Agnes and was slumped in the armchair, still looking a bit worse for wear.

'Where've you been? Gossiping with the old woman, I suppose.' He coughed. 'Well, where's me dinner?'

'I need to go to the shops first – and I need some money.' She held her breath. She had enough hidden away in a tin on the top shelf, but she didn't want him to know about it. To her surprise, he fumbled in his jacket pocket and drew out a few coins. 'Here you are then.'

'I didn't think you'd been paid,' she said.

He touched his finger to his nose. 'You think too much. Plenty more where that came from.'

She almost asked him what he meant but closed her mouth, picking up the hessian bag she used for the potatoes and hurrying out the door.

As she made her way through the narrow streets and alleyways to the grocers, she couldn't stop thinking about Lenny's last words to her. It was true he never seemed short of money, so what had he been up to? He had mentioned having a bit of business with his mates. She hadn't dared question him at the time, telling herself he was probably doing a job for one of them, earning a bit on the side.

The questions and doubts swirled in her brain. Little things came back to her – there was that time when everyone working in the docks had been searched, and Lenny and Joey had been cleared along with everyone else in their gang. But Emily suddenly recalled the smirk on Lenny's face when he told her, his triumphant glance at Joey. Had he been guilty and got away with it?

The more she thought about it, the more convinced she became that Lenny was up to something criminal. But who could she confide in? Sergeant Brent, her father's old friend, was the obvious person to go to. But she had no proof. And suppose Lenny found out she'd betrayed him? No, she would keep her suspicions to herself – for now anyway.

She managed to keep up a cheerful flow of conversation with Mrs Collins as she got her groceries and then went along to the greengrocers, filling her bag with potatoes and carrots. No meat today. She couldn't face Mr Burston, the jolly butcher who always cheered her up. She would make do with the bacon she already had at home.

As she turned the corner into the lane leading to St Paul's Close, she spotted

Gladys, her other neighbour. She didn't feel like stopping and chatting but she couldn't avoid the other woman.

'Emily, how nice to see you. I've just popped in to see Agnes. She's not too good today.'

'I know, I went in earlier. Her arthritis is getting worse. This damp weather doesn't help.'

Gladys nodded. 'And how are you, dear? Missing your brother, I suppose. How's he liking the navy?'

'He wrote a while back, seemed to be all right. But now he's at sea, it's hard to keep in touch.'

'Of course, dear. But how are you managing? You know - without Joey's money and now, Lenny...' She paused and her face reddened.

'Lenny? What do you mean?'

'Not working.'

'Oh, well, he's taken the day off, not feeling too good.'

'Oh, I see. Just today, is it? Only I heard he'd lost his job.'

Emily gasped but quickly recovered. 'I'm sure you've got that wrong, Gladys.' She gave a little laugh. 'How these rumours fly around,' she said. 'Well, I must be getting home with this shopping. Lenny will be waiting for his dinner.'

She hurried away before Gladys could say anything else. The woman must have it wrong, she thought. Lenny had been leaving home each morning at the usual time, and he had money. Well, she'd tackle him about it right away. She took a deep breath and marched across the courtyard.

The words died on her lips as she entered the cottage and saw Lenny in his usual place, sitting in Dad's chair. What shocked her was the sight of Cissie sitting on his lap. Her long blonde hair was loose about her shoulders, and Lenny was stroking it with the hairbrush. Most shocking was the expression on his face.

'Cissie,' she said sharply. 'You're old enough to do your own hair. Get down.'

Her sister scrambled off Lenny's lap and ran over to her. 'You were gone a long time,' she said. 'Did you forget we were finishing school early today?'

She had forgotten – something about having a new boiler fitted and sending the children home at dinner time. 'I'm sorry, Cissie. I had a lot of shopping to do.' She had no idea how she managed to stay so calm.

'I expect you were gossiping with the neighbours too,' Lenny said, glaring at her. 'It doesn't take that long to get a few groceries.'

Emily didn't reply, just carried on unpacking her bags and putting the shopping away. She couldn't get the scene she'd just witnessed out of her head. On the face of it, things looked innocent enough, but Lenny's face said it all. She had seen that look before, but directed at her. Her stomach churned, but she said nothing.

'I'll have your dinner ready soon,' she said. 'And what about you, Cissie – are you hungry?'

The little girl nodded and picked up a carrot. 'Can I help?'

'Let me finish doing your hair first, princess,' Lenny said.

'She wants to help,' Emily said. 'Let her.'

Lenny shrugged and leaned back in the chair.

Together Emily and her sister prepared the meal, Emily conscious of Lenny's gaze on them, her thoughts in turmoil.

She managed to dish up a reasonable meal, despite the churning in her stomach. Fortunately, Cissie didn't seem to sense the atmosphere, eating her dinner and chattering away about her school day. Emily could hardly swallow and found it hard to answer.

As for Lenny, he ate with his usual appetite, his hangover seemingly cured. He finished and pushed his plate away. 'Got to go out,' he said.

'I thought you were supposed to be ill. That's why you're off work,' Emily said.

'Well, I'm feeling better now, aren't I? And I've got a job to do.' He shoved his chair back so hard it almost fell over. Muttering a curse, he grabbed his jacket and went out, slamming the door behind him.

'Why is Lenny so cross?' Cissie asked.

'I don't know, love. Don't worry, it's nothing you've done,' she said.

'I know. He doesn't get cross with me, especially if I'm nice to him. He says he loves me.'

Such innocence! But Emily knew what he meant by being nice. She clenched her teeth. If he so much as ....

Maybe she was wrong, but she would watch Cissie carefully from now on. Surely there would be signs if anything untoward was going on.

She smiled at her sister and said, 'Shall we go over to see Agnes when we've done the washing up?'

Cissie nodded enthusiastically. 'And Kitty,' she said.

All thoughts of confronting Lenny about Gladys's earlier remarks had fled. Protecting her sister was foremost in her mind now. Could she confide in Agnes?

Chapter Twenty-Two

Cissie sat on the floor in front of Agnes's fire, playing with Kitty while Emily tried to summon up the courage to convey her suspicions to her friend. What if she was wrong? Could she have mistaken that look on her husband's face as he stroked and brushed Cissie's hair? It was that which had made her think his actions were not as innocent as they might appear to anyone else.

She looked across at her little sister – not so little now – growing up fast but still a child. Cissie still seemed her usual happy self, no sign that she was being molested. Had she overreacted, Emily wondered.

Agnes smiled. 'How she loves that cat,' she said. 'I love to hear her chattering away to her. It's as if Kitty understands every word.'

Emily roused herself from her dark thoughts and said, 'I'm sure she does.' She sighed. 'I worry about Cissie sometimes.' She could not bring herself to say more, and Agnes did not pursue it.

'She's fine, growing up to be a lovely girl. You've been a good influence on her. It must be hard growing up without a mother and then losing your dad.'

'We had Joey. I know he's younger than me, but when Dad was ill, he was the man of the house.'

'Pity he decided to join the navy,' Agnes said.

'Well, now I've got Lenny.' Emily put on a cheerful voice. She couldn't burden her friend with her troubles.

But Agnes just said in a flat voice, 'Yes, Lenny.' Then, appearing to change the subject, she said, 'Gladys popped in to see me this morning.'

'Yes, she told me. That was kind of her.'

'I saw her talking to you in the yard.' Agnes paused. 'I know she's a gossip. Did she say anything about your husband?'

Emily forced a laugh. 'Oh, yes, some nonsense about Lenny losing his job. I told her he was not well, just having a day off.'

Agnes nodded, then leaned forward and touched Emily's knee. 'I didn't want to be the one to tell you – but Gladys was right.' She lowered her voice, glancing at Cissie. 'He was dismissed a few weeks back.'

Emily gasped and raised a hand to her lips. 'Why?' she whispered.

'Bad time-keeping, missing shifts. Didn't you realise he wasn't working?'

'No. He always worked odd hours. And he always has plenty of money. How could I have known?'

'Are you going to tackle him about it?'

'I don't know.' Emily put her head in her hands. 'Oh, Agnes, what can I do? He'll talk his way out of it.'

Agnes shook her head. 'You say he always has money – where's that coming from then?'

'He might have got another job and not told me.' Emily knew she was clutching at straws.

'Perhaps.' Agnes sighed. 'Look, love. You can always come to me if you're worried about anything, and I'll look after Cissie if you want me to.'

'Thanks, Agnes. You're a good friend.' She turned to Cissie. 'Come on, love. Time to go home. Say goodbye to Kitty.'

With Lenny still out, the rest of the afternoon passed pleasantly enough, although Emily tensed at every sound, dreading Lenny's return. She found Cissie's reading book from school tucked down the side of the old armchair. 'I wondered where that had got to,' she exclaimed. 'Cissie, come and sit by me, and we can practice your reading.'

'Don't want to,' Cissie said.

'Why not? You like reading.'

'Lenny says it's a waste of time.'

'Of course it isn't. Besides, you always liked reading. Come on, we'll read together.'

Cissie dragged her feet but eventually climbed into the armchair and snuggled down next to Emily, who opened the book and pointed to the picture of a cow. Cissie giggled and read, her finger following the words on the page – 'The cow jumped over the moon.' She looked up at Emilly, laughing, 'That's silly,' she said. 'Cows can't jump.'

'How do you know? Have you ever seen a cow?' Emily teased.

Cissie shook her head.

'Never mind. When we get some nice weather, I'll take you to see some. They live in a field just outside the town.' Emily suddenly realised it was getting dark and jumped up. 'I must get on,' she said. 'Lenny will be home soon.'

Cissie dropped the book and started to get up from the chair. 'No. love. Stay there and read to me.' She handed the nursery rhyme book to Cissie. 'Try one of the others. What about Jack and Jill?'

She was pleased when Cissie settled down to read while she got on with her chores. She lit the lamp, then checked the fire in the range. It was almost out. She would have to go out to the shed and bring some wood in. It was usually Lenny's job, but he had neglected to fill the basket for the past couple of days. Too busy with his bits of 'business', she thought bitterly.

'Carry on with your reading, Cissie. You're doing very well,' she said. She picked up the log basket and opened the door, letting in a blast of cold air.

She tutted with annoyance when she entered the woodshed. The logs, which had been stacked neatly, were now scattered across the floor. She smiled grimly, picturing Lenny staggering about last night, trying to find his way out. Pity the whole lot hadn't fallen on him.

She filled the basket and made an attempt to stack the scattered logs neatly.

Back indoors, she soon had a good blaze going and decided to use up the last of the bread to make toast for Cissie and herself. They sat in front of the range, holding slices of bread on forks up to the bars. The smell of the toast made Emily's mouth water, and she realised she had hardly eaten for the past couple of days.

They were enjoying their food, still giggling about the cow jumping over the moon, when the door flew open.

Emily swung round to see Lenny standing there, his eyes glittering as he stabbed a finger at her. 'Have you been in the shed?' he shouted.

She nodded and found her voice, gesturing towards the range. 'The fire was out. I needed wood.'

'It's my job to get the logs in. I'm the man of the house, and don't you forget it.'

Emily had no idea why he was so angry, but he was scaring Cissie, and she couldn't have that. She straightened her shoulders and looked him in the eye. 'You should have been here to do your job then,' she said.

'I've been working – to put food on the table,' he snapped. 'I can't be in two places at once.'

Emily did her best to appease him. 'Lenny, I didn't mean to upset you. I know you work hard for me and Cissie.' It wasn't the time to confront him with her suspicions.

The anger seemed to drain out of him. 'Well, I don't want you going in the shed. It's dark in there. You might hurt yourself. So, keep out. All right!'

She didn't believe he really cared for her safety, but she spoke quietly. 'Yes, Lenny. I understand. I didn't think.'

'Well, just get on with my tea. I'm starving.' He took off his boots and sat in the armchair.

Cissie stood by the table, staring at him with frightened eyes. He smiled and beckoned to her. 'Sorry I shouted, princess,' he said.

She frowned. 'I don't like it when you're angry.'

'It's not your fault. How could I get angry with my princess?' He reached out and touched a lock of her hair.

Emily's gut curdled but she bit her lip. 'Come and help me get the tea ready, Cissie, love,' she said, surprised at how normal her voice sounded.

Cissie ran to her side but turned to smile at Lenny. How Emily hated that man. But she dared not speak out. Cissie had been upset enough already.

* * *

For the next few days, Emily didn't dare go near the shed and really there was no need. Before leaving the house each day Lenny filled up the log basket and made sure there was enough kindling to get the fire going each morning.

But she couldn't get out of her head the way he had reacted to her fetching the wood herself. What was he hiding? It was the only reason she could think of for keeping her out. Joey had always fetched the logs, and since he'd left, Lenny had taken on the extra chore, but he often forgot, leaving Emily to do it. Why was he now so concerned for her safety? It didn't ring true.

Cissie was in school, and Lenny had disappeared on his mysterious 'business', so Emily was able to finish her chores quickly. Agnes, despite saying that she was giving up her laundry job, had taken in some washing for one of the officer's wives and Emily had promised to help.

'Thank goodness it's a bit brighter today,' she said, as together they loaded the sheets into the boiler.

'Spring's on the way,' Agnes said. 'And this warmer weather is much better for my arthritis.'

'You mustn't overdo it though. I thought you were going to give up.'

'I'll try to keep going a bit longer, especially if I have you to help.'

Emily hesitated and Agnes, noticing, said, 'What's wrong?'

'It's Lenny – he doesn't want me working.' She sighed. 'I'm sorry. He says he's earning enough now, so I don't need to work.'

'It's all right, Emily. I understand. I'll probably have to give up soon anyway. I think Gladys will take on my customers if you can't. She's fed up with working in the dockyard ropery and scrubbing pub floors.'

Emily was relieved. She hated letting her friend down. But she hadn't told Lenny she was still helping Agnes, and she dreaded his reaction when he found out.

'Anyway, love. What's your Lenny doing since he left the dockyard? Must be a good job if he doesn't want you working.'

'I'm not sure exactly. He did tell me, but I can't remember the name of the firm. He works long hours though, out in all weathers.'

Agnes gave her a hard look, but she didn't comment, and Emily knew her friend didn't believe her. What could she say, though? She couldn't tell Agnes she had no idea what her husband was up to. She had her suspicions, something to do with the woodshed, she guessed.

They got on with the washing, finally getting the sheets rinsed and put through the mangle. It was hot, heavy work with little energy for conversation. When they'd finished and the laundry was blowing on the line stretched across the yard, Agnes suggested they have a drink and a rest, but Emily didn't want her friend to return to the subject of Lenny's job. 'I'm sorry, I must get going. Lots to do before Lenny gets home.'

She didn't even stop to make Agnes a cup of tea but hurried across the yard, pausing at the woodshed. She looked around nervously but there was no one in sight. She would be brave and defy Lenny. She must find out what was hidden in there. But when she approached the door, she saw a shiny new padlock hanging from the hasp.

So, he didn't trust her to keep her word. Her suspicions were right then – he was hiding something.

When Cissie got home from school, Emily did her best to conceal her worries. It was hard with so much on her mind. She hadn't slept well last night, still aching from Lenny's latest assault on her body. He didn't seem to care that it was painful for her, only thinking of his own pleasure. She had heard it described as making love, but where was the love? Usually, she was able to close her mind to what was happening, taking her thoughts back to happier days when she was content surrounded by the love of her family. Now, she only had Cissie and worry for her constantly occupied her mind.

Today, though, as she listened to Cissie's happy chatter about her school day, foremost in her mind was curiosity about what was hidden in the woodshed and why Lenny was so determined to keep her out.

She was so lost in thought that it was a few moments before she realised Cissie had grown silent and was sitting on her bed, sucking her thumb. It was a habit she'd grown out of a couple of years ago. She sat down beside her sister and put her arm around her.

'What's wrong, lovie? Have you got a pain?'

Cissie shook her head.

'Well, you look upset. Tell me.'

'It's nothing, Em. I'm a bit tired that's all.' She wiped her thumb on her skirt and looked towards the door. 'Will Lenny be home soon?' she asked.

'I don't know. Depends where he's working today. Why?'

'I just wondered when we'll have our tea. I'm hungry.'

'Well, we don't have to wait for Lenny. I've made some scones. We can have them with jam. Would you like that?'

Cissie brightened immediately and scrambled off the bed.

Emily smiled, her worries fading for a moment as she told herself there really couldn't be anything troubling her sister if she was enjoying her food.

Feeling extravagant, Emily buttered the scones before adding the jam. Whatever her feelings about Lenny she could only be grateful that at least they ate well now. Watching Cissie tucking into the treat, she started to relax a little, but a niggling at the back of her mind persisted in intruding.

Why was Lenny always flush with money? If only she knew where and who he was working for. No use asking him. He was adept at fobbing her off and, if she persisted, he would become angry. She was learning that life was easier if she avoided upsetting him.

Cissie finished her second scone and asked, 'Are you saving some for Lenny?'

Emily laughed. 'You can have another one if you like.' She buttered another and passed the plate to Cissie. 'I don't think Lenny will be home for a while, but I'll cook him something. Don't worry, he won't go hungry.'

'I'm not worried. He should come home at a proper time if he wants his tea.'

'Cissie, what's got into you? It's not like you to be so...'

'I don't like him, Em. He doesn't treat you right,' Cissie interrupted.

'It's nothing to do with you, love. I don't understand. You used to be so fond of him.'

'That was when I was little. I was just a baby then. But he's changed, or I've grown up. He can't get around me by giving me presents and telling me he loves me.'

Emily was shocked. Cissie had never been so outspoken before. She took her sister by the shoulders and looked into her eyes.

Cissie stared back. It was true, Emily thought - her sister was growing up. She had been treating her like a five-year-old, but she would be leaving school in a couple of years.

She gripped Cissie's shoulders, her stomach churning. 'What do you mean – getting round you?'

'He's always wanting to cuddle me, to sit on his lap. And he gets cross if I won't'.

Emily forced a laugh, although she had never felt less like laughing. 'Is that all?'

Cissie nodded. 'He comes home early sometimes when you're working with Agnes. I don't like it when you're not here.'

Emily didn't like it either. Cissie hadn't been specific, but Emily was convinced that Lenny's behaviour toward her sister was not right. Maybe it hadn't gone too far – yet. And Emily would make sure it didn't. From now on, Cissie must never be alone with him. 'You can always go over to Agnes if I'm not home. She loves you to keep her company.'

Cissie nodded. 'I hope Lenny goes straight to the pub when he finishes work. It's nice just the two of us,' she said.

Emily hoped so, too. She felt a bit better after talking to Cissie but she still wasn't sure that was the whole story. Cissie was so innocent and probably didn't realise what Lenny was up to, but she couldn't probe any further for fear of scaring her sister. She would just have to be extra vigilant.

* * *

Lenny didn't come home at all that night. Emily was relieved but couldn't sleep, her ears alert for any sound. Where was he, and what was he up to?

He still hadn't appeared the next morning, so Emily sent Cissie off to school with instructions to go straight to Agnes's at dinner time. 'If I'm out delivering laundry, she'll feed you.'

Cissie didn't mind. It meant more time to play with Kitty and listen to Agnes's stories of the olden days.

Emily made the beds and washed up the breakfast things, giving one last look around to make sure nothing was out of place. Lenny liked a tidy house.

She greeted Agnes with a smile, determined not to let her friend see the worries consuming her. 'All ready?' she asked after the usual greetings.

Agnes pointed to the pile of freshly ironed sheets on the table. 'Finished last night,' she said.

'You managed all right, then?'

'Of course I did. I always liked ironing, and I can do it sitting down.' She chuckled. 'Not so hard on the old knees.'

Emily loaded the laundry into the big basket and hefted it onto her hip. 'Just this for the Admiral's wife?' she asked.

'Yes. The housekeeper will pay you. I've told most of my customers I'm packing it in, but she persuaded me to do this one lot for her as she's got guests coming to stay.' She sighed. 'Shame, but I just can't manage any longer.'

'You've been saying that for months. Can't believe you're really giving up.'

'Sorry love – doing you out of earning a few pennies. Still, Gladys will probably need a hand – that's if Lenny don't object.'

Emily didn't answer as she made for the door. 'I have a few errands to do while I'm out, so is it all right for Cissie to come to you for her dinner if I'm not back?'

'Of course, love. She's always welcome - you know that.'

Emily manoeuvred the heavy basket through the door and said goodbye. She had taken on the deliveries when Joey's friend Bobby had followed him into the Navy. She missed her brother's friend almost as much as she missed Joey. He had always been a friendly and helpful lad, if inclined to be a bit cheeky at times.

As she passed under the archway, she saw Gladys talking to a group of neighbours.

They looked across at her but didn't speak, and she wondered what they were talking about. One of the women was a notorious gossip, and Emily always tried to avoid her, but Gladys was a friend. Surely, they hadn't been talking about her. No - more likely Lenny was the subject of their gossip. He wasn't popular in the close.

Perhaps they knew more than she did about his mysterious job.

She couldn't stop now, but she was determined to speak to Gladys later.

She turned into the High Street and proceeded towards Mile Town, entering the Dockyard and Garrison complex past the guard house at the Garrison gate and making her way to Admiralty Terrace. It was a pleasant walk down the avenue between the trees, now just starting to show green buds. Despite carrying the heavy basket, she never minded doing the deliveries even in bad weather. It was good to get out of the close for a while.

By the time she reached the tradesman's entrance to the Admiral's house, her arms were aching. She handed over the laundry to the housekeeper and, relieved of the heavy basket, she made her way back home with a spring in her step.

For a few brief moments, her anxiety abated, and she started to enjoy the walk. It wasn't often that she escaped from the narrow lanes and alleys of Blue Town. All too soon, she would be back in the close confines of St Paul's Close with its gossiping neighbours, her errant husband and, most of all, the worry for her sister.

She was so lost in thought that she didn't hear someone calling and jumped when a hand fell on her shoulder.

'Hey. In too much of a hurry to speak to an old friend?'

Emily turned, recognising her father's policeman friend, looking very smart in his uniform with its silver buttons. 'Oh, Sergeant Brent. How are you?'

'Busy – and it's Bill, remember?'

'Bill – yes. I haven't seen you for ages.'

'As I said, I've been busy.'

'Is there a ship in for repairs, then?' Emily knew that when a navy ship was in dock, the sailors were given leave. They crowded the many public houses in the area and got into fights with the locals. Police leave was cancelled until order was restored.

Bill shook his head. 'Not this time. First, it was pilfering from the dockyard; now, it's burglaries.'

Emily gasped and put a hand to her mouth. 'Not round here, surely. People in this neighbourhood don't have anything to steal.'

'True. But these chaps are more ambitious. They're targeting the big houses on the island – you know up Minster and Eastchurch way.'

Emily wasn't sure where those places were. She had never ventured beyond the moat that cut Blue Town off from Mile Town and the rest of the island, and she had only occasionally gone over the Well Marsh with Joey and Bobby to gather mushrooms.

'We think it's a gang out of London.' Bill patted her arm, 'Anyway, nothing for you to worry about, Emily. They won't come into your part of town.'

'Thank goodness for that.' Emily shifted the basket to her other arm and said goodbye, hurrying home with a lighter heart. A gang from London – nothing to do with Lenny, then. How could she have been so suspicious? If only he weren't so secretive she would have been spared all this worry. She'd have words with him when he got home.

Chapter Twenty-Three

Emily wasn't concerned when she saw the two policemen enter the close a few days later. They must be investigating the burglaries Bill had told her about. She had been reassured that Lenny wasn't connected with them when Bill had mentioned London gangs. As far as she knew, her husband had left London years ago and had lost contact with his old friends.

She thought that petty theft was more his style, and he had probably been guilty of pilfering from the dockyard, although he hadn't been caught – yet. She gasped at the thought that perhaps that was what was hidden in the shed.

She watched from her window as the policemen went from door to door asking questions and receiving shakes of the head. They would come to her soon. Good job Lenny wasn't home. She could truthfully say she didn't know why the shed was locked and she didn't have the key.

They knocked on Gladys's door, and she came out of the house, wiping her hands on her apron. Emily couldn't hear what they were saying, but she bit her lip as her neighbour nodded and pointed to the sheds on the other side of the courtyard.

They walked across and opened each door, glancing in before moving on to the next. They stopped when they reached the locked one and stared at the padlock. One of them shook it and shrugged.

Would they try to force it open? She let out a breath as they turned away from the shed, but stifled a gasp as they walked towards her cottage.

Thank goodness Cissie was at school, she thought when they banged on her door. She debated not answering but Gladys knew she was home. Taking a deep breath and trying to still the trembling of her hands, she opened the door.

She didn't know either of the policemen, a sergeant and a constable. If only it had been Bill conducting these inquiries.

'Mrs Lennox, is your husband at home?'

'He's at work,' she said.

'And where would that be?' the sergeant asked.

'I – I don't know,' she stammered.

'You don't know where your husband works?' It was clear the sergeant didn't believe her.

'He does jobs all over the place. I'm not sure where he's working today.'

'What time does he get home?'

Again, she had to admit that she wasn't sure, only to receive another disbelieving look.

'Well, Mrs Lennox, we need to search your shed, as we have the others in the close. Perhaps you could unlock it for us.'

Emily found herself stammering again. 'I haven't got the key.'

'Never mind. We'll come back later.'

The constable reassured her. 'Nothing to worry about, Mrs Lennox.'

The sergeant shot him a fierce look. 'I must warn you that if he isn't home when we return, we will have to break the door down.'

Emily gasped and clapped her hand over her mouth.

The two men walked away and she closed the door, sinking to the floor and stifling her sobs. Lenny was guilty of something, if not the burglaries. Why lock the shed if he had nothing to hide? And why hadn't she been brave enough to ask what they were looking for?

She wiped her eyes and realised that Cissie would be home for dinner very soon. She had to start cooking straight away. No time to run over and ask Agnes's advice. She hoped Lenny wouldn't come home wanting dinner. She hadn't made up her mind whether to tell him of the visit from the police. A voice in her head told her to keep quiet, not to warn him. Let hm be there when they returned. If they found something incriminating in the woodshed, his arrest might solve all her problems.

She mashed potatoes and chopped onions, mixing them in with leftover corned beef. She spread it into an enamel pie dish and put it in the oven. By the time Cissie came in it would have a nice crisp brown topping.

Cissie's eyes lit up when Emily took the dish out of the oven. 'Ooh, my favourite,' she said, pulling her chair up to the table.

Emily smiled. 'You always say that whatever we have for dinner.' She was amazed that she was able to act normally, keeping up a cheerful flow of talk.

'I like coming home for dinner,' Cissie said, taking another mouthful of pie.

'I like having you home.' It was true but she had felt embarrassed telling Mark Thompson that Cissie could no longer stay for school dinners. Another of Lenny's rules. He begrudged paying for school meals when Emily was cooking for the family anyway. She hadn't dared protest that it was her money she was using.

She smiled at Cissie. 'Didn't you like school dinners then? You never said.'

'They're all right. But it's nice to be home.' She paused, took another mouthful of pie, then said. 'It's best when Lenny's working and it's just you and me.'

Emily agreed. She had noticed that Cissie's affection for Lenny had cooled a lot in the past few months. She still had her suspicions about his behaviour and was constantly vigilant. It was a relief that Lenny spent more time in the pub nowadays although she dreaded him coming home the worse for drink.

He was also out a lot during the day, although Emily now realised he wasn't really working. His 'little bits of business', which was where the money came from, took up much of his time. Criminal business as she was now almost certain.

She urged Cissie to finish up her dinner as it was now almost time for her to return to school. She didn't want her sister to be here when Lenny decided to come home. She would send her over to Agnes's if he turned up before the police did.

The afternoon passed slowly, Emily constantly on the alert for Lenny's return or the police banging on her door. She tried to keep busy but kept going to the close entrance, looking out for signs of the police or Lenny.

She finished tidying the room for the tenth time and went outside. It was a beautiful day and she would have loved to go for a walk down by the estuary shore but she dared not leave the house. As she wandered across the yard to the archway, Agnes banged on her window and beckoned her inside.

'What's the matter? Are you all right?' Emily asked.

'I'm fine. It's you I'm worried about,' Agnes retorted. 'Look love, I know what's up and wandering in and out, looking out for him won't help.'

'I don't know what to do, Agnes.'

Agnes banged her hand on the table. 'Well, what you're not going to do is warn that excuse for a man about the coppers being here this morning.' Everybody in the close knew about the police visit.

'I wasn't thinking of doing that,' Emily said. She sighed. 'The sergeant said they'd come back later and break into the shed. I don't want them here when Cissie's home.'

'Maybe they won't find anything.'

Emily gave a cynical laugh. 'You don't really think that. Why else put a padlock on the door?' She walked to the window and glanced out. No one about.

'I could do with a cup of tea,' Agnes said suddenly. 'I'll let you make it. I've overdone the housework today.'

'I'm so sorry. I should have offered,' Emily busied herself with the kettle and teapot and set a tray with cups and saucers and a jug of milk. She put it on the small table beside Agnes's chair, apologising once more for her thoughtlessness.

Her friend brushed the apology away. 'Just sit and enjoy your tea. You'll hear soon enough if the police turn up again. It's not your fault. None of the neighbours blames you.'

Emily sipped her tea in silence. What was there to say?

Agnes felt in her apron pocket and pulled out a couple of sheets of paper. 'Here, I almost forgot. I heard from Tom, my eldest.

It's been months. He's doing well in Canada since he left the navy – sent me some money.'

'Lovely,' Emily said.

Agnes read out the letter, and Emily, conscious that her friend was trying to distract her from her worries, leaned forward and concentrated. Tom was indeed doing well, having started a chandlers' shop in a coastal town. As Agnes recounted stories of her son and grandchildren, Emily thought about Joey. He wrote when he had the chance, but his letters were just half sheets of paper, saying he was well and hoping she and Cissie were too. How she wished she had someone to write her long, interesting letters. Her thoughts drifted to Harry, the convict lad who had stolen her heart. No longer a convict now, she thought, hoping he had made a new life for himself in that far away country.

She was a married woman, she chided herself. She shouldn't be thinking of another man, especially as she knew she would never see him again.

Agnes's voice startled her. For a moment, she had been in a dream world. 'Emily love, it's getting late,' she said. 'Shouldn't Cissie be home by now?'

'I told her to come here if I wasn't home,' Emily said, standing up and going to the window. 'She must be at home – I can see a light.'

She said a hasty goodbye and hurried across the courtyard. Flinging the door open, she gasped. Cissie was home – but so was Lenny. How had she not heard him?

Her sister was sitting on his lap, but this time, she wasn't snuggled up to him. She was sobbing and struggling to get away. Her hair was loose, and her dress was rucked up around her waist.

Emily seized the poker and rushed at him, her arm raised. 'Leave my sister alone,' she roared.

He stared at her, his arms still around Cissie. 'What's got into you, Em? Can't you see she's upset? I was trying to comfort her.'

'Comfort? Is that what you call it, you animal?' She raised the poker higher but stopped herself, fearful of injuring Cissie. 'Let her go or I'll...'

He cowered back in the chair. 'Please, Em, you've got it all wrong.'

Cissie took the opportunity to scramble down and ran across to Emily, who still kept hold of the poker but stroked her sister's hair. 'Are you all right, lovie?'

Cissie nodded. 'Go to Agnes. She'll look after you. I'll come over in a bit.'

Lenny started to protest. 'I don't want that old bag knowing our business. Stay here, Cissie.' He leaned forward and reached out a hand. 'I didn't mean any harm,' he whined. 'Please believe me, Em.'

'Cissie – go,' Em commanded, waiting until her sister had left the room. 'Now, I'll deal with you – you bastard,' she screamed, bringing the poker down.

A thunderous knock on the door distracted her and deflected her aim. Instead of landing on his head, the poker glanced off his shoulder, bringing a howl of pain.

She was ready to strike again when the door burst open, and the poker was wrested from her hand. 'It's all right, Emily, love. You can leave him to us now,' Bill Brent said.

Emily collapsed against him, sobbing. 'I nearly killed him,' she wailed.

'But you didn't. Sit down, love, take a breath.' He nodded to the two constables who had accompanied him. 'Watson, Keen - take him away, but first, look in his pockets for the shed key.'

PC Watson, the younger one, found it and handed it to Bill. He then took Lenny's other arm, and he and PC Keen marched him out into the courtyard, where several of the neighbours were gathered.

Emily staggered to her feet and went to the door, watching as her husband was taken away. Beyond the entrance to the close, she could see the horse-drawn wagon that would take him to the cells beneath the magistrates' court.

She sighed and turned away when Bill spoke.

'I'm going to search the shed – we have a warrant, for the house also. Come with me. I need a witness.'

'I need to make sure Cissie's safe. She's with Agnes.'

'She'll be all right for a bit. Best she stays there till we've finished our inquiries.'

Emily agreed reluctantly and accompanied Bill across the yard to the woodshed. As he fitted the key into the padlock, he said, 'Weren't you suspicious when he locked the shed?'

'Of course I was. But he explained – I had to believe him. I couldn't face the thought of being married to a criminal.'

Bill nodded sympathetically, then opened the door and peered into the gloom.

'There's nothing there,' Emily said.

'Wait.' Bill opened the door wider, propped it open with a log and stepped inside. He pulled a torch from his belt and switched it on. He pulled a few logs from the pile stacked near the far wall, revealing a hollow space containing a large leather holdall. He grunted with satisfaction. 'Just as we thought,' he muttered.

'What is it?' Emily called from the doorway.'

Bill backed out of the shed carrying the bag. He glanced across to the watching neighbours. 'Best take this inside,' he said.

Emily followed him back to the house, flushed with embarrassment. She hung her head. Surely, Gladys and her cronies didn't think she was involved in Lenny's crimes.

'I need to take this to the station,' Bill said, placing the bag on the table.

'Aren't you going to open it?' Emily asked.

'No. I need to have an independent witness.'

Emily frowned. 'Oh, I see.'

'It's not that I don't trust you, but I have to go by the book.' Bill hesitated, looking embarrassed. He cleared his throat and said, 'I ought to take you in as well.'

Emily gasped. 'Please. No.'

He reached out and took her hand. 'It's all right, Emily, I'm not going to. I've known you long enough to be sure you're not involved. Besides, we've got his mates. One of them shopped him. He was double-crossing them. That's why he put the lock on the shed. Wanted to do them out of their share. He got greedy, and they didn't like it.'

'Serve him right,' Emily said.

Bill nodded. 'I must take this to the station,' he said, picking up the bag. 'You'll probably have to come down and make a statement, but tomorrow will do.'

'Thank you, Bill. I promise you - I had no idea.' It wasn't strictly true. She'd had her suspicions but never any proof.

'I know, love. Stop worrying. Go over and fetch Cissie. She seemed pretty upset when I arrived.' He paused and looked intently at her. 'By the way, why were you threatening Lenny with the poker? Are you sure you hadn't found out what he was up to?'

Emily shook her head. She couldn't tell him what she had witnessed. He would have to question Cissie, and it would upset her even more. 'Of course not - I told you. He was being nasty to Cissie - called her a spoilt little minx. I couldn't bear to see her upset, so...'

Bill smiled. 'Bit drastic though, wasn't it? Good job, I turned up when I did.'

Emily grimaced. 'I just lost my temper. What with him losing his job... It all got on top of me.'

'I understand. Don't worry. We've caught Lomax, that's the main thing. We still need to search the house in case he's hidden anything here.'

'There's nowhere to hide anything,' Emily protested.

'We have to do it, but I'm sure I can trust you not to touch anything,' Bill said. 'I'll be back later with a couple of my colleagues.' He picked up the holdall and started for the door. Just as it opened, Constable Keen burst in, panting.

'He got away,' he gasped.

'What? How?'

'He tripped, and as we helped him up, he managed to get hold of a knife he had hidden in his boot,' The policeman held his hand up to show blood dripping down his wrist. 'Watson's gone after him.'

'Did you see which way he went?'

PC Keen shook his head. His face was pale, and he grasped his wrist, breathing heavily. 'We should have searched him.'

'Too late now. You'd better get that seen to,' Bill said, pointing at Keen's injured hand. He thrust the bag at him. 'Take this back to the station and tell the inspector what's happened. Round up a few of the men to go after Lomax.'

Keen rushed outside, and before Bill could follow him, he said to Emily, 'I've got to go after him. Look after Cissie. I'll be back later.'

Then they were gone, leaving her pale and trembling.

* * *

Emily leaned against the table, her heart pounding. How on earth had Lenny managed to escape with two burly policemen holding him?

It had been a shock to hear that he carried a knife. If she had known, would she have dared attack him with the poker?

Maybe not, she thought. But she had been so mad. A small smile crept across her face as she recalled him cowering away from her as she raised the poker. A bully and a coward, she thought.

But he had managed to escape. She was almost glad and hoped he'd get clean away. She dreaded having to stand up in court and give evidence against him. She remembered her ordeal all those years ago, seeing Harry in the dock.

291

A thought struck her. Suppose he came back here. He would need money to get very far away. Although she was convinced he hadn't hidden anything in the house, he knew where she kept her tin of savings.

Suddenly, she was afraid. The police had taken the knife, but Lenny was still capable of violence. She grabbed her purse and flung a shawl over her shoulders, running across the yard and almost falling into Agnes's cottage.

Cissie was sitting on the floor in front of the fire, playing with the cat. She scarcely looked up, but Agnes struggled out of her chair and threw her arms round Emily.

'I saw him being arrested. Thank God,' she said. Then, seeing the look on Emily's face, she frowned. 'What's wrong, love?'

Emily shook her head, glancing down at Cissie.

Agnes took the hint and said, 'Tea's in the pot. Pour yourself a cuppa. Looks like you need it.'

'Thank you, Agnes.' She poured a cup and sat down beside her friend. 'It's been quite a day,' she said quietly.

Agnes said equally quietly, 'You must be so relieved. I guess they found enough evidence. What was in that bag they took out of the shed?'

'I don't know – Jewellery I expect.'

'Why aren't you looking more pleased?'

Emily hesitated. 'He's on the run,' she said, 'managed to get away from the police.'

'Oh, my God. That's terrible. I hope they catch him soon.'

'I'm sure they will,' Emily said, with more confidence than she actually felt. She didn't confide her fear that Lenny might come back looking for money. Surely, he would want to get as far away as possible.

Cissie was still engrossed in her game with Kitty, but she looked up and said, 'Has Lenny gone away?'

Emily nodded.

Cissie frowned. 'He won't come back, will he?'

'I don't think so.' Emily couldn't tell her sister the truth.

'Will Joey come home now Lenny's gone?' Cissie asked.

Emily sighed. Poor Cissie looked so hopeful. 'No, lovie. Joey's a sailor now. He can't come home when he wants to. Still, we'll write to him, shall we?'

Cissie nodded and went back to playing with the cat.

Emily and Agnes exchanged a look. 'Such an innocent,' Agnes murmured. She leaned towards her friend. 'Why was Cissie so upset when she came over - she wouldn't tell me.'

'I can't talk about that now – not in front of her. Later, perhaps.' And perhaps never, she thought. It was so hard to think about, let alone discuss with anyone, even her closest friend.

Chapter Twenty-Four

Lenny had been on the run for several weeks, and there had been no sightings of him. Bill kept her up to date on the manhunt, which had been scaled back, the authorities convinced he had escaped the island.

On a recent visit, Bill said, 'My boss thinks he's probably in London by now.'

'I hope so,' Emily said. 'I never want to see him again.'

'He's still your husband,' Bill said.

'Don't remind me. He's not the man I thought he was.'

'I know. He had a lot of us fooled. Still, he should be supporting you still.'

'I don't want his money – especially if it's dishonest money.'

Bill nodded and leaned forward to touch her hand. 'How are you managing though?' He hesitated. 'If you need any help...'

'No thanks. I've taken over Agnes's laundry work and Joey sends me a bit now and then. We're all right, Cissie and me.'

More than all right, she thought. She no longer felt nervous, lying awake listening for Lenny breaking into the house. At first, she had pushed the table up against the door in an effort to keep him out – just in case he returned. But she had been heartened by Bill's words. Lenny wouldn't come back now. It was too risky with every policeman on the island on the lookout for him. The rest of the gang had been caught very quickly and were now awaiting trial.

Emily was starting to feel happy and secure again. Although she still missed Joey, she had Cissie to care for, and that was enough.

Gradually, the nightmares brought on by Lenny's ill-treatment as well as what he had done to her sister, began to fade. Cissie, too, seemed to be recovering and, for the past two days, had insisted on walking home from school by herself.

Taking on Agnes's customers meant longer hours working, but Emily didn't mind. Agnes helped when she felt well enough, and during the school holidays, Cissie often gave a hand too.

Life in the close felt like it had when Emily and her family had first moved in – a close-knit community of neighbours who were always ready to help each other. Thanks to the support and friendship of Gladys and Agnes, the other women who had looked askance at her during her marriage to Lenny began to accept that she had never been involved in his criminal activities.

Often, during that summer, the women of the close would bring their chairs outside and sit together chatting and doing their needlework. Sometimes Emily could almost forget that she had ever been married, that her life with Lenny was just a bad dream.

* * *

Cissie had gone back to school after the holidays, and Emily and Agnes were enjoying the last of a late sunny afternoon, sitting outside with their drinks. It had been a long day with a huge load of laundry washed and dried. Emily enjoyed the work when they could hang the sheets outside to dry. All too soon, winter would be upon them with its daily struggle against the cold, mist and dampness.

'Summer's nearly over,' Agnes said, echoing her thoughts. 'We won't be able to sit out like this much longer.'

'Let's make the most of it then,' Emily said, shading her eyes against the sun.

'Not looking forward to winter. Me poor old knees will start playing up again soon as we get some cold and rain.'

The other neighbours had already gone indoors to prepare the evening meal for their families. Emily knew she should do the same but she wanted to enjoy the fine weather for a bit longer. And she decided to wait for Cissie to return from the shop where she had gone to get some flour. It was good to be able to trust her sister to do the errands and Cissie was proud to be able to help.

She sat up straight when she heard Cissie's high voice. The sun was in her eyes,

296

and she felt a brief flicker of alarm. Who was she chatting to? She let out a breath as she recognised Bill Brent. Did he have news?

Cissie put the bag of flour in her lap and leaned in for a hug before rushing indoors in search of Kitty.

Bill squatted down in front of Emily and took her hands. 'I'm sorry, Em,' he said.

'You've caught him?' she whispered.

Bill nodded. 'Yes, he's been found.' He took a breath. 'His body was found in one of the dykes over on the marshes. Drowned.'

'You said he was in London.'

'Probably, I said.'

'Are you sure it's him?' Emily asked.

'Positive. I'm really sorry.'

'I'm not. He got what he deserved'.

'Emily!' Agnes exclaimed.

'Well, it's true. When I think what I suffered...' She choked on a sob.

Agnes reached across and patted her arm. 'I know, love. Sorry.'

'Who found him?' Emily asked.

Bill coughed. 'You don't need to know the details.'

'But I do. I want to know everything.'

'All right, but it's not very pleasant.'

Agnes stood up and offered Bill her chair. 'Sit here. I'll go and make some drinks and keep Cissie occupied. You don't want her coming out and hearing this.'

'Thanks, Agnes.' Bill pulled the chair closer and sat down. 'We'd already caught his mates, so we knew he wouldn't be anywhere near their known haunts. He'd be desperate to get off the island, so we kept tabs on the ferry. No sign of him.'

'He was running away over the marshes?' Emily asked.

'Seemed so. We'd already searched that area so we assumed he'd got off the island. He must have slipped and fallen in where it's quite deep, got tangled up in the reeds.'

Emily gasped and put her hand over her mouth. Much as she had come to hate Lenny, she couldn't help feeling a little sad at his demise.

'Who found him?' she asked.

'A couple of lads were fishing for eels. The body got caught up in their fishing line.'

'Will I have to identify him?

'No, love. I wouldn't expect you to do it. It wasn't a pretty sight. He'd been in the water for weeks. Must have happened the day he gave us the slip'.

Emily clapped her hand over her mouth. 'How awful,' she murmured.

'Anyway, one of his mates identified him, although it was certain who it was. There'll be an inquest, though - nothing for you to worry about,' he hastened to reassure her, then stood up to go. 'Do you want me to tell Cissie?'

'No thanks. I'll tell her.'

Bill nodded and took his leave after assuring himself that Emily was all right.

Chapter Twenty-Five

The ship docked in the Pool of London on a fine September morning after a storm-tossed voyage which had taken weeks longer than usual.

Harry hefted his bag onto his shoulder and strode down the gangplank breathing deeply of the warm, fresh air. It had been a dreadful few months. The passengers kept below decks for weeks as the ship braved the incessant unseasonal squalls. There had been times when Harry had deeply regretted his decision to return to England as he lay on his bunk, fighting the nausea and listening to the screams and moans of his fellow passengers. He had made a good life for himself in Australia – a hard life but nothing compared to his early days as a street urchin in the slums of London, even worse on the chain gang as a convicted felon. Only the hope of meeting up with Emily again had impelled him to make this dangerous voyage, but in his worst moments, he had to admit it was a foolish hope. He was still determined to return to Sheppey, though, and his heart leapt as they made their way up the estuary, passing the island on their left, the masts and spars of the dockyard ships just visible in the morning mist.

Now, here he was, feet firmly on dry land and hope rising in his breast once more.

He stopped one of the stevedores unloading the ship and asked if he had any idea how to get to the Isle of Sheppey.

The man laughed at his query. 'Mate, what do you want to go there for?'

Harry explained he was looking for his family. A white lie but he couldn't confide in a perfect stranger how he'd fallen in love with a girl he hardly knew. He wasn't even sure if she would remember him. Well, there was only one way to find out.

'Your best bet is the steam packet,' the man told him. 'They call in at Gravesend and other places along the estuary. Not sure about Sheerness, though.' He showed him where the boats docked by Tower Bridge.

Harry wasn't keen on setting foot on board a ship again after his recent experiences, but it was probably the easiest way to get where he needed to be.

He thanked the man, hefted his holdall onto his shoulder and strode off along the river path.

* * *

Emily pushed the cart piled with clean laundry along the High Street. Since she'd purchased a handcart from the junkyard in one of the little back streets to replace the

300

cumbersome basket, she could get the collections and delivery done much more quickly. She liked this part of the job best: getting out of the close and visiting her customers. Of course, she never met the officers' wives who lived in the posh houses, but she got to know the maids and housekeepers she dealt with and even became friends with some of them.

She and Agnes were doing very well, especially with Gladys helping when they were extra busy. Nowadays, she seldom thought about her brief marriage and its tragic ending. She still missed her brother and longed for him to come home, but life was good.

Today, she was feeling especially light-hearted. She had counted up the money in the cocoa tin and found that, after setting aside the rent money and paying Agnes and Gladys their share, she could keep her promise to Cissie.

It was her sister's twelfth birthday, and she had begged to go to the Oxford Music Hall in the High Street. Several of her friends had been, and she couldn't stop talking about it. Cissie was no longer the shy, withdrawn child she had been and was even making friends at school. She was a great help to Emily too, taking on the bulk of the daily shopping after school when her sister was extra busy with the laundry. Emily was proud of the way she had recovered from the traumas of the past few months. She deserved a treat.

She was just passing the Music Hall and stopped to look at the poster pasted to the wall. Although she knew very little about the latest songs and singers, the poster looked colourful and exciting. She was really looking forward to the evening.

As she turned away, she came face to face with Mark Thompson. She hadn't seen him for a while and greeted him with a smile.

'I see you're interested in the show. Are you thinking of going?'

Emily nodded. 'I've already got my ticket.' She started to walk away, pushing the empty cart.

'It's good to see you, Emily. You're looking very well.' He walked beside her, glancing down at her hands resting on the handles of the cart. 'It's a pity you're still doing manual work, though.'

'I have to earn a living,' Emily said sharply.

'I know and you could do so much better if you would come back to the school.'

'I'm happy with my present job.'

'I wish you would re-consider. After all, I know it was your husband's wish that you didn't take up my earlier offer.' He smiled. 'You no longer have to consider Mr Lomax – you're free.'

It was the smile that hardened her heart. How dare he presume... She was about to retort when he said, 'We're both free.'

Fury exploded within her, and she almost spat. 'Mr Thompson, I must say again – I don't want to work for you. Please stop bothering me.' And she stalked away, thrusting the cart in front of her and almost catching his leg.

She was furious – with herself as much as anything. She had to admit that when they'd first met, she had been attracted to him, but after learning that he had a sick wife, she firmly rejected any notion of a relationship with him. By the time his wife died, she was married to Lenny, but that hadn't stopped him from pursuing her. If it hadn't been for his kindness to Joey and later to Cissie, she would have avoided contact with him altogether. Perhaps he had read more into her gestures of friendship than she'd meant.

By the time she reached the close, she had calmed down, and when Cissie greeted her excitedly she took a deep breath and hugged her sister. 'Yes, love, we really are going to the music hall and Agnes is coming with us.'

'Really, but she can't walk far. How will she get there?'

Emily pointed at the handcart. 'She's going to ride – and we're going to push.'

Cissie giggled. 'Have you told her?'

'Yes, and she took a bit of persuading, but I talked her round.'

'We must put some pillows in to make it comfortable for her – and a blanket,'

'I've already thought of that. Now, come on, help me get the tea ready. We don't want to be late.'

They prepared the meal together, Cissie unable to contain her excitement.

'Calm down, love,' Emily said. 'Run over and fetch Agnes. She's going to eat with us.' Cissie flew out the door, and Emily quickly laid the table and dished up their meal of beans on toast with a sprinkle of grated cheese. It wasn't much of a birthday meal, Emily thought, but it was one of Cissie's favourites.

When everyone was seated, Emily said, 'Eat up quickly, girls.'

Cissie giggled and lifted a forkful of beans to her lips. 'I can't wait. I'm so excited.'

'So am I,' said Agnes. 'I can't remember the last time I went to the music hall.'

When they'd finished eating, Cissie cleared the table and placed the plates in the sink while Emily arranged the cushions in the cart.

'We'll leave the washing up till later, Cissie. Come and help me.' Together, they helped Agnes into the cart, made sure she was comfortable and set off.

The doorman greeted them cheerfully. 'You can leave the cart in the foyer,' he said. He and a couple of men in the queue lifted Agnes from the cart and took her to her seat. Emily had worried that her friend might be embarrassed by the attention, but she seemed to enjoy herself, bowing and waving to the waiting crowd.

'Just like the Queen,' Cissie whispered. They settled into their seats just as the introductory music began and they all leaned forward in anticipation. The show held them spellbound as act followed act.

Then came the highlight of the evening. Bella Forde, a new singer rapidly becoming famous, glided onto the stage, her hands clasped demurely in front of her, and began to sing. The sad song about a lost love brought a tear to Emily's eye, and as she stole a glance at Agnes, she saw that her friend was similarly affected.

Thunderous applause greeted the end, and then, with a twinkle in her eye and a cheeky grin, Bella started on a rather risqué song that brought the house down.

The show was almost over, but before the final curtain, Bella led the audience in singing several popular songs, including 'Daisy, Daisy' and 'After the Ball'.

When the applause had died away after several encores, the curtain fell, and people started to leave their seats.

They made their slow way up the aisle and Emily went ahead to fetch the cart.

As she pushed the door to the foyer open, she spotted Bill Brent and his wife. 'Didn't know you were coming tonight,' she said. 'Did you enjoy the show?'

'It was marvellous,' Mrs Brent enthused.

'Shall we walk you home?' Bill asked. 'There's a few rowdies about.'

'That's very kind.' Emily pointed to the cart. 'We brought Agnes with us – she can't walk far. She's waiting with Cissie.'

Bill told her to stay with his wife while he fetched Cissie and the old lady.

As she and Mrs Brent stood chatting about the show, Mark Thompson appeared at her side. 'Good evening, Emily. I've come to see you and your friend home. It's not safe for ladies on their own.'

'No need, Mr Thompson, thank you. Mrs Brent's husband is escorting us.' She was careful to keep her tone neutral. Why, oh why, had she told him she was coming to the show?

At that moment, Bill appeared pushing the cart with Agnes seated in it, Cissie skipping alongside.

Emily smothered a grin as she saw the expression of horror on Mark's face. He hastily said goodbye and hurried away.

'What's up with him?' Bill asked.

'I don't think he wanted to be seen with us,' Emily said.

'Stupid man,' Mrs Brent said. 'What's he got to be so superior about?'

The Brents walked with them as far as the entrance to the close, Cissie skipping along and humming songs from the show.

Agnes was almost asleep, and Bill offered to help her into her cottage. They settled her into bed and said goodnight.

Emily and Cissie both thanked Bill and his wife and went indoors.

'Mr Brent is a nice man,' Cissie said.

'Yes, we're lucky to have such good friends. Now, off to bed with you.'

Emily had a quick tidy-up before following her sister upstairs. What a lovely evening it had been. The delight on Agnes's face had been worth the struggle to push her to the theatre in the handcart. As for Cissie, she would remember her birthday for a long time. Emily firmly pushed the encounter with Mark Thompson out of her mind. She would not let him and his snobby attitude spoil what had been a perfect day.

Chapter Twenty-Six

Harry leaned on the rail, listening to the churning of the paddles as they cleaved the waters of the Thames Estuary. He'd had to wait almost a week before he could get a place on the steamer.

As they left London Bridge, Harry spotted the pilot cutter drawing alongside. When they reached Gravesend, the packet boat pulled in to the shore, and the pilot transferred to the steamer. A nearby passenger told Harry that between here and the merging of the Thames estuary with the River Medway, there were dangerous currents and sandbanks.

As the paddles started turning once more, the man said, 'We'll drop the pilot when we reach open water.'

Harry gazed about him curiously. He had little memory of his earlier journey to the island, kept below decks in chains with his fellow prisoners. Those few years on the hulks had been a nightmare, terrorised by Toothless Tony and his gang. Getting caught during their mad attempt at escape had turned out for the best, though.

He would never understand why Emily and her family had helped him, but he blessed them every day. And now, here he was, on his way to find her and thank her. He hadn't had a chance to show his gratitude at the time. He prayed that she would remember him. It had been more than six years, after all.

Lost in thought, he gradually became aware of a change in the rhythm of the paddles and he noticed the boat was changing direction. Were they here at last?

'Are we stopping?' he asked his fellow passenger.

'Sheerness Pier coming up. That's your destination, isn't it?'

Harry nodded, turning his head to see the towering walls of the dockyard and the outline of the pier beyond.

'It's changed a bit,' his companion said. 'The old hulks that were moored alongside have been broken up. They don't send prisoners to Australia anymore.'

Harry shuddered at the memory and didn't reply, just grabbed his bag and began to push his way through the throng of passengers lining the rail. Only a couple of men disembarked with him and they hurried off to their destination, leaving him looking around him, not sure where to go.

He descended the steps from the pier onto the road and turned left, following the dockyard wall and scrutinising the rows of shops, ships' chandlers, and pubs on the other side of the road. Lots of pubs, he noted. The wooden buildings, some painted tar black, many of them sporting the blue paint which gave the town its name, were separated every few yards by narrow alleyways.

He remembered that beyond the houses was the treacherous marsh where he had stumbled in the mist and dark, cold, hungry and terrified. He'd finally found his way down one of these alleyways leading out into a maze of mean streets and courts. How was he ever going to find the place where he had hidden and been given shelter by the Williams family? It would take days to explore them all. He continued along the High Street, passing a smart white building. It seemed out of place among the shabby shops and pubs crowding the street.

A flash of memory made him hunch his shoulders and scurry past. How could he forget the magistrate's court where his fate had been decided all those years ago? He shuddered at the memory of the days spent in its basement cells. Nothing to be nervous about now, he chided himself. I've done my time. I'm free. Straightening his shoulders, he decided to try asking for the Williams family in one of the pubs. In a small community like this, someone was bound to know them.

He entered the 'Crown', the first one he came to, ducking under the low lintel and stepping down into a dimly lit bar area. Several sailors leaned on the bar, tankards of ale in their hands. They wouldn't be any help, Harry thought, glancing around. Two elderly looking men sitting at a small table in front of the fire seemed a more likely prospect.

Harry wandered over to them and saw they were playing dominoes. He leaned over and said, 'Enjoying the game fellers?'

'What's it to you?' the older one snapped.

Before he could think of a suitable reply, the other man said, 'No need to be so grumpy, Will.' He looked up at Harry, noting the holdall he carried. 'Just off the boat, mate?'

Harry nodded. 'Can I buy you two a drink?'

Will cheered up immediately and said, 'Mine's a pint.'

His mate said, 'I'm Al. The same, please.'

Harry went to the bar, ordered three pints, and then returned to the table.

'Thanks.' Al lifted his glass, and his friend Will did the same.

'Not seen you in here before,' Will said. 'Been at sea, have you?

Harry nodded.

'You're not from round here though, are you?' Al said.

'No. But... I'm looking for some old friends. I can't remember their address, but I know they lived in Blue Town. The Williams family,' he said, reluctant to use Emily's name.

'Williams, eh? Don't remember them,' Will said.

'Yes, you do Will. Joe Williams – he worked in the dockyard.' He turned to Harry with a frown. 'You're out of luck, young feller. He died some years ago.'

'Oh, yes,' Will interrupted before Harry could speak. 'Terrible accident in the dockyard. I remember now.' He took a swig of his beer. 'Good bloke, he was.'

Harry's heart sank. He hardly dared to ask. 'What about his family?'

Al thought for a moment. 'I know he'd lost his wife. I expect the children went to an orphanage.'

Harry plied them with more questions but couldn't discover anything specific. The conversation meandered around reminiscences of the men's years working in the dockyard and the people they had worked with.

They finished their beer and seemed anxious to get back to their game, so Harry thanked them and left. He suspected he would have to visit many pubs before he discovered anything more about the family – and the beautiful girl – who had helped him.

He refused to believe that Emily would have been sent to an orphanage after the death of her father. The youngest girl – yes. But the boy Joey would be grown up by now. And Emily had been on the verge of womanhood. It seemed more likely she and her brother would have been sent out to work – or, dreadful thought – to the workhouse.

He spent the afternoon wandering up and down the alleyways and narrow streets, stopping to ask anyone he met for news of the Williams family. As evening drew on, he almost lost heart, but he refused to give up. He'd find a bed for the night and start again tomorrow.

* * *

After a sleepless night spent in a cheap lodging house, Harry welcomed the dawn and started his search again. He breakfasted in a shabby café on bacon, fried bread, and a mug of strong tea. As he ate, he questioned the owner and a couple of dockyard workers.

The café owner shook his head, but when Harry mentioned the accident which had killed Joe Williams, he and the other two customers nodded.

'Terrible that was,' the cafe owner said. 'But he wasn't killed. That was the worst of it. He was bedridden and lingered on for a couple of years. His daughter nursed him.'

Harry gripped his mug of tea to stop his hand shaking. 'His daughter?'

'Lovely girl. Pity she married that Lomax. No good wastrel. Prop'ly pulled the wool over her eyes.'

Harry hardly took in the last words. Married? His Emily married?' He couldn't believe it – didn't want to believe it, despite repeatedly telling himself that she must have met someone in the years that had passed. And why not? How foolish to imagine that she even remembered him, let alone waited in hopes of seeing him again.

The café owner was looking at him strangely, and Harry pulled himself together. 'Does he still live hereabouts?' He couldn't bring himself to mention Emily's name.

'Don't know. He was in here a while back – Lenny Lomax, her husband – boasting he had some money coming, talking about going back to London. I heard the police were after him.'

Harry's heart sank. To come all this way only to discover that the girl he'd kept in his heart all these years was not only married but to a criminal. How could she have fallen for someone like that? Fate could not have dealt him a worse blow.

He drained his mug of tea, paid the man, and thanked him for the information. He stumbled out into the street, looking this way and that, undecided where to go. Nothing for it, he supposed. His dwindling funds meant he would have to find employment soon. He could probably get some labouring work in the dockyard, but the thought of staying here, besieged by memories, with no hope of even seeing the girl he loved, made up his mind for him. He would return to London.

*   *   *

Cissie was turning the mangle while Emily fed the sheets between the rollers and dropped them into the basket. She glanced across the yard to where Agnes sat dozing in her chair. Her friend was having a bad day today. Sadly, bad days were becoming more frequent. It would soon be too cold for her to sit outside and watch the comings and goings in the close. Emily dreaded the coming winter, knowing how the cold and damp would affect Agnes.

She pushed her dismal thoughts out of her mind and smiled at Cissie. 'It's so good to have you helping,' she said.

'I could help all the time if you'd let me leave school,' her sister replied.

Emily shook her head. 'Schooling's important,' she said.

'I'd rather be working.'

'But Mr Thompson says you're doing so well.' Despite her dislike of Mark Thompson, she had to admit he was a very good teacher and always did the best for his pupils. He had told her more than once that he would make sure Cissie got a good position when she left school.

Thinking of her own thwarted ambitions, Emily had sworn that her sister would not end up doing menial work as she had. Not that she regretted taking her mother's place and caring for her siblings.

She was proud of the way she had brought them up.

When Cissie protested that she couldn't see the point of staying on at school, Emily didn't reply. They carried on with their work, both sighing with relief when the last sheet was done and ready to hang on the line.

Agnes woke up and tried to get out of the chair, protesting that she wanted to help.

'Don't get up. We're nearly finished. Besides, it's time for dinner,' Emily said. She had left a stew simmering on the stove and directed Cissie to go and add a couple of potatoes to the pot.

'You don't have to feed me, too,' Agnes protested.

'Nonsense. There's plenty for three.' She grabbed the peg bag and proceeded to drape the sheets over the line. She fetched the clothes prop from the corner of the yard and hoisted the washing up high where the sheets could catch the breeze.

'All done,' she said. 'Now, come on. Those spuds should be done by now.' She helped Agnes out of the chair and held her arm as she hobbled across the yard.

When they got indoors, Cissie was laying the table, and Emily picked up a ladle to check on the stew. She took a small taste and smiled.

'Lovely,' she said. 'Now sit down and let's tuck in.'

There was silence as they made short work of the delicious stew, to which Emily had added carrots, onions, pearl barley, and floury dumplings to bulk out the small amount of meat.

Agnes pushed her empty plate away with a satisfied sigh. 'You could get a job as a cook,' she said. 'Much better than doing other people's washing.'

'Don't start, Agnes. I'm quite happy with things as they are.'

'You might be, but I'm not. Look, Emily - I've got to face facts. I keep saying I'm going to give up, but this time, I mean it. You know how I was today – left it all to you and young Cissie.' She smiled at the younger girl. 'And a very good job you did too love.'

'They're your customers, Agnes. They rely on you.'

'They don't care who does the work so long as it gets delivered on time. Besides, you can manage quite well without me.'

'I don't think so. What about when Cissie's at school and Gladys is working at the pub? I don't think I could cope on my own.'

Before Agnes could reply, Cissie said, 'You wouldn't be on your own if you let me leave school and be your assistant.'

'We've discussed this before. I want you to stay on.'

Cissie folded her arms and glared at her sister. 'Well, I don't want to.'

Emily gasped. It was so unlike Cissie to defy her.

They sat glaring at each other while Agnes struggled to stand. 'I'll leave you two to sort it out between you.' She leaned on the back of the chair and then turned to Emily. 'But before I go, I must say, your sister has a point. She's confided in me that she hates school and struggles with her lessons. Why not let her leave and work with you?'

'But Mr Thompson said...'

'You don't understand, Em,' Cissie interrupted with a sob in her voice. 'He only tells you I'm doing well to please you. He wants to keep me at school, so he has an excuse to speak to you.'

'What do you mean?'

'He likes you – I think he wants to marry you now Lenny's dead.'

'Cissie, how could you say such a thing?'

'Well, he's always saying how clever you are and what a good job you've done with me and Joey.'

'And so you have, Emily. He's right about that,' Agnes said. 'Please, love. Give it some thought.' She limped towards the door, waving Emily back when she went to help. 'I can manage. Stay here and sort things out with your sister.'

When she'd gone, Emily sat down heavily, and Cissie began to clear the dinner things away. Lenny had always insisted on clearing the table and washing up as soon as the meal was finished, and she had not yet got out of the habit.

'Leave that till later. Agnes is right. We need to have a chat.'

Cissie put the plates on the draining board and came over to put her arms around Emily. 'I'm sorry I upset you,' she said.

'And I'm sorry I upset you.' She hugged Cissie and said, 'You're right - I don't understand. I thought I was doing the best for you. Perhaps you'd better tell me...'

'I'm not clever like you. I don't read so well, but I loved you reading to me and Joey when we were little. And sums – they don't make sense to me.'

'Why didn't you tell me? And why did Mr Thompson say you were doing well and he wanted you to stay on at school?'

'Like I said, he likes you. He wants to please you.' Cissie gazed into Emily's eyes. 'You won't marry him, will you, Em?'

Emily laughed. 'Marry him? Definitely not.'

'I thought you liked him.'

'I did at first, mainly because he was kind to you and Joey. But then he started to get too friendly, if you know what I mean.' Cissie nodded. 'And he was married. I couldn't...'

'Let's not talk about it anymore. And don't worry, I've been married once – no more.'

'Good,' Cissie said. 'But you do understand now, why I want leave school.'

Emily sighed. 'Yes, I do. Perhaps you're right.' She held out her hand and grasped

Cissie's. 'Welcome to the working world. And no slacking.'

Cissie laughed and gave her sister a hug. 'Partners,' she said. 'Can I go over and tell Agnes?'

'And leave me to do the rest of the clearing up?' But there was a smile in Emily's voice and she nodded. 'Go on, then.'

She poured hot water from the kettle on to the dishes, added washing soda and picked up the dish mop. As she began to clean the dried-on stew, the door flew open.

'Em, please come. It's Agnes.' Without waiting for a reply, Cissie ran back across the yard.

Emily followed without drying her hands, her mind in turmoil. She should have seen her friend home, not let her walk across the slippery cobbles on her own.

Agnes was lying on the stone flagged floor, blood pouring from a cut on her forehead. Cissie knelt beside her, trying to place a cushion under the old lady's head.

Emily knelt down too and lifted her friend's hand. She could feel a pulse and sighed with relief. Just then Agnes's eyes opened. 'Silly me, I tripped,' she whispered.

'Let me help you to sit up. Where does it hurt?'

'Just my head.' Agnes gave a shaky laugh. 'No bones broken.'

Emily turned to Cissie. 'Fetch a cloth and some warm water,' she said.

Cissie obeyed and together they got Agnes into her chair. While Emily bathed the cut on her head, Cissie fetched a blanket and tucked it around her.

'Would you like me to stay with you?' Cissie asked.

'I'm all right. No need to make a fuss, just a little cut. I caught my head on the fender.' Agnes protested.

'You need to take it easy,' Emily scolded. 'Let Cissie stay until you feel better.'

'She just needs an excuse to stay and play with Kitty,' Agnes said with a chuckle. 'Still, you could make me a cup of tea.'

Satisfied that Agnes wasn't badly hurt and would soon be back to her old self, Emily said she had things to do at home but left Cissie to keep an eye on the old lady.

She would speak to Gladys and the other neighbours and let them know that Agnes wasn't too well. They would all rally round and look after her. Agnes was popular with everyone in the close and they had also become more friendly with Emily too, since Lenny had died.

She could see that Gladys was home and knocked on her door. She quickly described what had happened and assured her that Agnes was only a bit shaken up. 'Cissie's staying with her for a while.'

'I'll pop over later if you like,' Gladys said.

'Thank you.' Emily went on to tell her that Agnes had decided to give up taking in washing and that she would be dealing with her friend's customers.

'It's about time she packed it in. She's not been too well for some time,' Gladys said. 'How will she manage for money though?'

'One of her sons sends her a bit from time to time. She'll be all right.'

'I'm sure we'll all help out when needed. Don't want the poor old thing ending up in the workhouse.'

Emily nodded in agreement. 'By the way, Cissie is going to leave school and work with me,' she said.

'She's a good girl. You'll make a good team,' Gladys said. 'I'm pleased.'

'I hope you'll still be able to give a hand when we're busy,' Emily said.

'Of course. I'm always glad to earn a bit extra.' She pointed to the sheets blowing in the wind. 'They look nearly dry. Shall I get them in for you?'

Emily thanked her and went indoors to finish her chores. She'd still have the ironing to do, a task she hated. Maybe she could get Cissie to take it on as part of her new job.

She had just finished putting the dishes away when there was a knock on the door. It was Gladys.

'Is it Agnes?' she asked anxiously.

'She's all right, sleeping at the moment. It's just that I forgot to tell you earlier. Some bloke came into the pub this morning asking about your dad. He was chatting to one of the regulars, who told him your dad had died. I was busy behind the bar, or I would have spoken to him. When I looked over later, he'd gone.'

'I wonder who it was.'

'He didn't give a name. An old friend, I heard him say.'

'Someone from our old life in London, perhaps.' She thanked Gladys and closed the door, leaning against it until she had caught her breath. It couldn't be – could it? He was in Australia, surely. And Dad had never spoken about their old London life. No one would be asking about him after all this time.

It must be Harry. Or was she just dreaming? Convicts who'd served their time did occasionally return to England. Why wouldn't Harry? Her mind drifted back six years to the frightened boy hiding in their shed. Her heart had gone out to him even before she knew what had happened to him. And after the court case and Bill Brent speaking up in his favour, she had been convinced that, despite being a convicted criminal, Harry Jones was, at heart, a good person, forced into a life of crime by circumstance. She had never forgotten him, and she dared to hope that he would never forget her.

Chapter Twenty-Seven

Harry spent another, mostly sleepless, night in the lodging house and woke with the determination to have one last effort at tracing Emily and the Williams family. He was sad to learn that Joe had died and devastated at the news of Emily's marriage. If he could be sure she was well and happy, he would be content and go back to London. But the man had said her husband was a criminal. Suppose she needed help.

He would also like to make sure that the younger siblings – children when he had met them – were being cared for. Joey, of course, would be a grown man by now. But the thought of sweet little Cissie in the workhouse was more than he could bear.

Before he gave up the search, he would do his utmost for the family, including Emily, married or not.

He passed the magistrates court again and walked past with his head down, stifling the memories. The High Street was busy with shoppers, mostly women huddled in shawls against the cold wind. They barely glanced at him, although he peered at each one as they passed. Would Emily be out shopping at this time of day? She would have changed, but he knew he would recognise her at once.

As he carried on down the High Street towards the Dockyard entrance. he heard the church clock strike and guessed that the 'dockies' would be finishing the early shift. They would come pouring out of the gate on their way home for their midday meal. He leaned against the wall and watched.

He would stop every one of them and question them if that's what it took.

The trickle of men hurrying past him thinned out, and Harry sighed. He had stopped several of them, but they had either ignored him or shrugged and shaken their heads.

He walked back towards the Red Lion, where he had already made inquiries the day before. There was a narrow alleyway at the side, which he had at first taken for an entrance to the pub's yard. He was about to enter the pub when he saw a young woman holding a child's hand, turning into the opening. Wondering where it led, he decided to follow.

A memory struck him. It had been dark when he had found his way off the marshes that dreadful night, but he had stumbled down a similar alley – maybe not this one, he thought, but one that was very like it. It had led him to a maze of narrow streets and from there to the courtyard where he had hidden, cold, wet and terrified.

He shivered at the thought, but a flicker of hope intruded. He came to the end of the alley and walked out into a street of wooden houses that all looked alike. There was a shop on one corner and a pub on the other. Emily's home couldn't be far away.

In this maze of streets, it would be hard to recognise the house where she had lived – that's if she was still living here. He would just have to explore every lane and courtyard.

As he hesitated, trying to decide which way to turn first, he spotted two men walking towards him. His heart leapt into his mouth. He would know that uniform anywhere. Without stopping to think, he ran back into the alley, ignoring the shouts from behind.

At the end of the alley, he paused to catch his breath. Why had he run? He had nothing to fear from the police. He was no longer that frightened boy in thrall to Toothless Tony's gang. He was a free man with the papers to prove it.

Cursing his stupidity, he waited for them to catch up with him. He should have gone to the police station in the first place. That policeman who had been so good to him was a friend of the Wiliams family. Surely he must know where they lived.

The younger of the two policemen reached him first. 'What you been up to then?' he asked, pushing Harry against the wall.

'Nothing.'

'Why run then?'

Harry couldn't answer. He was still trying to catch his breath after his dash up the alley.

The other man joined them and looked intently at him. 'Do I know you?' he asked.

Harry shook his head, but the policeman said to his fellow officer, 'I do know him. You're too young to remember the London gang who escaped from the hulks.' He turned to Harry. 'I remember though – we caught you in St Paul's Close hiding in one of the woodsheds, didn't we? You had ginger hair in those days. And you've filled out a bit since then.'

Harry nodded. He had just realised that this man – a sergeant now by his uniform - was the one who had helped him, spoken up for him in court. 'I can't remember your name, but I want to thank you for what you did for me all those years ago.'

'Aren't we going to arrest him then, Bill?' the young policeman asked.

'Course not. He hasn't done anything.' He turned to Harry. 'I guess you've come back to find Emily.'

'I heard she's married.' He choked on the words.

'It's a long story. That family's been through some bad times.' He turned to the other man. 'It's nearly the end of your shift. Why don't you report back to the station? I'll carry on questioning the suspect.' He winked at his mate.

'Suspect? But you said...'

'I suspect he's just returned from the penal colony in Australia. I need to ask him some questions. He's not dangerous. So off you go.'

The young man hurried away, looking back over his shoulder before turning the corner.

Bill laughed. 'Come on, I can't drink on duty, but I can buy you a pint.'

Harry's face cleared. 'He called you Bill. I remember now. You're Constable – sorry, Sergeant - Brent. I never forgot you and what you did for me.'

'I guess you never forgot Emily either,' Bill said with a smile.

'That's why I came back.' Harry's face fell. 'Too late though.'

'Don't lose heart, lad. It's a long story,' Bill said, leading the way into the Red Lion. He went up to the bar and greeted the barmaid. 'Hello Gladys, get this young man a pint of ale, will you?'

Gladys stared at Harry. 'You were in here yesterday, weren't you? Looks like you've found someone to answer your questions.'

Bill grinned. 'He's got quite a story to tell, and so have I. See that we're not disturbed, please, Glad.'

He carried Harry's beer to a table in a secluded corner and they sat down.

'Well lad, I'm dying to hear what's happened to you since I last saw you, but I'm sure you're impatient to hear about Emily and her family.'

Harry nodded, biting his lip. 'I heard her father died and she got married. That's all.'

'Very sad about Joe Williams.' Bill went on to tell Harry about the accident and how Lenny Lomax had wormed his way into the family in the guise of friendship. 'Everyone thought he was a good bloke, helping his mate and looking after the family when Joe couldn't earn any money.'

'This Lomax – that's who she married?' Harry asked.

Bill grimaced. 'Turned out he was a real bad 'un. We suspected for some time he was involved in a spate of burglaries. Even when he lost his job, he always seemed to have plenty of money. Emily, poor girl, never suspected, carried on working hard to support her little sister.'

'What about her brother, Joey? Didn't he do anything to help her?'

'He fell out with Lenny, joined the navy.' Bill sighed. 'I always suspected Lenny didn't treat Emily well, especially after Joey left. But she never complained.'

'Do they still live around here? I'd like to see her, though perhaps I shouldn't, seeing she'd a married woman.'

Bill reached across the table and grasped Harry's hand. 'Hang on, lad. I haven't finished. Whoever told you she was married didn't finish the story. He knew the police were after him, and he tried to get away over the marshes.' He paused. 'Well, you know yourself what it's like out there in the mist and the dark.'

Harry nodded. 'I remember. So, did you catch him?' The hope he'd fleetingly felt faded. Lenny was probably in jail, and Emily still tied to him for life.

'No, we didn't. But he turned up later – drowned in a ditch.'

It took a moment for Bill's words to sink in until he saw the grin of satisfaction on the policeman's face.

Harry felt as if a huge weight had been lifted off his chest. He half rose from the chair.

'Hang on there. I know you want to see her, but there's plenty of time. She won't run away. Finish your beer. I need to bring you up to date before you go rushing off.'

Reluctantly, Harry sat back down and picked up his tankard. Bill was right. Suppose Emily had forgotten him, didn't want to see him. It would be such a shock for her. 'Do you know if she ever got my letters? I wrote many times, hoping.'

'I think she would have told me if she ever heard from you.'

'I wasn't sure of the address.' Harry slapped his forehead. 'I'm an idiot. Why didn't I think of writing to you at the police station? I could have told you I was coming back.' Preferably before she tied herself to that no-good swine, he thought.

He sipped his drink, listening avidly as Bill told him of Emily's efforts to support her little sister by taking in washing. 'She's worked really hard. And Cissie's grown up into a lovely lass.'

'I would have thought her brother would have stayed to help,' Harry said.

'You can't blame Joey. Emily tried to keep the peace but - all of them in that tiny little cottage – it all got too much. In the end, Joey decided to leave before things got out of hand.'

'So, she's still living in that little place?'

Bill nodded.

'Does she remember me?'

Bill laughed. 'She remembers a skinny little lad with flaming ginger hair. Don't worry, though. You've changed, but she'll know you. I recognised you, didn't I.'

Harry was suddenly assailed by doubt. 'I don't know. What will I say to her?'

'Don't get cold feet now. You've finished your beer, so let's get going.'

Out in the autumn sunshine, Bill grasped Harry's arm and hurried him through the streets to St Paul's Close. As they approached, Harry recognised the arch leading into the courtyard and its rows of small cottages along two sides. A washing line stretched across the yard hung with sheets and pillowcases, blocking their view of the houses on the far side. He could see the row of privies and woodsheds at the back, and he shivered, remembering that night huddled behind the pile of logs.

As they crossed the cobbled yard, a gust of wind caught the sheets, revealing a young woman fighting to pin the washing to the line, her fair hair whipped up by the wind.

'Emily,' Harry whispered, his heart thumping. But the girl turned at the approach of the two men, and he saw at once that it wasn't her. So like Emily as he remembered her, but she was too young. It must be her sister, Cissie.

The girl let go of the sheet and cried out, 'Emily, visitors. It's Sergeant Brent and a friend.'

The door opened, and there she was. Yes, it was her, older, more mature, but still his sweet Emily with her silky blonde hair and those incredible blue eyes – just like the opal he had stashed in his bag. He couldn't wait to see her face when he gave it to her.

He took a step towards her, but she didn't seem to notice him.

'Bill, what are you doing here? Not on duty, I hope,' she said, noticing his uniform. She turned to Cissie. 'Don't let that sheet drag in the dirt.'

'Never mind the sheet, Em. I've brought someone to see you.'

She glanced at the man, his face half in shadow in the lee of the arch, confusion in her eyes. But only for a second. Then those eyes widened, and her hand went to her mouth. 'Harry – is it really you?'

He nodded, speechless. They stepped closer and stood, gazing at each other in silence for what seemed like endless moments.

'Emily,' he whispered.

'Harry – you've come back.'

Then they were in each other's arms, clinging on as if they would never let go.

Lost in those precious moments, they were not aware of Cissie staring open-mouthed. Bill gave her a nudge and winked. 'Time to get the kettle on,' he said, steering her towards the house door.

Chapter Twenty-Eight

It was a dream come true. Harry could hardly believe it. His Emily, here in his arms – and amazingly, seeming delighted to be there. There had been times over the past years when he had tried to forget her, telling himself how foolish he was to pin his hopes on a girl he hardly knew. But then he recalled her kindness to him, her belief that he was not a bad person despite being a convicted felon, and hope would rise once more.

And deep in his heart was the memory of his last glimpse of her - her smile as she watched him hustled in chains through the streets to the ship. That smile had sustained him through his darkest moments.

Dusk had fallen in the little courtyard and still they clung together, whispering their love to each other. So much to say, so much to catch up on.

The door to Emily's cottage opened suddenly, spilling lamplight onto the cobbles, and they sprang apart.

'Better come in out of the cold,' Cissie called. 'Bill's just going.'

'Emily, I'd better go too,' Harry said. 'I'll be back tomorrow. There's still lots to talk about.'

'Please don't go yet, Harry,' Emily pleaded, clinging to his hand.

Bill appeared in the doorway. 'Let him go, lass. He won't run away.'

'But I've nowhere to go,' Harry said. He didn't fancy going back to the dingy lodging house and had hoped Emily would let him stay with her, but his conscience told him that wouldn't be right.

'You're staying with me,' Bill said. 'The missus won't mind. Now come on, say good night to your sweetheart. You'll see her in the morning.'

It took all Harry's self-control to kiss Emily goodnight and break away. He followed Bill through the arch into the street, turning at the entrance to look back. Emily still stood there, one hand to her lips, the other raised in a wave.

They had scarcely spoken, except for sweet murmurings of love, but there was so much more to say, long stories to be exchanged of the years between. Harry strode beside Bill, his mind going over everything that had happened since the steamer had docked at the pier. His companion, seeming to sense his need for silence, didn't speak until they reached the house behind the police station where Bill lived.

'Here we are. Come on in, lad,' Bill said, opening the front door.

'You sure it's all right for me to stay?'

'It'll be fine. The wife's used to me bringing home waifs and strays.'

As he spoke, a door opened at the end of the passage, and Bill's wife appeared. 'You're late, love,' she said.

'Sorry, dear. Been a bit busy.' He ushered Harry into the light. 'Brought someone home – needs a bed for the night. I don't suppose you remember Harry Jones? He were just a scrap of lad when we last saw him.'

'The name's familiar, but... Anyway, you're welcome, son.' She stepped forward and shook his hand. 'I'm Dorothy – Dolly.'

'Thank you for letting me stay, Mrs Brent.'

As he moved into the lighted room, she looked more closely at him. 'Ah, yes. Harry Jones. I remember now. My Bill spoke up for you in court. You were transported. What brings you back then?'

Harry wasn't sure he liked people knowing his convict background. He was trying so hard to put all that behind him.

Before he could think of a reply, Bill said, 'Now then, Dolly. Give the lad a chance to sit down before you start quizzing him.'

She was all apologies. 'I'm not thinking. Forgive me. I'm sure you must be hungry – you, too, Bill. I'll fix you some supper.'

Harry nodded gratefully. He'd had nothing to eat since the greasy breakfast in the workman's cafe that morning and the half-drunk pint of beer with Bill.

The two men sat at the kitchen table while Dolly bustled around preparing a meal of eggs and bacon with fried bread, the tantalising smell causing Harry's stomach to rumble.

Dolly poured mugs of tea and dished up the supper.

When she put the plates on the table, Bill said, 'Get that down you. And then it's off to bed with you. It's been quite a day. We can talk in the morning.'

Harry nodded, his mouth full. He then took a slurp from the mug and pushed his plate away. He was dead tired, mostly from the emotional events of the day, but he didn't think he would sleep.

Dolly smiled. 'I can tell you need your bed. Don't worry, I always keep the spare room ready for unexpected visitors.'

Harry stood up and went to pick up his plate.

'Leave that. Up you go.' She led the way upstairs.

When Harry tried to thank her, she waved him away and left him to get into bed.

He lay in a half-dream, re-living his emotional reunion with Emily, finally falling into a deep, dreamless slumber.

* * *

Cissie burst out laughing as she watched Emily pacing up and down the small room.

'What's got into you, Em? Please, sit down and relax.'

'I can't relax. I just...'

'So, this is what being in love does to you?' Cissie teased. 'I've never seen you like this before.'

'I can't help it. 'Emily crossed the room and seized her sister's hands. 'Oh, Cissie. I've dreamt of this so often, but now it's happened...'

'Why so worried? I thought you'd be happy.'

'I am – it's just. Oh, dear, Cissie. He doesn't really know me, and once he hears about Lenny and...'

'You are not to blame for what Lenny did. I'm sure Harry will understand that - Bill will put him straight anyway.' Cissie hugged Emily. 'Be happy, Em. He came back – he loves you.' She grinned. 'I suppose you'll be getting married now.'

'No, no. I said I'd never re-marry, and I meant it. I couldn't go through that again.'

She threw herself down in the chair – Dad's chair – and covered her face with her hands. How could she explain to her innocent little sister?

But Cissie surprised her. 'He hurt you, didn't he – Lenny?'

Emily nodded. 'I tried to hide it from you.'

'I know, but I could tell.' She shook her head. 'I don't understand how he could be so cruel to you and so nice to me.'

'I don't understand either.' Emily sighed. 'Let's not talk about him.' It had suddenly struck her that, young as Cissie had been during her marriage to Lenny, her sister had been more aware of what was going on than she had realised.

'All right then,' Cissie agreed. 'But give Harry a chance – it might take time to get to know each other properly. You've waited this long...'

'When did you get to be so wise?' Emily asked, hugging Cissie again.

Cissie laughed. 'I had a good teacher. Now, I'm hungry – how about some supper.'

Later that night, as the sisters lay together in the big bed Emily had shared with

Lenny, she began to tremble. She had often imagined how it would be if she and Harry ever got together. He would be gentle, loving – nothing like the beast she had married. But how could she be sure? She had so little experience of men.

Cissie reached out and stroked her arm. 'You all right, Em?' she whispered.

'I'm fine. Go to sleep.' And she was fine, Emily told herself. She would not let thoughts of the past spoil her happiness. She closed her eyes and re-lived Harry's kisses – fierce, demanding, yet at the same time gentle, loving.

* * *

Harry woke early to grey light filtering through a gap in the curtains. For a moment he couldn't remember where he was and he sat up quickly, gazing around the unfamiliar room. Had he been dreaming? Gradually, the events of the previous day flooded back, and he threw back the covers and jumped out of bed.

Emilly, dear sweet Emily – he'd found her. Their reunion had been everything he had dreamt of over the past years. But why was he here in this strange house? They should be together.

Now fully awake, commonsense took over. He was in the police sergeant's home. He could hardly believe that Bill Brent and his wife had made him so welcome. From below came the sounds of a household going about its morning business.

He dressed quickly and went downstairs. Mrs Brent – Dolly as she had insisted he called her – was stirring a pan of porridge on the stove. Without turning around, she said, 'Morning, son. Sit yourself down. Sleep well?'

'Yes, thank you. Where's Mr Brent?'

'At work. He had to go in to report on yesterday's shift.'

For a brief moment, Harry was alarmed. The habit of being wary of authority was hard to dispel. He constantly had to remind himself that he was free now and had done nothing wrong.

Dolly put a bowl in front of him and ladled a good portion of porridge into it. She smiled, pointing to the jug of milk. 'Help yourself.'

Harry ate quickly, anxious to be on his way. He hoped he could remember the way back to the close. He had to see Emily to reassure himself that they would be together from now on. Surely, nothing could separate them now.

He scraped the spoon around the bowl and pushed it away. He was about to stand up when Dolly sat down opposite him. 'In a hurry, aren't you?' she said.

'I need to go,' Harry didn't say Emily's name.

'I understand. Bill told me some of your story last night after you were in bed. There's no need to rush off...' She held up a hand. 'I know you want to see her, but there's plenty of time. Wait till Bill gets back. He needs to talk to you before...'

'What about?' Harry interrupted,

'Nothing to worry about, son. There are things he wants to discuss before you meet up with Emily again.'

'What things?' Harry's mind whirled. Surely nothing could stand in the way of him and Emily getting together now? Perhaps her husband wasn't really dead? What else could it be?'

He stood up and began to pace the cramped room. He threw open the back door and stared out into the small backyard, which had a view of the back of the police station and just a tiny glimpse of the sky. He had become used to the wide skies and open spaces of Australia and had begun to feel hemmed in by the narrow streets and courtyards of this little town. He took a deep breath. He could bear it if it meant being with the love of his life. He turned and went back indoors, apologising to Dolly and taking his seat at the kitchen table once more.

* * *

Bill finished writing his report on the previous day's shift and put it on the inspector's desk.

'I've got some free time due,' he said. 'OK if I take it now? I know it's short notice but...'

'I see. Family business?'

Bill nodded. It wasn't a lie. He'd always thought of Emily and her sister as family.

He left the police station and hurried down the side street to his home at the back, hoping that Harry was still there. He didn't want soft-hearted Emily to invite him to stay with her. He had nothing against the young man but recalled what had happened when Lomax had ingratiated himself with the Wiliams family. It had taken Bill a long time to realise what a rotter the man was. He had fooled them all for a time, and then it was too late. He wouldn't let it happen again.

He knew in his heart that Harry was sincere, but he couldn't take a chance. He threw open the back gate and marched across the yard,

Harry was sitting at the kitchen table and leapt up when Bill entered. 'I want to see Emily,' he said.

'All in good time, lad.' Bill turned to his wife, who was rolling pastry at the other end of the table. 'Any chance of a cuppa, love?'

Dolly smiled. 'Of course, love. Just let me finish this.' She lined the pie dish, dusted flour from her hands, and went to the stove.

Bill sat down beside Harry. 'I know you're keen to be with the lass, but you must understand. You turning up out of the blue was a shock for her. It's not long since her husband died.' Bill, of course, knew that Emily's marriage hadn't been happy. The poor girl had hardly been able to hide her relief at the news of his death.

'I know,' Harry said, 'but I've heard things since I've been back here.' He grinned. 'She didn't seem like a grieving widow when we met yesterday. You were there – you saw.'

Bill nodded. 'He was a wrong 'un all right, and she's well rid of him. But I promised her brother I would look out for the girls when he went away. I don't want Emily to make another mistake.'

Harry leaned forward and looked earnestly into Bill's eyes. 'She won't. Look, Mr Brent, while I was on the chain gang and later working on the sheep station, I thought of Emily every day, every waking hour. It was the thought of her that got me through the bad times, that made me determined to do my time and get back here to find her again.'

Bill could not doubt the man's sincerity. His first impression of Harry Jones all those years ago had been correct. The lad had ended up as a convict through force of circumstance, coupled with the harsh penal laws that did not allow second chances.

'So, what happens now? he asked.

'I love Emily. I want to marry her – if she'll have me.'

Bill relaxed and grinned. 'Oh, I'm sure she will.'

Harry leapt from the chair. 'I'm going round there now.'

'Hang on, lad. Have you thought about her sister – Cissie? Are you willing to take her on too?'

'Of course. She'll be my sister too, won't she?'

'And what about work? Emily barely makes enough from the laundry to keep the two of them.' Bill deliberately put obstacles in Harry's way to be certain the lad was sincere.

'I'll find work somehow'. Harry's voice rose. 'I don't expect her to keep me. What do you take me for?'

'All right, simmer down.' Bill was now satisfied that things would work out for

Emily this time. Harry was a hard-working lad who would treat her right.

Before, he would agree to take him to Emily, though he told Harry he would have to stay with Bill until the wedding. 'And that won't be until you've got a job and I'm satisfied you can care for both girls. They've had a hard time of it and deserve a better deal.'

Chapter Twenty-Nine

Harry woke early on his wedding day. So much had happened since he'd stepped off the packet boat at Sheerness Pier. Until that wonderful moment when he'd caught sight of Emily, he had scarcely dared believe that they would be together again. How many times had he told himself she would not remember him after all this time?

But she had fallen into his arms, and the years had dropped away. He was sixteen again and in the throes of first love.

He lay in bed watching the light strengthen as the sun rose. He had so much to thank Bill and his wife for. They had taken him in and treated him like a son.

It was thanks to them that he had a job and a home for him and Emily. He hadn't seen her for two weeks, and he wouldn't see her until she entered the church on Bill's arm. It had been hard to contain his impatience, and he had to admit it would have been even harder if he had stayed in Blue Town, so near her home.

His new job had taken him to the other side of the island, and he had returned yesterday evening to spend his last night as a single man in the home of his dear friend Bill.

He got up and dressed in his new clothes, bought from what remained of his Australian earnings.

He knotted his tie and put on his jacket, patting his pocket to make sure the ring was safe. Bill had put him in touch with a jeweller who had set the blue opal into a silver ring and sold him a plain gold band – an engagement ring and a wedding ring on the same day.

He went downstairs where Dolly was, as usual, busy at the stove. She turned with a ladle in her hand and smiled. 'You're looking smart today. Must be a special occasion.'

Harry laughed. 'You could say that.'

Bill came in from outside dressed in his uniform, its silver buttons polished to a brilliant shine.

'Look at you two,' Dolly said. 'Better let me go and get ready too. Don't want to be outshone by you two.' She placed two plates on the table and disappeared up the stairs.

Harry looked at the breakfast Dolly had cooked and sighed. 'I don't think I can eat anything,' he said.

'Better try. You don't want to upset Dolly.' Bill grinned. 'You're not that nervous, are you?'

'Not really. It's just, I can't believe it's really happening.' Harry picked up his knife and fork and started to eat, finding to his surprise that he was quite hungry. He'd almost cleared his plate when Dolly came downstairs and paused in the doorway.

Both men gave exclamations of approval. 'You're a fine figure of a lass,' Bill said, taking her hand and kissing it.

Dolly dipped a little curtsy.

Harry smiled. In her emerald-green velvet dress and matching hat perched on her abundant curls, she certainly was, but, he was sure, not a patch on his Emily.

There was a knock on the door, which opened to reveal Dolly's brother, Stan, the farmer from nearby Minster who had given Harry a job and a cottage to go with it.

'Glad you're here, Stan. You need to be getting to the church,' said Bill. 'Don't want to be late.'

'I'm ready,' Harry said. 'It's good of you to stand as my best man, Stan.'

'Pleasure, son. I'm a poor substitute for my brother-in-law but I'm sure you understand his first commitment was to Emily.'

'Of course. You've all been so good to me – I feel like I've got a real family.'

'Well, I'm off. See you all in church,' Bill said.

* * *

'Keep still, Em,' Cissie said. 'I need to fix your headdress.'

'There's plenty of time,' Emily said, but she sat up straight and let Cissie finish getting her ready. She smoothed down the pale blue dress with its border of embroidered flowers, pleased with how well it looked. It had been the dress her mother had got married in. She'd had to do a few alterations to make it fit. Thank goodness she hadn't worn it for her wedding to Lenny. She blessed the instinct that had made her choose something different.

She swallowed a lump in her throat, remembering how Mum had looked when all dressed up to go dancing. It was one of the few memories she had from their life in London.

'Don't look so sad, Em. This is your wedding day.' Cissie paused, frowning. 'You weren't thinking about Lenny, were you?'

'No, of course not. I was thinking of Mum – and Dad, wishing they could be here with us.'

'Me too, although I hardly remember Mum, but it's lovely that I'm wearing one of her dresses too,' Cissie said.

'And you look gorgeous in it. That lilac colour suits you.'

'I keep thinking of Joey. I so hoped he would get leave so that he could give you away.'

'I hoped so, too. But we're lucky to have Bill, he's such a good friend,' Emily said.

'He'll be here soon. I think I can hear the cart now,' Cissie said. 'It was so good of Mrs

Brent's brother to lend us the horse and cart to take us to the church.'

'Better than walking, although it's only a short way.' Emily went to the door, gasping with pleasure.

No longer looking like a plain old farm cart, the sides were almost hidden by the flowers attached to them. More flowers were woven into the horse's mane and bridle and the leather harness had been polished to a gleaming shine.

Bill jumped down and took Emily's hands, kissing her on the cheek, then turned to Cissie and did the same. 'My lovely girls.' He looked up at the sky. 'Such a beautiful day for a wedding.'

'Where's Agnes?' Emily asked. 'I hope she's well enough to come.'

'She's already at the church. I took her and Gladys a while ago.'

Cissie giggled. 'Thank goodness for the farm cart. I couldn't imagine Emily pushing Agnes in the handcart dressed in her finery.'

Emily smiled. 'I would have if it was the only way to get her to the church. I couldn't get married without my best friend.'

Bill helped the girls into the cart and shook the reins, clicking his tongue at the horse. As they turned out of the close, all the neighbours came out to see them off.

Emily's heart swelled. How fortunate they were to have such wonderful friends and neighbours. She felt a little sad as she took one last look at the tiny cottage where she had been happy most of the time, looking after her young siblings and caring for her father. It had been a real home full of love despite the bad times with Lenny.

Her thoughts turned to the future. Harry was waiting for her at St Paul's Church, and within a short time, they would be husband and wife, starting a new chapter of their lives and making a new home together.

She would miss Cissie but she would return often to visit her sister, who was moving in with Agnes, leaving their little cottage to another family.

The church came in sight, and Bill turned round. 'Here we are lasses.' He pulled the horse to a stop and helped the girls down, handing the reins to a boy who waited by the church wall. 'Look after him, lad, and there's sixpence for you when we come out.'

The boy grinned and bobbed his head.

Emily took Bill's arm, and Cissie followed them down the church path. As they neared the porch, Emily heard the swell of the organ and her heart beat faster. She wasn't dreaming. She was about to marry the man of her dreams.

Epilogue
Two Years Later

'Home, home, sweet sweet home...' Emily sang as she hung the washing on the line. It was a song she'd heard on her first visit to the music hall in Blue Town, and she thought of it every time she looked back at the farm cottage with its hollyhocks growing up the walls, hens pecking in the grass and the green countryside beyond.

She pegged the last sheet on the line and watched as the washing snapped and fluttered in the breeze.

She picked up the empty basket and called to her little daughter who had been playing on the grass nearby.

'Time for dinner, Sally, sweetheart.' She scooped the little girl up and ran across the grass, the pair of them laughing.

Emily paused by the back door and turned to look out over the fields that sloped down towards the marshes. In the distance, the sun sparkled on the water of the Swale, which divided the island from the mainland. It was a view she never tired of. This really was a place to call home.

In the distance, she spotted Harry walking steadily behind the horse-drawn harrow. 'Look, Sally. There's Daddy.' She pointed, and Sally stuck her fingers in her mouth. 'Dada,' she murmured, then wriggled to get down.

'He'll be home for dinner soon,' Emily told her, smiling. She still felt a little lift of her heart at the thought of him coming home to her, and she looked forward to the cosy evenings when Sally was in bed.

Harry had taken to farm work from the start and never tired of telling her how happy she made him. The birth of their little daughter cemented their love, and she was now looking forward to telling him that Sally might soon have a little sister or brother.

When she had first arrived at the farm, she had been a little worried that Harry wouldn't settle. The proximity of the marshes must surely bring back haunting memories of the gang and their attempted escape.

But when she had tentatively questioned him, he had assured her that the past now meant nothing to him. He loved the open spaces and the wide blue skies, which reminded him of a bit of Australia – 'apart from the weather,' he said with a laugh. 'But that's all in the past. This is where I want to be – with you and our darling little daughter.'

He admitted that he had begun to feel stifled by the cramped little houses and

narrow streets of Blue Town.' But I would
have stayed there if that was the only way I
could be with you,' he said. 'But, as long as
I'm with you, I'm happy.'

Emily kissed him. 'That makes two of
us,' she said as she silently blessed Bill and
his family for making her new life possible.

The End

After 22 years of handling other people's books while working as a library assistant, Roberta Grieve decided it was time to fulfil a long-held ambition and start writing her own. On taking early retirement, she began writing short stories and magazine articles with some success. She then turned to novels, and her first, 'Abigail's Secret,' was published in 2008. Since then, she has had seven more historical romances published, as well as eight short novels published as large-print paperbacks. 'A Place to Call Home' is her fifteenth novel for Books We Love.

Roberta lives in a small village in South Norfolk, and when she is not writing, she enjoys painting and taking part in village life.